Charlie Fightmaster
and the
Search for Perfect Harmony

Joe Siple

Black Rose Writing | Texas

First printing / First Hardcover printing

ISBN: 978-1-68433-748-4 (Paperback); 978-1-944715-89-2 (Hardcover)
PUBLISHED BY BLACK ROSE WRITING
www.blackrosewriting.com

Printed in the United States of America
Suggested Retail Price (SRP) $18.95 (Paperback); $23.95 (Hardcover)

Charlie Fightmaster and the Search for Perfect Harmony is printed in Book Antiqua

*As a planet-friendly publisher, Black Rose Writing does its best to eliminate
unnecessary waste to reduce paper usage and energy costs, while never
compromising the reading experience. As a result, the final word count vs. page count
may not meet common expectations.

For Dad, who taught me that baseball
— beautiful as it is —
is about more than just the game.

Charlie Fightmaster
and the
Search for Perfect Harmony

The Curveball

One of the oldest off-speed pitches is the curveball. With grips and delivery methods as varied as the pitchers who throw them, curveballs historically have a "twelve-to-six" movement as opposed to the sideways darting of a slider, or the modern cut-fastball. It's often thrown when the pitcher is ahead in the count and has the luxury of tempting a batter to chase a pitch out of the strike zone.

While it can be effective at any time, the curveball is most powerful when unexpected.

Chapter 1

The crack of the bat echos off Fenway Park's upper deck. Subdued cheers and a spattering of applause mean the Red Sox have recorded the third out of the inning. Ordinarily, my father and I would dutifully document it in our scorebook. We would stand for the seventh inning stretch and order a hot dog or a beer from the vendor.

Instead, we're trying to hide.

I hurry along the concourse, through the floating scent of hotdogs and nacho cheese, passing a gruff voice calling out "cold beer here!" and I try to blend in with the sea of jersey-clad fans.

A security guard sits on a padded stool so I lower the rim of my cap, blocking my eyes from his view. The door I've scouted is within sight, twenty steps away. I try not to focus on it, but my eyes betray me, drawn like a beacon.

"This way," I say, and my father follows at my heels.

As thirty-thousand fans begin singing "Take Me Out To The Ballgame," I slow my pace, scan the area for anyone who might be watching—including the nearby security guard—then quickly twist the knob of the door and duck inside. As soon as my father rushes in I quickly pull the door closed behind us, and we're alone.

The room is pitch dark. After a few moments, I notice a thin sliver of light along the bottom of the door. I open my eyes wide against the darkness and slowly, objects begin to appear, as if out of a mist. There's a rake, a large trash can, and a shelf holding bags of diamond dry. The room smells strongly of chalk.

"You've done this before, Charlie?"

My father's voice is a whisper but I can still hear the excitement in it. A hint of incredulity at what he has allowed his son to convince him to do, mixed with the anticipation of a new adventure. I'm sure my father hasn't done anything so illegal in many years.

"Not exactly," I say. "But a guy I played with in the Mexican League spent ten games with the Sox last year. He told me about it."

"He was on the big league team? Then wouldn't he be allowed to…do whatever it is we're going to do?"

I'm not sure how much to tell my father. There's no mistaking the hint of fear in his voice and I don't want to scare him more than necessary. But still, I'm not going to lie to my dad.

"This isn't exactly allowed," I say. I consider explaining more, maybe giving him some reassurance that we won't go to jail if we get caught. But since I'm not sure that's true, I change the subject. "Pippin would love this," I say.

I can almost hear my father smile. "Pippin would love anything as long as you're there."

Outside the dark closet, the game continues. We follow it through its sounds. The Sox go down in order in the bottom of the seventh. There's a pitching change in the top of the eighth. When the final out of the game is recorded, the stadium speakers play music as tens of thousands of footsteps flicker the light at the bottom of the door.

Eventually the footsteps slow, then stop completely. I sit with my back to the door, my shoulder next to my father's, as the noise outside slowly fades. Still, we wait. After two hours, when it sounds like everyone has left, I put my ear to the cold metal and wait several minutes, hearing nothing. I motion my dad to follow, open the door a crack, and poke my head out.

The stadium lights have been turned off. The concourse is empty and one man from the grounds crew pushes a rake around home plate, then slams the flat end against the dirt. After looking at it from various angles, he nods his approval and disappears into the dugout. Finally, the entire stadium is deserted.

"This way," I say.

I creep out of the closet and through the concourse, keeping close to the wall, as far from the field as possible, in case someone is still down there. I feel like a criminal and have to remind myself that the only crime we're guilty of is trespassing.

And it's an amazing place to trespass.

I allow us a moment to take it all in. Even with the lights off, the green of the grass seems to emit a glow that casts the entire ballpark in a halo of beauty. It radiates off the seats, making the entire stadium feel sacred.

My dad and I are all alone in Fenway Park.

I lead him through the concourse, behind home plate, along the third base line, and all the way to the left field corner. I take one more look around, in case any security guards are still watching. When I'm satisfied that the stadium is, indeed, empty, I jump over a small barrier by the foul pole. A few steps later, I'm behind the base of a giant, thirty-two foot wall.

"The Green Monster," my father whispers reverently.

I scan the back side of the enormous wall. Rungs of an old, rusted ladder lead all the way to the top.

"Ready?"

My father's mouth drops open and his eyes flick high into the air. "Ready for what?" he says.

I smother a smile and follow my father's gaze to the top of the giant wall. Then I wrap my hands around the rusted metal of the ladder and begin to climb.

. . .

It must have been the nickname — The Green Monster — that gave me nightmares as a child. It didn't matter how much my father reassured me or how much reverence was in his voice when he spoke of it, in my eight year-old mind, the only thing I could picture was something out of the books he would read to me at bedtime. *Where the Wild Things Are* or *Jack and the Beanstalk*. Something dangerous, with sharp thorns or fangs.

I never imagined that twenty years later I would sit atop the wall with my father by my side. And my imagination was the only place I thought I'd share the news I'm about to share with him.

"Now that's quite a sight," my dad says.

I try to hold the moment. I breathe the humid Boston air—city fumes mixed with equal parts popcorn and ballpark franks. I put my weight on my hands and scoot further out onto the wall, toward my father, careful not to get a sliver in my palm. Our feet dangle into fair territory.

"I brought you up here for a reason, dad. I've got some big news."

Careful to keep my balance, I chance a glance at my father, who's still looking at home plate. Still lost in visions of Fisk and Yzskrimski, or maybe Smokey Joe Wood and the Babe himself. I wonder if he heard me. He hasn't moved an inch.

I shake out of my jacket carefully—the giant wall is flimsier than I expected—and drape it around my father's shoulders. This will be one of the biggest moments of my life and I want desperately for it to be perfect. I square my shoulders to my father, careful not to rock the wall, and smile.

"I got the call," I say. "From the Twins. I'm going to be a Major League baseball player."

The furrow in my dad's brow is the last thing I expected. I've spent years planning this moment so it would be perfect—and it is. We're on baseball's holy ground, seeing it from a perspective almost no one sees. My dream to play for our hometown Twins is finally going to come true, after so many years, so much hard work. And yet, the old man's stare never leaves home plate.

Old man? When did I start thinking of him as an old man? He was always one of the fittest dads. The one that could still throw a decent BP and hit fungos for hours, while other kids' dads sat in lawn chairs with their hands folded over their beer-bellies. It wasn't that long ago. Doesn't seem that long ago, anyway.

"You'll never guess how they did it," I say. "It was amazing. They sent Hudson to tell me."

This finally seems to get my father's attention. "Hudson White?"

"Yeah." I try to shake the pangs of jealousy I always feel whenever I think about my friend who has become a star. There's nothing to be jealous of anymore. I'm going to get my chance, too. Finally. "The

Twins had an off day and they sent him because they know we were tight in A-ball."

A few more moments pass and my father still gives no indication he understands. But what is there to misunderstand? This is life-changing news. The dream of so many American boys. I can't fathom why my father hasn't responded with more excitement. Or did he, and I was too wrapped up in my own thoughts to hear him?

"We need to live our lives for the people in it. It's the people that matter." My father pats my knee and nods, as if satisfied with his random comment. "You know that, right Charlie? It's the people."

"I fly out in the morning. To California. They have a three game inter-league series with the Dodgers."

We, I realize. Not *They*. *We*.

My father's chest rises with a deep breath and he closes his eyes, as if trying to cling to the moment. When he finally speaks, it isn't about my promotion to the big leagues.

"Remember Nomar's home run?" he asks.

I stare at him like he's crazy, then shake my head and say, "Of course, I remember."

The Nomar Garciaparra Home Run. A four-hundred-fifty foot blast from the shortstop—the same position I play. It was the first Monthly Game, the beginning of a ritual.

The rules of the Monthly Game are simple: Once a month during the season, we meet to watch a Major League ballgame. We pick a game close to where my minor league team is playing and I take the twenty year-old Ford Escort he bought me, used, for my high school graduation and meet for nine innings of quality time.

"The home run would have whisked right by our ears here," my father says. "Or maybe sailed high over our heads. And that triple play the Braves pulled off down in Atlanta? Remember that? Where had you played the night before? Memphis? Or was it Durham?"

"Dad? You heard what I said, right? I got the call. Right after last night's game. Hudson almost started crying when he told me we're going to be teammates again."

My father still doesn't react. He takes another deep breath as if resetting something inside himself. "My son, the professional baseball player. It's been fun to watch you."

"Dad?" I say. And I wait until he looks at me this time. "What's going on?"

"Nothing. What do you mean?"

"Come on. I just told you I'm going to play in the big leagues and you haven't even cracked a smile. I know something's up. Just tell me."

He clasps my arm hard. At first I think it's for stabilization. But then he looks into my eyes so deeply it makes me uncomfortable.

"Okay," he says. "You're right. It's..."

He takes another deep breath and I can see the war inside him. I wait him out, knowing that whatever's going on, if it's big enough to affect this moment, I need to hear it. When he finally says it, it's just one word.

"...Pippin."

I feel a thud in my chest. And immediately I know one thing beyond a shadow of a doubt: my Major League debut will have to wait.

• • •

I rest my hand on the steering wheel of the Escort as the sun touches the horizon. My dad is asleep in the passenger seat and it's a struggle to focus on the road. One thing dominates every thought.

Pippin.

My father tried not to overstate the struggles my little sister is facing, but it wasn't hard to see the truth. Her only friend moved away a month ago. Her nervous tick has gotten progressively worse. Her confidence and self-worth seem nonexistent. And my dad has always been ill-equipped to raise a girl on his own. I'm slapped with the memory of my mother leaving, but bat it away quickly.

I can count on two fingers the things that could have kept me off that plane to California: getting run over by a semi truck, and hearing that Pippin needs me. The sense of protectiveness I feel toward her has always been overwhelming. Some people might think I couldn't possibly know her that well, since I left home when the Twins drafted me at age eighteen—meaning she had only been two—and haven't been home more than two months altogether in the ten years since. But those people wouldn't know what they're talking about. I love that kid more than anything in the world.

And she needs me now.

My dad squirms next to me, trying to sleep. Trying to find a comfortable spot in the passenger seat of the Escort. I'm convinced there isn't one, but he seems determined to make the discovery. Eventually, he gives in to reality, opens his eyes, then puts a hand to his chest while taking a sharp inhale of breath.

"You okay?" I say it casually, because my dad has always been okay. I was sixteen before I could run as fast as he could. Eighteen before I could throw as hard. But I'm not met with a noncommittal wave like I expect. Instead, he looks at me sheepishly, like he has a secret. Turns out, that's the truth.

"I wasn't going to tell you so soon, but since you're coming back…"

My heart races a bit and I brace myself for more bad news. "What is it?"

My dad looks straight out the windshield. "I have cancer," he says.

In that moment, my world changes forever. Again.

"What?" I say, because I can't think of what else to say. "You can't have cancer. You…"

My dad shrugs at my disbelief, as if he's familiar with the reaction. His must have been exactly the same. "I'd been having pain while breathing for a while," he says. "I guess I should have gone in sooner. By the time I did, it had spread."

"Wait, this is serious," I say, still trying to wrap my mind around it. "Are you getting chemo?"

"No," my father says, too nonchalantly for my liking. "That ship has sailed, I'm afraid. And if it's not going to cure me, I'd rather live out my remaining days with some semblance of a normal life."

"Dad, you have to get treatment. They're finding breakthrough drugs all the time these days. Even if they can't cure you now, if you can just stay alive—"

"Charlie," my dad says in that way of his that means the conversation is over. "I'm going to watch the sunrise, I'm going to spend time with my kids, and I'm going to coach the Stallions. I am not going to seek treatment."

After a long moment of silence, I say, "Why didn't you tell me on the scoreboard?"

"I didn't want you to come home for me. I've had a good life. If you decided to come home, I wanted it to be for Pippin."

So many emotions are bombarding me I can't seem to make sense of them. "How long?" I finally ask.

"They didn't want to guess, but when I pushed them, they said a couple months. It's pretty advanced."

Another wave of shock sweeps over me. "Dad," I say, but I have no idea what he needs. "I'm so sorry."

"I'm sorry, too," he says, nestling his face into the pillow against the window. "I'm sorry I didn't buy you a more comfortable car."

•   •   •

The rest of the drive takes place somewhere outside my consciousness. All I can think of is the fact that one day ago, I was going to be a Minnesota Twin. Now, I'm headed back to Sweetwater where my sister is struggling and my father is dying. Twenty-four hours can make a world of difference in a life.

The drive is almost done, thank God. Boston to Minnesota is no small trip. I keep one eye on the road and scoot toward my father. I reach for the pillow that fell from between his head and the passenger-side window. The car swerves as I snatch the pillow and try to gently stuff it back between the cold window pane and my father's sleeping face.

"Where are we?" he asks, groggily opening his eyes.

"Not sure. Almost to the border. Sorry I woke you up."

He waves me off. "I don't have many minutes left. No reason to sleep them away. The Minnesota border?"

"Yeah. Want some dinner?"

"No thanks. Not much of an appetite these days. When was the last time you were in Sweetwater? Christmas?"

"I think so."

I don't mention that it was Christmas three years ago. That I've spent recent off-seasons playing in leagues from Cuba to the Dominican, trying to prove I have what it takes. I wonder if my father remembers this, or if he's starting to lose it a little bit, mentally. I've heard that can happen when people get old and sick. I just never thought it could happen to my dad.

"What'd the Twins say?" my father asks.

"Not much. I told them I had a family emergency and that I needed some time. They understood. Said they'll have to fill the spot with someone else, of course. Whenever I go back to Triple-A, I'll have to hope for my break all over again, I guess."

"I'm sorry," he says, but I just shrug. It's for Pippin, after all. I didn't have a choice.

"Emily Conley's been stopping by," my father says. My stomach flutters at the thought, but then twists. It feels like my insides are being wrung dry. When I don't say anything, my father continues. "She finally finished all that education, but she's still in Sweetwater for now. Sometimes she brings Mack around and we talk baseball. Sometimes she just checks on me. Nice girl." I can feel my father's eyes on me. "You remember her, don't—"

"Yes, dad. I remember her."

I didn't mean to be so short. It's the drive, most likely. Twenty hours of nothing but cornfields is enough to knock the sanest person off his rocker.

After another hour, the landscape starts to fill with towering oak and maple trees, and soon I see the shining lights of Sweetwater Ballpark on the horizon, and the looming presence of Mercy Hospital right next to it, so close they had to install shatter-proof glass in the bottom floors because so many windows were being broken by foul balls. I've never known which was built first—the hospital or the ballpark—but I've always wondered why the town didn't build the second structure farther away.

Now, I'm tempted to say something about the hospital to my father. To encourage him again to seek treatment. But I know perfectly well what he would say. *I don't want to live like that, just so I can claim to be alive.* Just like he said the first dozen times I suggested it since learning about his illness.

At the ballpark, high school-aged kids play a game under the glow of the lights. A green scoreboard marks the home field of my youth like a welcoming lighthouse. Someone swings a bat and sprints toward first base, causing an ache somewhere deep inside my chest. Part longing, part regret. It turns out giving up a lifelong dream isn't easy—no matter the reason.

"How've the Stallions been doing?" I ask.

"We can do no wrong," my father says. I notice a straightening of his posture and a brightening in his eyes. Why he takes the town's amateur team so seriously, I'll never understand. But coaching the team has been his passion for as long as I can remember. "We've got a new kid," my dad continues. "Moved because his grandma lives just outside town, by the old elevator shaft. Hits the stuffing out of the ball. And more. He's a five-tool player." He pats my leg and smiles. "We've got a real shot to break the streak this year. I just know it."

"Well, I'm glad to hear it. So you're hoping to keep coaching for a while?"

"I'll coach the Stallions until the day I die," he says. "Or at least, as close as I can get. Mack helped me set up a big recliner in the corner of the dugout so I can be more comfortable during games. We even have an agreement—if I fall asleep, the bat boy protects me from any foul balls into the dugout and Mack takes over managing until I wake up."

"Ha! I bet Mack loves that."

My dad laughs softly. "Last game, I pretended to sleep for a couple innings just to see what he'd do."

"And?"

"Not bad. He made a pitching change one batter too late, but it could have been worse."

I want to take my time driving through downtown. It's been so long since I've been home. But my father has been in the car far too long and surely needs a decent night's sleep. So I speed through town and pull into the driveway of our faded yellow, two-story house.

It looks terrible. It desperately needs to be painted and several windows look like they'll disintegrate if they're not replaced soon, but I hold my tongue. I help my dad out of the car and manage to fit all four of our bags in my arms. I stop on the sidewalk in front of the house and let the memories wash over me.

What I want is to keep focused on the front door and walk straight inside, but there's no way that's going to happen. So I at least try to be subtle, in case she's watching. I duck my head and peer under the brim of my baseball hat toward her house, across the street and four doors down.

Emily Conroy.

She's not there. She isn't watching me. In fact, there's a kid in front of the house, sitting on the steps. She must have moved. Why does that bother me so much? Did I expect her to let me know that she had moved on with her life? I try to laugh at myself but find I can't quite do it.

My father is staring at me with an odd expression on his face. "Lots of memories, huh?" he says. He pats my arm." Come on in and get some sleep. It'll be an early morning if Pippin has anything to say about it. She's bursting at the seams to see you."

•   •   •

I wake up feeling like a kid again. Dreams from the restless night mix with long-forgotten memories. The familiar scent of the sheets stirs something inside me but it isn't until I open my eyes that I remember where I am.

Sweetwater. In my childhood bed. I'm home. It has been a long time.

As I make my way toward consciousness, I look out the window at a yellow-winged bird. It chirps a beautiful morning song and I watch it for a long time. Finally, I reach for my cell phone to check the time. It's 9am—my dad must have made Pippin let me sleep—but what really wakes me up is the text waiting from Hudson White:

—**Hey man, I'm confused. You okay? People don't just pass up opportunities like this.**

I stare at the text for a long moment. Hudson has been nothing but good to me. And skipping out on the Twins was my own decision, so there's no reason to let envy take over. But it turns out doing the right thing doesn't alleviate the desire for the thing you want. And I want to be a Major League baseball player so bad I can taste it. Finally, I respond:

—**Just have some things I have to take care of. Shouldn't be long. Good luck in LA!**

Voice bubbles pop up on the screen, then give way to Hudson's response:

—**Thanks, Fighter. I think you're nuts, but I hope to see you in the dugout soon!**

I stare at the phone, fighting the strong temptation to call the Twins back and beg and plead for my spot on the roster. Instead, I make my way down a creaky staircase and into the kitchen. Before I reach the bottom step, a blur of pink and red lunges into me and nearly tackles me to the ground.

"Hey Pip-squeak," I say. "I'm happy to see you, too."

Pippin says something, but all I can hear is mumbling into my hooded sweatshirt. The mumbling continues as the force of her hug increases. When I ease her to arm's length so I can see her, Pippin wipes tears from her freckled cheeks, tries unsuccessfully to straighten her mess of red hair, and sniffles loudly. She tries several times to speak, but nothing comes out, so she lunges at me again and squeezes me in another suffocating hug.

I mess her hair and hug her back. When she's finally able to speak, she says, "Did you bring me anything?"

I try to give her a disappointed look. "When was the last time I didn't bring you anything?"

"Never," she says.

"Never." From my back pocket, I pull out a plastic-sheathed baseball card and hand it to her. Her eyes explode open.

"A David Ortiz card?"

"Autographed by Big Poppy himself," I say. I don't tell her about the effort it took to get that card. The last thing I want is for guilt to dampen her excitement. She lunges back at me and squeezes me so hard she shakes.

"Thanks, Charlie. This is the coolest thing ever."

Pippin follows me like a lost puppy as I drag a fraying, plaid recliner from the living room to the den, and set it next to the one already there. She watches my every move, silently at my side, her gaze flicking occasionally to the baseball card in her hand. I try not to scrutinize her too obviously, but I can see that my dad was right. The bags beneath her eyes weren't there last time I saw her. And the desperation in her hugs—that's new, too.

"Think he'll be okay with me moving this out here, Pip?" I say.

"They look like front-row seats to me," my father says as he appears at the door. He comes in and sits in the chair, letting out a little groan that tells me more than I wanted to know.

"Do you have last night's game recorded?" I ask.

"Sure do. Emily likes to swing by sometimes and watch. Maybe we should give her a call."

"We should," Pippin says. They're the first normal-voiced words she's said since I returned home—until now her excitement forced her voice up an octave. I'm startled now by how different she sounds. I fight a pang of guilt for letting so much time go by.

"Why does she come over so much?" I ask. I have no interest in seeing Emily Conroy, which would inevitably lead to reliving several of my past mistakes.

My father gives a half-shrug, as if he hadn't thought much about it. "She seems to have taken a liking to me, and her little boy thinks the world of Pippin."

Her little boy. So Emily has a son—maybe that had been the kid in front of the house. Maybe it is still her house.

I hate the burning sensation in my chest when I think of Emily with a kid. As much as I don't want to admit it, I know perfectly well what it is. Jealousy. As if I have any right.

To hide my discomfort, I fiddle with the remote control until I get the prior night's Twins game playing. I settle into the chair next to my dad and Pippin hops into my lap.

Again, I wonder at the time that's passed. Pippin's almost a teenager. But she snuggles into me like a toddler, which is just fine with me. This is what I came here for.

The fact that my little sister is in seventh grade baffles me. In just four years she'll be sixteen. Images of Pippin as a young woman flit around the edges of my consciousness, bringing a lot of questions with them. I wonder if she'll outgrow her awkwardness—both physical and social. I wonder if her teeth will straighten and if her clumsiness will fade, along with her nervous tick. And if none of those things happen for her, I wonder if there's any way she'll be happy.

I crouch down so I'm at eye-level with Pippin and really look at her for the first time. I try to watch her closely without making it obvious that I'm watching. I don't notice a single blink, much less anything that resembles the nervous tick that has made her the brunt of so much bullying, according to my father. Maybe she's made some progress.

"Are you staying here?" Pippin asks.

I've never once lied to my sister—even when I probably should have. But I decided long ago, when hard, unfair truths have to be told to an innocent girl at too young an age, the only way to earn and keep her trust is with complete honesty.

"For a little bit, kiddo. But eventually I'll have to go."

"Back to baseball?"

"Yeah." I pull her pigtails out like wings. "It's my job."

"You know, a real job requires education," Pippin says.

"Sounds like they've been preaching to you at school, huh?"

"I guess. But Emily says so, too."

"Yeah, well, don't tell her I say so, but Emily doesn't always have any clue what she's talking about."

"Maybe not," says a voice from the entryway to the den. "But at least she's here more than you are."

I fight to contain the butterflies in my stomach, but it's a losing battle.

Emily.

At least I think it's Emily. It's been ten years since I've seen her and she was only sixteen at the time. She was a girl then, at a time when most of her classmates had grown into young women. She had kept the innocence of childhood along with the face and even the curve-less body. But the woman walking to the recliner next to my father is exactly that. A woman. I know her voice and those silvery-blue eyes but other than that, I wouldn't recognize her.

"I didn't know you were here," she says. "I'm sure you have things to do so I'll let you be."

I try to stop her. I say something like "wait" or "hang on," but I can't figure out which, mesmerized as I am by how much she's changed. In all the best ways. She deftly sidesteps around me before I can get my thoughts straightened out. Next thing I know, the front door slams and she's gone.

Pippin's grin reaches each of her ears. "You want to marry her. I can tell."

I try to think of a response, but can't come up with anything appropriate for twelve year-old ears.

"Some women sure know how to hold a grudge," my father says. "I don't care to know what you did to her when you two were in high school, but..." He whistles as if impressed. As if whatever I did, it must have been unusually cruel. The thought makes me sad and I try not to think about the past.

"Does she just show up unannounced?"

"She knows she has an open invitation," my father says.

I drop down into the recliner next to my father, thankful for the baseball game. Twins and Indians. Bottom of the fifth, Twins up a run.

I'm hoping to watch a couple innings in peace. Maybe figure out how I can help Pippin, then make it back into professional ball and ultimately to the Major Leagues. I just need to figure out how to make all that happen from Sweetwater, Minnesota.

But a few moments of privacy aren't in the cards. There's a knock on the front door and Pippin sprints to open it, so I follow her reluctantly.

It's Emily again, looking thoroughly tortured and averting her eyes with impressive resolve. Behind her, Mack Conroy sports the tight Sweetwater Stallions shirt and too-short coaching shorts I've come to expect.

"Charlie, you know my dad," Emily says through the screen door. "He heard you were back."

"Charlie Fightmaster," Mack says. He opens the screen door, takes my hand, and squeezes it without shaking. I wish he'd let go, but I'm not sure how to pull my hand away without being rude. "Boy, am I glad to see you."

"It's nice to see you, too, Mack."

"Can I come in?"

"Of course. My dad's got the Twins game on."

Pippin excuses herself to "research" in her room, whatever that means, and I lead the way back into the den, where Mack greets my father. Emily moves to a corner of the room, as if she's trying to get as far from me as possible. The old men chat about the Twins game and their prospects for the season, but predictably turn to their own team — the Sweetwater Stallions.

The two have coached the team for two decades. In fact, it's how I met Emily in middle school. I still remember her shagging foul balls from the parking lot and bringing them back to the dugout, where I sat in awe of the players, soaking up as much baseball as I could and watching my dad coach.

I didn't hear the last thing that was said because I've been staring at Emily, but when she looks at me, I realize it's because I've been asked a question and everyone is awaiting my response.

"What? Sorry, I was...distracted."

If I didn't know better, I'd swear Emily's cheeks tint red. Mack bounces on his toes, making his turf shoes squeak against the hardwood floors.

"I said it sounds like your old man was too polite to say it, but it sure would be great if you joined the Stallions. Being that you're here, and all."

I laugh and nod, until I realize all three are staring at me, expectant. "Wait, are you serious? Me? Play with the Stallions?"

Still, no one speaks, but when I look at Emily I'm met with one of the most vicious glares I've ever seen from her—and that's saying something. My father looks to the television, as if hurt by what I said.

"I know it's just town-ball," Mack says. "But I'm sure your dad has told you we've got quite a line-up this year."

I didn't mean to be insulting, but seriously? I've just been offered a Major League contract. Now they're asking me to play with accountants and insurance salesmen on Sweetwater's town team? Legally, I could do it. Since I'd be playing for free, I wouldn't be breaking my contract. But why would I?

"I'm sure the line-up is great, Mack. And dad, you know I'd love to play for you." I turn back to Mack, unable to look at my dad. "It's just that I'm only going to be in town for a while. To make sure dad's okay, spend some time with Pippin. And then I'm going to head back. I figure if I'm playing by June and have a good summer, I could be a September call-up."

"The Twins are holding your spot?" Mack asks.

"Not the big club, obviously," I say, fighting back the regret that comes with the answer. "But my Triple-A spot is still there."

"How long will they hold it? They have to play games too, don't they?"

I lean over and scratch at my knee. "Well, yeah."

"So they bring someone up from Double-A, he gets hot, next thing you know, they don't have a spot for you. Seems like you should be thinking of other possibilities."

For a moment, I want to lash out at Mack. Ask why he thinks an assistant town-team baseball coach can tell me what to do. Nothing impressive has ever come out of Sweetwater's baseball scene except my Triple-A run. And Bud Crawford, of course. But Bud Crawford is on such a different level and his career was so long ago it hardly counts. Bud Crawford is like Babe Ruth—so legendary no one can claim him. He's an entity all to himself.

"I think we could have a mutually beneficial situation," Mack says. "We've got three pitchers on our staff who throw ninety-plus, and a high school kid named Raimel who might be as good as you were at his age."

I turn to my dad, but his gaze never leaves the television. "Look, Mack, I understand you have a good team this year —"

" — Best Sweetwater's seen since the days of Bud Crawford —"

" — But I just don't think it's for me. I mean, no offense, to any of you, but it's town ball."

Mack nods as if he's absorbed a body blow but is fighting on. "We could break the streak. Win our first state championship in fifty years. You could be a part of that. It would be quite an accomplishment."

"The only accomplishment I'm interested in is tipping my cap to my dad from the batter's box of a Major League baseball stadium. I'm sorry, but I'm just not going to play for the Stallions."

Mack purses his lips and nods. A man defeated. Too many body-blows. I just hope I wasn't too insulting. My father still hasn't said a word since we started talking about the Stallions. Not until Mack plops into the recliner next to him and turns his attention to the Twins game. Then, as if they rehearsed the whole thing, my father finally speaks.

"Well it's too bad," he says, rocking comfortably in his recliner. "Because that kid Raimel has scouts from every Major League team just swarming around the stadium. You know, just in case your old team can't hold your spot."

I freeze and feel my pulse quicken. I hope no one else can hear it thumping like a drum. I risk a glance at Emily, but she seems interested in something out the window.

"Practice starts at seven-thirty this evening," my father says, his attention back on the television. "Just in case you were wondering."

Productive Out

If a batter doubles to lead off an inning, a manager may opt to have the following hitter bunt the runner to third base. If, however, the coach doesn't want to take the bat out of the hands of the following hitter, he may allow the hitter to swing away. If the hitter gets on base, the strategy worked. But it is also a success if the hitter is retired, but manages to advance the runner to third base with less than two outs via a ground ball to the right side of the infield, or a long fly ball that allows the runner to tag up. While not the best-case scenario, this is considered a productive out.

Chapter 2

Seven-thirty. I have until 7:30pm to decide if I'm going to humiliate myself and show up for a Sweetwater Stallions practice. The thought scares me. Have I really fallen so far, so quickly? But if there are Major League scouts around — and if I can't be sure how long I'll be in Sweetwater or if I'll still have a team to play for when I leave — it might be the smart thing to do.

For my career, anyway. Certainly not my ego.

In the meantime, I figure it's a good chance to do what I came here for and spend some time with Pippin.

So I make my way to Sweetwater Middle School. Or at least, it used to be Sweetwater Middle School. Now, the sign out front includes a long list of letters signifying the half-dozen small towns that Sweetwater has combined with as attendance has continued to drop.

I walk through the same front doors I entered as a student and start down the hall, looking for the science fair. It's not hard to find, with "Summer Science Fair: District Finals" signs posted every five feet. I make my way to the gym and begin looking for Pippin.

I know she's in here somewhere, but the entire gym seems dominated by a cluster of very sparkly, very loud, and very skimpily dressed girls, flirting with very awkward, very short, and very pimply middle school boys. I can't believe what the girls are wearing: the designer jeans with holes showing more skin than denim, and crop-tops showing enough of the girls' pre-teen bodies to make me uncomfortable. Did girls wear that when I was a student here? Maybe I'm just getting old.

I scan the gym, keeping my eyes as far away from the cluster of girls as possible, and notice Pippin in the far corner, wearing baggy pants and a long sleeve Sweetwater Stallions sweatshirt, despite the heat. She's adjusting something on a table that holds a three-sided poster board and a model volcano.

For a few moments, I stay where I am and watch her work from a distance. The kid's been dealt a bad hand and has spent her entire life living with the consequences. She isn't like other kids and it kills me to see it.

I was fortunate when it came to timing and genes. I was nearly an adult when our mother left; Pippin had just turned one. I had some athleticism, girls thought I was good-looking, which made me confident. Pippin didn't get any of that. Through some cosmic luck of the genetic draw.

So how's she supposed to make her way through life? When stress and misplaced guilt about our mother's departure resulted in a nervous tick of excessive blinking, what history of love did she have available to summon? Our father has been there every step of the way, but he was never equipped to raise a girl by himself. The scales have been uneven, with Pippin's vibrance, intellect, and innocence on one side, and the other side piled high with our mother's departure, insensitive kids, a tendency toward clumsiness, and curly red hair with freckles that do nothing for the slightly off-center look of her eyes. I don't even want to consider the next couple years, as Pippin faces the changes of puberty without a mother. And soon, we now know, without a father. I don't know what will happen to her, so for the moment, I try not to think about it.

Pippin is so engrossed in her science fair project, she doesn't notice me until I tap her shoulder.

"Charlie!" she shrieks. She restrains herself from lunging into another hug. "I knew you'd come. I just knew it. Look at my project."

She drags me to the volcano. "This is an exact replica of Paricutin."

"Who?" I say. "Oh yeah, wasn't he a pitcher back in the dead-ball era?"

Pippin giggles, which sounds just like the chirp of the yellow-winged bird I saw outside the bedroom window this morning. "It's a volcano that appeared in a cornfield in Mexico overnight."

"A volcano appeared overnight? I thought it took a really long time for volcanos to form."

"Most people assume that," Pippin says. "And most of them do. That's why I chose this particular volcano. It was five stories tall within a week."

"That's really cool, Pip. What you've done here is seriously amazing."

Pippin's shrugs her shoulders, then slouches. "Thanks." I don't understand her sudden lack of enthusiasm, but before I can ask, she gets a crinkle in her brow. "You're going to go to baseball practice tonight, aren't you?"

"I haven't completely decided yet," I admit.

She huffs a disgusted breath. "How are the Stallions going to break the streak and win the state tournament if you're wasting all your time at middle school science fairs?"

I hold my hands out, as if to slow her down. "First of all, I'm not wasting anything. Being here with you is exactly where I should be. Even more than that, it's exactly where I want to be." Pippin blushes and tries to find something to look at. She ends up trying to hide her smile at the volcano. "And second of all," I say. "What's this fascination with the Stallions? Why do you want them to win a championship so bad?"

Pippin's shrug suggests it's not a question she's ever thought was very relevant. "They're the Stallions. And they've always been so bad. I want them to win state more than anything in the world."

"Come on, Pip. There's gotta be something you want more than a Stallions state championship." A voice comes over the loudspeaker, announcing that the final round of judging has begun. After several loud clicks and a deafening burst of feedback, I turn back to Pippin. "Think hard. Imagine it. The Stallions win state. Really, go ahead and picture it."

I'm not sure I should have started this little exercise because judging by the grin spreading across her face, there might actually be nothing in the world she wants more than a championship for this silly baseball team. Even her eyes look happy — and they're closed.

"Okay, that was pretty good, right?"

"The best. For sure."

"Great. Now, think of something that would make you feel even better."

"Nothing would."

"There has to be something. How about finding treasure worth a million dollars?"

"Nope."

"What if in the treasure there's a genie in a bottle that will grant you three wishes?"

"Okay."

"Great!"

"As long as the first wish is a Stallions state championship."

"Oh my god, kid, you're killing me here."

Pippin giggles, like she's enjoying my frustration. But finally, she shows me some mercy. "Okay, maybe there is one thing."

"I knew it. What is it?"

"Actually, two things. Wow! This is kind of fun to imagine."

"Bring it, kid. What've you got for me? What would be better than a Stallions state championship?"

Pippin's smile widens even further. "Beating Skyler Shepherd in the state middle school science fair."

"Alright, well you're in the right place," I say.

"Yeah, and the second one is even better."

"Well what is it?"

"It's actually what I've decided I want to do with my life."

"And what's that?"

Pippin's eyes flutter a bit and she turns her face away. It's that lack of confidence my father told me about. The fact that it's even happening with me is distressing. She's always been an open book with me. "Come on." I gently elbow her ribs. "Just tell me. You know I won't judge. What, do you want to be the Fat Lady in a circus or something?"

"No," Pippin says, and I soak up her bird-call giggle.

"A poop-scooper at a dog park?"

"No!"

"Then what?"

"If I tell you will you promise not to laugh?"

"Cross my heart," I say, in my best twelve year-old impression.

She rolls her eyes, then prepares herself with a deep breath. "I want to be a baseball bat maker."

I try to say something like *Oh, that's great!* Or *You can definitely do that!* But the words won't come out of my mouth. Instead, I say, "A what, now?"

"I told you it was stupid."

"No, it's not stupid, Pip. It's just not what I was expecting." I study the callouses on my hands; a baseball bat's handiwork. "Help me understand," I say. "What do you mean you want to be a baseball bat maker? Like, real wooden bats? You want to work for Louisville Slugger or something? I'm sure you could do that."

"No."

A burst of laughter rings out from the gaggle of girls and Pippin's eyes momentarily flick toward them. "You know Arty Black?" she says.

"The singer? Of course. I saw him play three times when I was in high school."

"Some guy in Tennessee makes his guitars. Every one of them. Arty Black refuses to play with anything else, even though the ones this guy makes cost, like, a billion dollars each."

"Okay," I say, trying to follow her logic. "So what?"

"So do you think he couldn't go to some local music store and buy a nice guitar? Of course he could. But he doesn't. He won't use a guitar unless it's made by that guy in Tennessee." When I don't respond, she continues, getting more exasperated at my lack of understanding with every word. "People with money will pay a ton for something that's unique, even if they could get something really good at a store. I want to make bats that people want to use, even though they could get a Louisville Slugger from any sporting goods store. Because mine's going to be better."

"Interesting," I say. The last thing I want is to sound condescending, but if she thinks she's going to make better bats than a company that's been making them for over a century, a reality check now might be less painful than later.

"Think about it," Pippin says, her eyes growing wild with excitement. "Baseball players are super superstitious, right? And you know lots of professionals. So if I can make the perfect bat and you can convince someone to use it, and he gets a hit in his first at-bat with it, he'll never want to use another bat. Soon everyone will want one."

It's a bit of an exaggeration, but I see her point. I once stole three bases in a game, then went four weeks without washing my socks. Eventually, of course, I did wash them. But not because of the smell, which was nauseating to anyone in a fifteen foot radius. But because I was finally thrown out stealing. So yeah, baseball players can be a bit superstitious.

"I've done all the research," Pippin says, facing me earnestly now and ignoring her volcano. "Once I have the wood, I just need a good lathe, a roughing gouge, a skew chisel, a parting tool—"

"Hold on a second," I say. "I'm all for your idea, but I don't know if I'd be able to convince anyone to use a bat you made. I mean, what's going to make your bats so different from other ones?"

"You mean other than my unassailable skill and craftsmanship?"

"Yeah," I say, wondering what 'unassailable 'means. "Other than that."

"Quebracho."

I stare at her a moment, then say, "Gesundheit."

Pippin slaps her forehead and groans. "You've never even heard of Quebracho?"

"Are you trying to tell me there are people in the world who have?"

"Only everyone who knows anything about wood." Pippin forces her most patient voice as she explains to me what "everyone" knows. "Quebracho is the hardest wood in the world. It's a combination of Spanish words that mean 'axe-breaker.' It's found in the South American tropics, has a really pretty reddish-brown color, and is so strong they use it in heavy construction. And the best part is, the grains are interlocking, so it won't break when you hit a ball off the end of the bat."

"That all sounds great, Pip, but if it's that strong it's going to be—"

"—Heavy, I know. But I have a solution for that. I'm going to make the middle, between the handle and the barrel, extra thin. It's going to taper in from the handle more than any other bat, then back out to the barrel."

I try to picture the bat she's describing. The image that comes to mind is something out of a video game. "A bat like that would snap too easily. Right at the taper."

"If it was ash," Pippin says, exasperated. "Or birch or even maple. But not quebracho. Are you even listening to me?"

I'm out of my league in this debate. The smart move is to simply agree. "I guess if you want to be a bat maker, you should probably make some bats. You say you've looked into what you need?"

"The tools are easy to come by," she says. "It's the quebracho that's tricky. That's where you come in."

"Oh, I just come into your plan now?" I say. "I thought you already wanted me to get all my friends to buy one." I wonder if this entire interaction has been planned, and suddenly feel like a base-runner who realizes too late he's been decoyed—just before the fielder tags him out.

"That too," Pippin says. "But I need you to buy the wood because I'm a kid. I don't have a credit card. You do."

"Wait, you're wanting me to pay for this? How much is it going to cost?"

"Well, quebracho is one of the more expensive woods—"

"—Great—"

"—But it won't matter once we start selling them."

Yep, I've been set up. The kid's too smart for her own good. Or for my good, anyway.

"All right, Einstein," I say. "I'll buy you enough wood for a bat and we'll see how it goes, okay?"

"You drive a hard bargain, but okay."

We turn back to Pippin's volcano, and just as I'm about to ask a question about how quickly it formed, one of the sparkly girls steps right in front of me. "Hi Pippy," she says.

In her designer jeans and crop-top, the girl acts like I'm not standing here at all. And "Pippy?" I know I haven't been around much, but I've never heard anyone call my sister Pippy. Judging by Pippin's reaction, she doesn't consider it a term of endearment.

Pippin's eyelids begin to flicker. It's all I can do not to intervene. At the thought of someone hurting my little sister, my head feels like it might explode. But if I'm going to help her, I also need to know what she's dealing with on a daily basis, so I stand back and watch.

"Hi, Skyler," Pippin says. Her voice is barely more than a whisper and she doesn't look the girl in the eye.

"Mr. Lauritson just judged my project," Skyler says. "He says it was the best seventh grade science project he's ever judged. Have you seen it?"

Pippin's eyes flick to the group of girls still clustered by the awkward boys and Skyler's science fair project. "It's really good," Pippin says. "Congratulations."

"It's probably going to win at state in August. You probably didn't even make it to state, did you?"

Pippin looks at her shoes, shakes her head, and says, "Mine hasn't been judged yet."

"Well, when it does get judged, I don't think all that blinking is going to help. You might want to get that under control, you know? Just some friendly advice."

My vision blurs a bit and I take a deep breath to reign myself in. The bullying I'm used to seeing—the bullying of boys— is very different from this. It's more physical and the evidence is more easily seen, but I can tell by the look on Pippin's face that insults, manipulation, and innuendo can cause damage not just to a nose or a jaw, but to a psyche, to a person's sense of self-worth. It can result in more lasting injury than the worst shove or punch.

Just as I'm about to intervene, a man in a white shirt and striped tie approaches, holding a clipboard and pen. His smile to Pippin is broad and genuine and Pippin noticeably relaxes. Skyler scurries away like she's been caught at something.

"Pippin Fightmaster, I presume," the man says, which makes Pippin smile.

"Hi Mr. Lauritson."

I step to the side to let the judge have a good look at Pippin's volcano. He asks several questions—all of which Pippin answers thoroughly and articulately—then nods his approval.

"I'm proud of you, Pippin," Mr. Lauritson says.

"Do you think I'll qualify for state?" Pippin asks, and the sadness in her voice makes me have to work very hard not to hate that Skyler girl.

"I'll have to meet with the other judges to make it official," he says. "But just between you and me, you're definitely qualifying for state. The top three go, and with this score," he says, tapping a pencil to his clipboard, "you'll be at least third. Probably second."

Pippin glances over at Skyler's table and begins blinking furiously again. "Who's going to get first?"

Mr. Lauritson's gaze follows Pippin's and the slouch in his shoulders suggests two things: that Skyler will win first place, and that Mr. Lauritson isn't any more of a fan of that than Pippin is.

"She didn't even do her own work," Pippin says. "Her parents did the entire thing for her."

Mr. Lauritson looks like the effort to swallow his words is physically taxing him. "Well, it's true that I've never seen a seventh grader do work like that, especially one with her grades. But I can hardly go around accusing someone without proof."

Pippin's slouch mimics her teacher's. "Is there any chance I'll be able to beat her at state?"

Mr. Lauritson studies Pippin's project, as if desperately trying to discover a way in which she could overcome Skyler at the state science fair.

"To be honest, Pippin, I think next year you should be more daring. You're the smartest kid in class. Maybe the smartest I've ever taught." He pauses, as if trying to decide how to proceed. "If you don't mind my asking, what made you decide to do your project on a volcano?"

"Skyler told me she thought I should do volcanoes. That I'd have a good chance to win if I did it really well. She said judges love volcanoes."

Something flashes in Mr. Lauritson's eyes that mirrors the spark in my chest. "I'm sorry to say that's just not true. The truth is, volcanoes are overdone." He motions to Pippin's project, looking thoroughly impressed. "You've done the best you can do here—a really great job—but I think you need something a little more unique to have a chance to win at the state competition. Something judges don't see every year."

I'm speaking before I even realize it. "Did she qualify for state? Or did her project?"

Mr. Lauritson steps back, surprised by the random question by an unknown man. "This is my brother, Charlie," Pippin says, taking my hand, and Mr. Lauritson's manner immediately softens.

"Yes, I was just telling Pippin, she's qualified for the state science fair in August, which is right here at the school. It'll be official in just a few minutes."

"No," I say. "I mean, is it *her* that qualified, or her project. Like, can she display a different one at state?"

Mr. Lauritson looks thoughtful for a moment. "I guess I'm not sure. I would think she's earned the right to present a different project if she'd like, but I'll have to run it by the rest of the judges. Did you have something in mind?"

I catch Pippin's eye and we grin at each other. "Yep," I say. "Quebracho."

Heckler

A heckler is someone in the stands or on the opposing team who attempts to negatively affect a player's performance through distraction, humor, or insults. Techniques vary widely, but the common theme of all hecklers is the desire to see someone fail and, indeed, to be the cause of the failure.

Chapter 3

Right in the shadow of the 200-bed Mercy Hospital is the most beautiful place in the world. Sweetwater Ballpark. It's a living piece of baseball history, for one. Built in 1920, it arose during Major League Baseball's darkest days. The Black Sox scandal had thrown a dark cloud over the entire game, professional and amateur alike. It was as if Joe Jackson and his crew had cast doubt into every game, from the sandlot on up. The Babe was twenty-five years-old and a seasoned Major Leaguer, but had yet to become the Sultan of Swat.

But while the big leagues floundered, places like Youngstown, Pennsylvania, Pearl, Mississippi, and Sweetwater, Minnesota kept the game alive. Here, in Sweetwater, where fans never left the game, they built a one-thousand person capacity stadium, fielded two town-teams because so many young men wanted to play, and even became one of the first stadiums in the state to host games under the lights.

But even if Sweetwater didn't have any of that history, it would always have one thing no one else can claim as their own: Mr. 500. Seville "Bud" Crawford.

I pass through a gate decorated on either side with framed jerseys sporting Crawford's number 14, retired so no one in the state of Minnesota amateur baseball will wear it again.

I'm still not sure about this decision to attend a town-team practice, but I sling my Rawlings bag over my shoulder and walk onto the field and into the glow of stadium lights. It's only been three days since I last stood beneath lights like these, but I've missed it more than I thought possible. It takes some restraint to stop myself from kneeling down and kissing the beautiful infield dirt.

"Well, if it isn't Charlie Fightmaster."

I turn around, see Duane Jones, and cringe. This is exactly why I wanted nothing to do with this team. Duane was on my high school team — and he hadn't been any good then. If this is the kind of player my dad is putting in the line-up, I'll look bad just being in the same uniform. Not to mention, Duane has hated me ever since I took his spot during my sophomore year in high school. He was a senior at the time and made no secret of the fact that being banished to right field because of a younger kid made us mortal enemies.

"The legend returns home in all his glory," Duane says. "After a remarkable professional career." He moves two fingers almost together. "Oh so close to making the majors. But not quite."

I want to tell him about the offer from the Twins and how I turned it down, but can't figure out a way to do it that won't come off as insecure. The last thing I need is for Duane to smell weakness. "Well, we can't all be insurance salesmen," I say. I slap his shoulder a little harder than necessary. "Some of us have to travel the country playing the game we love."

Duane seems to flinch, almost as if I hit him. "Still an arrogant prick, I see," he says.

It's easier to let the comment go when I notice the wad of gum, blown into a large bubble, bouncing from the top of Duane's hat as he struts away, unaware.

I climb down the three concrete steps into the dugout, throw my bag onto the bench, and am greeted by three pairs of wide, awe-struck eyes. Kids, they seem like, although they must be in college. Probably home for the summer because this league is better than any wood-bat league their college coaches could put them in. It's not pro ball, but the truth is this league isn't bad.

"You guys responsible for the bubble?" I say. Their eyes widen even more and each points to the other. "I've always preferred pine tar in the glove. You might want to give it a try next time."

The three college kids burst into laughter, hooting and hollering like they've been waiting for this moment for a long time.

"Where's this Raimel kid?" I ask.

"Where he always is," one of the kids says. "Working on the tee." He flicks his head in the direction of right field.

I leave the dugout and pace along the right field line, making sure not to let my spikes touch the chalk. I allow myself a peek at the grandstand, but no one's there. I wonder if my dad exaggerated about the scouts to get me to the ballpark. If so, mine will be the shortest career in Sweetwater Stallions storied history.

I follow the crack of a bat that echoes through the empty stadium every few seconds. In the bullpen, a tall, lean kid smacks the baseball off a batting tee and into a net, then pulls another ball from a white bucket and places it on the tee. He repeats the process over and over, adjusting his stance to put the ball further back in his swing, then more out front.

I watch silently for a while, noticing the quick, quiet hands and the taut, powerful legs. I study the subtle weight shift and the long, arching follow-through, searching for a flaw. There's nothing. Whereas my swing has always been short and quick — intentionally so, as a way to hit a 95 mile-an-hour fastball — this kid has one of those long, flowing swings that make it look like he'll never get the barrel through the hitting zone until suddenly, miraculously, he does. It's as if none of the rules apply. The kid's swing is one of the prettiest I've seen in person. Which is startling, since he can't be more than seventeen.

I wait, watching and studying, until finally he hits a ball with slightly less than perfect precision.

"Stay behind that now," I say, walking up to him and placing a new ball on the tee. "Keep your hands inside it. You understand?"

"Yes, sir," Raimel says. He has a lean jaw and eyes that seem to study everything around him. "I got out front." The Spanish accent is thick and I wonder how long he's been in Sweetwater. And with a swing like this, how long he'll stay.

"Just a little," I say. Actually, I hadn't noticed him get out in front of the ball at all. And I wonder if he knows it and is helping me save face.

"I hear you've got the scouts drooling."

Raimel nods and for the first time, his studious eyes look at the dirt as he swipes his spikes. "They make me nervous. I sometimes wish they weren't here."

I look around. "They're not here now."

"They're always here," Raimel says, and uses his chin to point toward the parking lot.

I follow his gesture and notice some movement in the gravel parking lot. A large tented area is set up, occupied by dozens of old men wearing a variety of colors on their hats and eating hot dogs from the concession stand.

"Wow," I say. "Those are all big league scouts?"

"The one from the Cardinals is the nicest. But the Dodgers guy says they'll offer me the most money."

I try not to make it obvious that I'm watching the scouts. So many old men and stop watches and radar guns. I've never seen so many scouts in one place, even during my senior year in high school. This kid must really have something special.

They chatter among themselves and chew their hot dogs. Some glance over to Raimel at the tee, but there will be plenty of time to see what he can really do. Mostly, they appear to tell jokes and spit sunflower seeds.

But one of them, dressed in plain clothes instead of a warm-up jacket or a tee-shirt with the logo of a Major League baseball team spread across the front, sits as still as the early summer air. His head points toward us, but the distance makes it impossible to know what he's looking at.

"I have to hit more," Raimel says. "I have to work hard."

"Sure," I say. More players file into the stadium and the chatter in the dugout grows. In the parking lot, my dad steps out of his rusted car, grabs a bucket of baseballs from the trunk, and waves to the scouts on his way by as if their presence is completely natural. I guess he wasn't exaggerating.

"I better go help my old man," I say. "You should probably wrap it up soon."

I head back toward the dugout but can't slip the feeling of being watched. I glance back at the tent full of scouts. The old one in plain clothes sits just as still as before, only his head has followed me and remains pointed straight at me.

I fight a shiver and lift my chin in a nod of greeting, but the man doesn't seem to notice. Or if he notices, he ignores me. I can't pin down why the man's stare is so unsettling, but it is. I touch my pointer-finger to the brim of my cap. Surely the scout will acknowledge a greeting so obvious.

Standing in the shadow of the tent, the old man doesn't appear to move a muscle. It looks like he doesn't even blink as he continues staring straight at me.

· · ·

As I step into the batting cage and kick at the dirt, a flash of red catches my attention and my eyes are drawn to the grandstand. About half way up, Pippin is bouncing and waving at me like she hasn't seen me in years.

It's not something that would have happened in pro ball.

I can't help but grin and give her a little wave, which makes her jump even higher. Then she forces herself to sit down, apparently to watch me take batting practice.

Mack Conroy winds and fires. The red stitches rotate with the slightest counter-clockwise movement. I adjust for the small tailing motion, away to the outer half of the plate, and cock my hands in a backwards "C." I explode my hips open and whip my hands through the strike zone.

The crack of the bat echos through the stadium and the baseball sails into the air. I hold my backswing high over my right shoulder and enjoy watching the ball fly into a cluster of mature maple trees beyond the wooden, advertisement-covered right field wall.

The swing feels good. Three days off were just what my body needed. And having Pippin in the stands feels pretty good, too. I sneak a peek at her expression and it's just what I was hoping for—a mixture of joy and amazement.

Mack grooves another one right in my wheelhouse. I blast it over the wall again, this time to right-center. I know I should stay focused on what I'm doing, but can't help myself. I sneak a glance into the grandstand, this time at a cluster of impressed-looking scouts. It's exactly what I need—to keep the word out that I'm ready for the big leagues, as soon as I'm able to leave Sweetwater. At the very least, the chatter among scouts should keep my Triple-A spot nice and warm.

I turn my attention back to the pitcher's mound, but an old, gravelly voice from the grandstand distracts me. It's impossible to know for sure, but it sounds like it's directed toward me.

"Quit playing around out there," it says.

I step out of the batter's box and look toward the voice, more than anything else to make sure it wasn't talking to me. The plain-clothed old man who stared at me earlier is glaring at me now. I guess I'm staring at him, too, but not aggressively. I'm just trying to figure out if he was the one yelling, if it was directed at me, and if so, why? But I must look at him a little too long because he stands from his seat.

"You got some sort of problem?" he says.

I look away quickly, down to my spikes. I kick the dirt and try to figure out what I ever did to some random, old scout. There was a Diamondbacks scout who tried to get me to sign with them out of high school. They even offered me a few thousand dollars more than the Twins. Maybe he's holding a grudge.

Whoever it is and whatever his problem is, I don't have time for it. So I step back in and try to get refocused. Pippin yells, "Hit another home run, Charlie," and I chuckle. For her, I'd stand here and hit home runs all day, if my body would hold out.

But the good feelings don't last long. As Mack winds up and throws, the same man from before, in the same gruff voice, mutters just loud enough for everyone to hear. "Oh, shut up."

Something flares inside me. I take my eyes off the baseball and immediately find Pippin in the stands. Her entire demeanor changes. Her shoulders slouch, her head bends low, and she's not even watching me anymore. I drop the bat and stomp straight toward the grandstand.

"What'd you say?" I can barely recognize my voice through the fury.

"You heard me," he says.

"Yeah, I heard you. Who were you talking to?"

I expect the man to cower beneath my angry tone, but instead he stands and approaches the netting between him and the playing surface. "None of your business," he says. "Ball players are supposed to play ball, not play cute with the fans."

"That's my sister," I shout, waving my finger somewhere in the direction of Pippin. "And if you just told my little sister to shut up, then —"

" — Then what?" the old man says, stepping right up to the netting. "What are you going to do about it?"

In a flash, my mind conjures several images of Pippin: blinking uncontrollably in front of the popular girls. Looking dejected when her science teacher told her Skyler would likely win the state science fair. And burying her face in my chest when she first saw me, needing me to protect her.

Before I can think to stop myself, I lunge at the man. He's a couple feet above me and on the other side of the netting, but I grab his shirt near the collar. He grabs me right back, wrapping his surprisingly strong hands around my forearms and pulling. I'm shocked at what's happening — both at what I did and at the old man. But my shock doesn't last long.

Something yanks me away and throws me backwards, off the net. I crane my neck to see who has me. It's Mack Conroy. He squeezes my arms in a full-nelson and drags me away. Then he spins me around and shoves me hard toward the dugout, where my father stares at me in amazement. Mack grabs my shoulder and guides me roughly onto the bench.

"You want to tell me what in God's name you're doing out there?"

"Did you hear that guy?" I say. "He told Pippin to shut up."

"And he shouldn't have," Mack says. "But you can't go attacking him like that."

"Why? Because he's a scout? I don't care. That doesn't mean he can talk to Pippin like that."

Mack points behind him without seeming to care what direction his finger is aimed. "That's no scout out there."

For a reason I can't pinpoint, something like a hole finds its way into my stomach and grows, slowly at first, but then faster, as if feeding on my sense of dread. Then, as if to confirm my worst fears, Mack shakes his head and says, "That man you just attacked? That's the greatest baseball player to ever come out of this state. Son, you just attacked Bud Crawford."

The Slump

A slump is when a baseball player is struggling in one or more aspects of the game, although it typically refers to a prolonged lack of hitting success. Slumps are inevitable in baseball. Even the best players in the history of the game have experienced slumps.

While in the middle of a slump, it seems to the player that nothing he does turns out right.

Chapter 4

The next morning, I wake up with Mack's words ringing in my head.

Son, you just attacked Bud Crawford.

Bud Crawford. The one and only Bud Crawford. The biggest legend in Sweetwater. Maybe even the whole state of Minnesota. He wasn't only a Major Leaguer, but an All-Star, until he blew out his arm just after the All-Star break his rookie year, ending his professional career and sending him home to Sweetwater, where he became the most successful amateur player in state history. He hit more than five hundred home runs and became something like a myth to Minnesota baseball fans. And I physically attacked him.

It's hard to regret it too much, though, when I remember why I attacked him.

Pippin.

Somehow, thinking of Pippin makes me think of my mother. It's not something I think of often, since she's been gone for twelve years. I was three days shy of my sixteenth birthday when she left. My dad and I were in the back yard, playing catch and swatting mosquitoes in equal amounts. Pippin was rolling around on a screened-in Pack-N-Play near the house, shaking a rattle and attempting to push herself into a sitting position. The sun disappeared behind the cornfield on the horizon but its rays provided just enough light to see a baseball.

My mother stepped out the sliding glass door that led to the back yard and announced in a voice so small I could barely make it out, that she was leaving. She'd had enough changing diapers and wanted to live a real life while she could. She picked up the blue leather suitcase she shared with my dad and drove off in their recently acquired station wagon.

"Where's she going?" I asked my father.

He stared down the empty road for what felt like a very long time before admitting, "I don't know."

"When will she be home?"

"I don't know, Charlie."

A mosquito buzzed near my ear and I swatted at it. "For dinner?"

She didn't come home for dinner.

For years, we didn't talk about her. Pippin grew up with a father and a near-adult brother. She didn't know it was different from most people until she went to kindergarten. By then, I was gone, playing Single-A ball in the Twins organization. But every time I visited my childhood home, we acted as if my mother could return at any moment. Whoever set the table for dinner put out four plates. When we drove somewhere together, I sat in the back seat with Pippin, leaving the front passenger seat open. It was like we were saving a spot for her in every aspect of our lives, in case she ever decided to return.

"Where'd mom go?" I finally asked, home from Single-A ball one Christmas. I was twenty years-old. Recently, our attempts to keep alive the possibility of her return had lost the hopeful feeling it once had. It had long ago begun to seem childish.

"I don't know," my father said.

"She didn't tell you?"

"She wasn't happy here."

And that became the standard answer any time I asked about her. "She wasn't happy here." I must have heard it a dozen times, but I never dared to ask the next question — Why?

I never asked because I already knew the answer. It was Pippin. By being born — an unplanned pregnancy — she had stolen the freedom our mother saw so close on the horizon of her life. Having a child so late had crushed her dreams and killed her spirit. It wasn't anything Pippin had done. It was simply the fact that she was. That she existed at all.

Eventually, I came to realize my way of thinking had been wrong. Sure, changing diapers and cleaning spit-up was the last straw for my mother, but if I had been a better child, an easier child, she never would have been pushed to the brink to begin with. The picture became clear—my mother's decision to leave wasn't Pippin's fault at all. It was mine. Pippin just suffered the consequences.

For a while, everyone in my life seemed to think I needed their advice. "Hold on to the good memories," a teammate told me. "Don't take it personally," my favorite uncle said. And then, after years had passed and the absence of a Mrs. Fightmaster had become normal to everyone outside the family, people began to tell me to move on with my life. The statute of limitations had run out. My permission to be sad, to question why, to feel her absence in my life, had expired.

I learned to ignore them. I pretended not to hear. I lashed out. People didn't understand where the anger came from. Adolescence, some people said. Others decided it was a manifestation of my supreme arrogance, surely due to my success on the baseball field. But that wasn't it at all.

I'd simply had enough of people talking about my mother, or me, or my father. No one ever talked about Pippin. No one every worried about Pippin. No one thought to stick up for Pippin.

And now, after attacking Bud Crawford, I can't summon any shame. If anything, I'm proud to have gone after him. It was way past time someone stuck up for Pippin.

Thinking of Pippin, I go to her room and nudge her shoulder. "Hey. Want to go get some of that wood you were talking about?"

"Quebracho?" Pippin says, her sleepy eyes widening.

"Whatever you call it. Let's do it."

Pippin pops out of bed, hurriedly brushes her teeth, and grabs an apple from a basket on the counter. Minutes later, we're walking the streets of Sweetwater, toward Edmond's Lumber.

"Have you ever considered how amazing language is?" Pippin asks between bites of apple.

"No, I can't say I've really thought about it," I say, trying to suppress a grin. The kid spends so much time with her nose in a book I'm pretty sure she already has more knowledge swirling around in her brain than I ever will. But to hear a twelve year-old kid use the words she does — and articulate the thoughts she has — is nothing short of amazing.

"I'm not talking about English, Spanish, or Mandarin," Pippin continues. She follows at my elbow, so close I have to keep moving to the edge of the sidewalk so I don't run into her. It's like she wants to walk in the same space as me. I have to admit, I love it.

"I'm talking about how, if you share the same set of words with someone, people are able to shape their lips and tongue a certain way and vibrate their vocal cords and send sound waves through space. Then another person is equipped to take those sounds in, interpret them, and manufacture in their own mind the exact same image you have in your mind. It's like telepathy, if you think about it."

"Huh," I say, scratching my temple in sincere confusion.

After a few more minutes of pretending to understand Pippin's thoughts, we arrive at Edmond's Lumber. The first thing I notice is the smell. It's a swirling rotation of scents, from cedar to maple to cut oak.

We go to the desk and I shake the hand of the man behind the counter. It's rough and calloused, like my own I suppose, but the man's hands are also laced with too many cuts and scars to count. "Hi," I say. "I'm Charlie Fightmaster."

The man smiles through a thick lumberjack beard. "Don't I know it. I'm Mark Edmond's dad."

"From Little League!" I say, remembering the stocky first baseman who was built like a lumberjack even as a kid. "What's he up to these days?"

"Working the forest up in Alaska for a bit. Said he wanted more adventure than we have here. Anyway, I was sorry to hear the news. Today's been a rough day for our Sweetwater Stallions, hasn't it?"

I look at Pippin, who seems just as clueless about what could have happened to my new baseball team in the past eight hours. Have I been suspended for attacking Bud Crawford and not yet heard about it? Or kicked off the team before I even receive a jersey? Turns out, it has nothing to do with me, but it definitely is bad news for the Stallions, and for me.

"You haven't heard?" Mr. Edmond says. "Raimel's gone."

"Gone?" I say. My first thought is of deportation, but it turns out to be much better news — at least for Raimel.

"He went in the third round yesterday, to the Braves. Rumor has it he got a six-figure bonus, signed on the dotted line, and headed out to Rookie Ball this morning. Didn't waste any time, did he?"

Memories from my own draft day flash in my mind. The anticipation of sitting by the phone, waiting for the call. The elation when the Twins took me in the second round. Strange how draft day — one of the best days of my life — continues every year for high school and college kids, but I never think about it anymore. I hadn't even realized it was draft day.

The phone interrupts us and Mr. Edmond puts his finger up to ask for a moment. As he chats with a customer on the phone, I notice Pippin's desperate expression.

"You're going to leave now, aren't you?" she says. "And the Stallions won't have any chance of winning state."

She looks like she's about to cry — which breaks my heart like nothing else can — so I motion to Mr. Edmond that we'll be back and lead her out the front door so we'll have some privacy.

"What's wrong, Pip? Are you seriously that concerned about the Stallions? I thought we decided there are more important things."

"We decided there are two more important things," she says, pouting. "It's still number three."

I try to think of something to say, but come up empty.

"I know you think it's just town ball and it doesn't matter," she says. "I'm not stupid, I get it. But this was supposed to be the year. I've watched them for so long — and dad has coached them for so long. And they've always been middle-of-the-pack. They've only even made the state tournament once since I was born. And this year the state tournament is here at the ballpark. And it could have been different. With you, it still could be. But if you leave…"

I study the agony on her face. I can't pretend to comprehend why an amateur baseball team means so much to her. Sure, she's been the Stallions biggest fan for as long as I can remember, but it still seems like an overreaction.

But then I remember what I should have been thinking all along. That she isn't like me. In her world, maybe how the Stallions do makes a huge difference. Maybe watching them lose can ruin her day, and seeing them win a championship could give her a happiness I'll never be able to understand. And if I'm going to help her with any of the things she says would make her happiest, this one's probably my best shot. Plus, it's not like the Twins have given me a deadline yet.

I wrap my finger under her chin again and look straight into her sad, brown eyes. "I'm not going anywhere right now," I say. "Scouts or no scouts, I'll play with the Stallions until the Twins say I have to go back or lose my contract, okay?"

"When will that be?"

"That's impossible to know. It could be soon, or maybe I'll be here all the way through the state tournament, and I can help the Stallions win it all."

Pippin frowns like she knows she's being appeased, but she wipes her tears and says, "That would be good."

"Now," I say. "Let's go see about this 'kay-brochy 'thing of yours."

"Quebracho," Pippin says through giggles.

Back in the store, Mr. Edmond has hung up the phone and is waiting for us. "So what can I help you two with?"

He addresses the question to Pippin, but she begins blinking quickly and looks away.

"Quebracho," I say, hoping I pronounce it right.

"Ah, so that was your voicemail." Mr. Edmond leans over the desk like their conversation is confidential and speaks to Pippin in a gentle voice. "If you don't mind my asking, what do you need such an exotic wood for?"

I give Pippin a moment to respond, but when it becomes obvious she isn't going to, I speak up before it becomes awkward for her. "She's going to make the best baseball bats in the state."

"Is that right?" Mr. Edmond says. Pippin nods, but doesn't make eye contact. "With quebracho? Now that's one interesting idea. Did you think of that?"

I know he's trying to be friendly, but I wish he'd stop. Pippin seems to tighten more and more—and blink faster and faster—with every question thrown at her. "She's a pretty smart kid," I say. "Is it all right if we pay for it here?"

"Oh, I don't think you understand," Mr. Edmond says. "We don't just happen to have a load of quebracho sitting around in the back."

"You don't?" It's not the first time since returning home that my heart sinks for my sister.

Mr. Edmond shrugs. "Afraid not. Quebracho's not so easy to come by. It only grows in a small region of Argentina and we don't get much of it anywhere in the U.S. But lucky for you, after I got your voicemail I spent some time scouring the interwebs and found a South American distributer who'll ship it here. Not cheap, of course."

"How much does it cost?" Pippin says, finally finding the courage to speak up.

"Well most of it's the shipping, but we're looking at several hundred dollars to get enough for some bats."

I see Pippin's posture deflate. Thinking about my checking account, I can't help but feel the same way. My signing bonus was substantial, but it was also followed by a decade of virtually nothing in the minor leagues. A few hundred bucks would pretty much wipe me clean. "Sorry, Pip-squeak," I say. "We tried."

"I'm sure we can find you a nice, hard wood to make a bat out of," Mr. Edmond says. "Maple's all the rage right now."

"Yeah," Pippin whispers. But instead of asking how much it would cost, she turns and leaves the store without another word.

. . .

I thank Mr. Edmond for his help and run to catch up with Pippin. The tears are back again, meaning I've once again failed my little sister. It's hard to stomach, knowing that I made her articulate her dream about the bats, and then wasn't able to come through for her.

"I know it's disappointing Pip, but like Mr. Edmond says, we can find something almost as good. It'll still be a great science fair project. You can still beat Skyler."

"I don't want almost as good!" Pippin shouts. "And maple won't beat Skyler, because it won't work the same. It's not interlocking, remember? So it'll break, just like you said. I just wanted this one thing to be how it's supposed to be. Nothing else is how it's supposed to be, why can't this one thing be?"

"What are you talking about, Pippin? Things aren't that bad."

"Yes they are! Mom left. You left, and you're going to leave again. No one wants to be my friend. I suck at sports. Daddy's sick. I can't make my bats so I'll never win the science fair. *Nothing's* how it's supposed to be."

I want so badly to comfort her, but I have no idea what to say. Everything she said is true.

"Is he going to die?" she asks.

I hold my breath, as if stopping my breath might stop time as well. Hasn't anyone talked to her about our father's condition? On top of everything else she's dealing with, now she'll have to face this? And no one has bothered to prepare her for it?

More than likely, someone has—our father, I'm sure. But Pippin probably didn't believe it. Not fully, anyway.

"Yeah," I say. "I'm afraid he's going to die."

Pippin nods in that way of hers. Like something clicks into place in her brain with a small bounce, where it's now understood and will be stored for later use. "When?"

When? What, does she expect me to say, *Next Tuesday at 9:47 in the morning?* Then I realize she probably does. With her dizzying vocabulary and uncanny ability to understand concepts I can't even comprehend, it's easy to forget she's just a kid.

"I don't know," I say. "But pretty soon."

"What's soon?"

I purposely haven't thought about it, but now I do. I consider the shadows under his eyes. The loose skin that hangs from his arms. The green veins growing more and more prominent on the tops of his hands. "Maybe a couple months. Or weeks. It's hard to know something like that. Hopefully not until after the season. We want him to see the Stallions win the state championship, right?"

Pippin slouches and looks away from me. I have no idea what to do. My Major League dreams fade a little each day I spend in Sweetwater. Pippin is obviously in a fragile state. My dad is dying of cancer. In fact, there's nothing in my entire life that feels settled. Nothing that feels solid and grounded. I guess Pippin is right. Nothing is how it's supposed to be.

"Tell you what, Pip-squeak," I say. "Give me a few days to see if I can scrounge up some cash, okay?"

"Cash for what?"

"Quebracho," I say, as if the answer should be obvious. "You heard Mr. Edmond. They don't just give the stuff away."

The uncertainty of my life doesn't change in the next moment, and our problems aren't suddenly solved. But for just a second, the light from Pippin's smile makes the world feel like a slightly better place.

•   •   •

I step into the dugout of Sweetwater Ballpark, unnaturally nervous for my first game with the Stallions. The last time I heard my metal spikes clink against the dugout cement, Mack had told me I'd physically attacked the biggest baseball legend in Minnesota history, and my father had looked on silently while his son made a fool of himself. This time, I'm met with the only thing that could possibly be worse — Emily Conroy.

She sits on the end of the bench, off in her own corner, scribbling something into a notebook on her lap. I can't imagine what she's doing here. Sure, she's Mack's daughter, but that doesn't give her the right to be in the dugout before a game. I need to take off my pants, slip a cup into my sliding shorts, and use a little powder to prevent chaffing. But I sure can't do any of that with Emily in the dugout. As more Stallions saunter in, I keep my head down and wait for Emily to leave.

A boy that looks a little younger than Pippin darts around the dugout, organizing game bats and batting practice bats and weighted warm-up bats. He wears the number "0" and appears to take his job as bat-boy very seriously. I watch him work for a while, impressed by his focus and his routine. After several minutes, Emily still hasn't moved.

The guys on the team mostly act as if she isn't there. A few of them sneak glances to the end of the dugout. Every one of their stares bounces to Emily's tanned legs and hover there long enough to make things uncomfortable. They strip into their sliding shorts with grins on their faces, obviously wanting her to look.

She doesn't. She keeps her eyes planted firmly on her book, continuing to draw or write or whatever she's doing. Finally, I realize she's purposely keeping her eyes down, not planning to leave any time soon. So I quickly get into my uniform. Next time, I'll change at home.

I tie my spikes, pull my cap low over my eyes, and grab my glove, but still Emily hasn't moved. On my way past her, I stop two feet away and slap the pocket of my glove, but I don't look away from the center field wall. Something about her intimidates me, if I'm honest.

"What are you doing here?" I ask.

When she doesn't answer, I can't help but crack a smile. Years ago she did the same thing—waited until I "had the courage" to look at her, as she put it. I give in—it seems I've always given in to her, although I know she doesn't see it that way. And I'm shocked all over again at how much she's changed. Everything but her eyes.

"It's nice to see you, too," she says.

"Sorry. But I don't like distractions at the ballpark. Unlike the rest of these guys, this is my job."

"You're saying I'm a distraction?"

I hate how women know just how to twist a guy's words. "The dugout is kind of a man's place," I say, which sounds more chauvinistic than I intended. "No offense."

"I don't remember you being so sexist."

"Sexism has nothing to do with it."

"No? Then what? You're so attracted to me you're unable to focus?"

I glare at her, using the bill of my hat to hide part of my face because something about facing her makes me uncomfortable. I wish she'd just go away.

"I'm afraid you're going to have to get used to me," she says. "I've been the official scorekeeper for the Stallions for the last three years and I don't intend to stop just because the new hotshot can't handle the presence of a woman."

I shake my head and leave without a word. I jog down the right field line to loosen up. Duane is there, playing catch with someone I don't know. Actually, I don't know most of the players on the Stallions, but that's just fine with me. I'm here for business, and to win a championship for Pippin. That's all.

"Still got a thing for Mack's daughter huh, Fightmaster?"

"Still an ass, eh Duane?"

I go further down the line to warm up in peace. An hour later, just before the game starts, I haven't said another word to a single teammate. I did say "hi" to the bat-boy, who looked up at me with wide eyes and replied with an excited, "Hi Charlie Fightmaster!" And I chatted with my dad briefly about the line-up. My name had been penciled in third, followed by Raimel in the clean-up spot. But both names were crossed out and now I'm fourth and Raimel is off chasing his own Major League dreams. I tell my dad we'll be fine without Raimel, to which he grunts something about "hell of a player."

When the game starts, I'm shocked to feel more butterflies in my stomach than I've had in years. I chalk it up to my desire to play well for my dad and Pippin. I make a nice play in the top of the first, ranging up the middle, spinning, and throwing a strike for the third out of the inning. So far, so good.

In my first at-bat, a tall left-hander seems to pitch around me, which I kind of expected. But if I expected it so much, it's hard to explain why I chase two pitches out of the zone. A high, two-strike fastball with surprising zip somehow gets by me and my first amateur baseball at-bat since high school is an embarrassing strikeout.

"It's okay," the bat-boy says as I restrain myself from throwing the bat. With more outward calm than I feel, I hand it to the boy, who takes it like he's receiving a gift from a prince. A prince who'd just struck out, of course.

They pitch me exactly the same in my second at-bat, and the result is miraculously the same as well. I walk on four pitches in my third at-bat, meaning I have to come up with a hit in my fourth if I don't want to start the inevitable process of obsessing about my hitless at-bats to start the season.

I jump on a first pitch fastball and hit a sharp line drive toward second base. A short, chubby man with a graying beard ranges to his right, but the ball hits off his glove and trickles toward second base. It isn't much, but an infield single could be the start of something big next game, as long as I stay confident. At least, that's the hope.

The five-hitter drives a ball that just clears the left field wall and I trot around the bases. Back in the dugout, I feel a strong desire to keep as much distance as possible from everyone else. I hadn't realized the pressure I'd feel to perform, and when I don't immediately live up to expectations, I'd prefer a hole to crawl into rather than a dugout full of guys wondering if I'm overrated. If maybe Triple-A ball isn't that impressive after all. If, compared to what they lost in Raimel, they received a downgrade.

But the only way to stay away from the guys is to sit next to Emily. Fighting every instinct in my body, I plop next to her and look straight ahead, not inviting conversation.

"It's just the first game," she says. "It'll get better."

I haven't noticed her say a word to anyone all game. Why start now? "One-for-three isn't that bad," I say. It is, of course, when the one hit is an infield single, combined with two strikeouts. And I'm supposed to be the professional.

"You're not one-for-three, you're oh-for-three."

"What are you talking about?" I say, genuinely confused. "I just singled."

She consults her scorecard as if she isn't sure and has to look it up. "No, that was an error on the second baseman."

"No way that was an error!"

Emily's eyes flash, but then she turns her attention back to the field as if the conversation is over. But it's not even close to over, unless she changes the ruling.

"That was the hardest hit ball all day, by either team."

"And directly at the second baseman."

"No, it was to his right."

"A half-step. All he had to do was reach out and catch the ball. But it hit off his glove and rolled away. E-4."

"You have no idea what you're talking about."

"What, you think because you played pro ball you know better than anyone else?"

"No," I say, feeling defensive. "Well, actually, yes. When you play over a hundred games a season, you know the game better than people who play fifty."

Emily rolls her eyes and I wonder how she can make me feel so stupid when I know I'm right. "Have you seen the guys playing pro ball?" she says. "Half of them are only there because they throw ninety or run a six-eight sixty. But they can't play ball and they sure don't know the game."

It's not true. Not in Triple-A, anyway. But she's getting me off the point. "It was a single, and you know it."

"It was an error, Charlie. Deal with it. Or maybe this game is too difficult for you. Maybe you should just run away and leave, like with everything else you've ever done."

She's standing over me now and everyone in the dugout is staring, which is horrifying. A pro ball player, quibbling over an error call in his first game? After striking out twice? As hard as it is, I know I need to let it go.

But then Pippin pops her head into the dugout.

This is all so foreign to me. Women in the dugout. Kids in the dugout. Not to mention failing miserably in my first game. But seeing Pippin shifts something inside me. I want so desperately to impress her, for her to look up to me. Suddenly, the embarrassment is more than I can take.

As Pippin disappears from the dugout, I grab my bag from under the bench, shove my batting gloves into it, and zip it shut. I brush past Emily, feeling her stare on me the whole way, and keep my eyes down as I leave the dugout.

I can't decide which is stronger, my fury or my shame. As my spikes grind against the blacktop of the parking lot, Emily's voice follows me like a taunt.

"The call stands, Charlie. E-4!"

Professional At-Bat

When a team is struggling, base runners can be hard to come by. Often what's needed to get a team back on track — in the absence of home runs, triples, and doubles — is for a hitter to go with a pitch and slap an opposite field single, or to work an 0-2 count into a walk.

These small successes, in the face of adversity, are often called "professional at-bats."

Chapter 5

I sit in the driver's seat of my car for the final inning and a half, trying to rationalize the fact that I walked out on my team. They were up by seven runs. They only had six outs to get. They were going to win no matter what I did. But as the sun disappears below the horizon, the darkness somehow illuminates the truth of the situation. I quit on my team. I left them during the middle of a game. It's something I've never done before—at any level, at any time in my life. What was I thinking?

I shrink down in the seat and pull the brim of my hat low. The game is over and several fans walk by, their voices growing until they're only inches away. I close my eyes and hope no one notices me. I imagine wrapping myself in a sleeping bag, over and over and over until every last bit of light is gone and no one could possibly see me any more than I can see them.

A tense moment later, a car door slams and the fans drive away. Many others follow, and about an hour after I started hiding in my car, several of my teammates haul their bags to their cars and leave.

The lights above the stadium turn dark with an echoing click, and the silhouette of my father hobbles to his car, carrying bags full of bats, balls, and helmets that I should be helping him with. And I would be, if I wasn't too embarrassed to be seen. Soon, my dad's gone too and I'm left alone at the ballpark.

I step out of the car and close the door softly behind me. My spikes click against the blacktop of the parking lot, and then the cement of the dugout.

My gaze lingers on the stadium and the beauty calms me. The immaculate grass, with checkered patterns mowed into a design by

Mack's riding lawn mower. The lights overhead, with the bulbs still illuminated slightly in a darkening shade of red. And the pristine outfield, where the old scoreboard still shows the final score:

Stallions: 10

Millers: 4

Funny. Until this moment, I hadn't even been sure we won.

I make my way to the outfield fence and slip the toe of my spikes into one of the chain-linked slots. I climb to the top, maneuvering my way sideways until I'm even with the scoreboard. It feels almost like Fenway, only in miniature.

A wooden platform sticks out from the scoreboard like a bench, probably used to change the lightbulbs. But it'll work perfectly as a place to sit.

I ease myself onto the wooden slab and lean my back against the warm lightbulbs of the scoreboard. As fireflies dart in the open field outside the stadium, I stare up at the stars and try to come to terms with all that's happened since my return home. Hearing about my dad's illness. Seeing Pippin struggle. Attacking Bud Crawford. And now, walking out on my team.

Before I can get too deep into reflection, someone enters the dugout. From four hundred feet away it's difficult to see who it is but the shape seems too small to be a teammate. I can make out the cursive writing on the front of a baseball uniform. Maybe a kid who just finished his Little League game? On more than one occasion as a kid I came to this field after games to dream about my future at the big ballpark. But this kid, whoever it is, seems to have a purpose. He doesn't go to the pitcher's mound or to home plate, like I did as a kid. He walks straight past second base, charting a direct course toward me.

As moonlight shines on him, I recognize the jersey as a Sweetwater Stallions' jersey and the kid as the Stallions 'bat boy. When he sees me sitting on the scoreboard, he jumps back in surprise. Then he squints and leans his body forward.

"Charlie Fightmaster?" The boy says in a squeaky, surprised voice. "Is that you?"

I duck my eyes under the brim of my hat. Here I am yet again being shown as a fraud. Triple-A players don't do things like sit atop a scoreboard in the middle of the night after a bad game.

But something about the kid's expression is...easy. Certainly there are lines of admiration in his squint, but somehow it comes up short of awe. I'm left with the feeling that I don't have to perform for this kid. That if I'm sitting atop a scoreboard in the middle of a dark baseball field, then sitting atop a scoreboard in the middle of a dark baseball field must be a reasonable thing to do. Maybe even a brilliant thing to do. After all, the peacefulness that surrounds the ballpark seems to overpower my numerous problems. At least for the moment.

A rattle of chain-linked fence reminds me I didn't respond to the boy. But he's unfazed, and climbing. I shift over to make room.

"Some kids on my team said you could have played for the Twins, but you chose the Stallions instead," he says, and sits right next to me. "Is that true?"

"Well—"

"It makes sense to me," he says, cutting off what was going to be a long explanation of why someone might give up such an opportunity. "I made my fourth grade Majors team, but the Minors team plays more games because none of the kids play on the club team, too. So I'm playing Minors just so I can play more games."

It's strange that both this kid and I gave up our own version of the "Majors," although for very different reasons. Again, he's unfazed by my silence and continues as if we're having a two-way conversation. "The best thing about the Major Leagues is that you get to play almost every day," he says. "But the best part about being a Stallion is that you get to play a lot and...well, you're a Stallion."

He says the word with complete reverence. Like being a Minnesota Twin couldn't hold a candle to being a Sweetwater Stallion. Before I can correct his misconception, he moves on.

"I'm Oz," he says.

"That's a great name," I say, finally able to get a word in. "My very favorite player growing up was Ozzie Smith."

"Really?" Oz says, his eyes growing to half the size of baseballs. But then his demeanor deflates a bit. "It's not really my name," he says.

"It's just what my mom called me when I was really little." He shrugs. "Some of my friends heard her call me that so they started to do it too."

I nudge him softly with an elbow. It's not something I'd typically do with anyone other than Pippin, but something about this kid reminds me of her. "It's still a cool name," I say.

The left side of Oz's lips crinkle into a bashful smile. "So anyway, what are you doing here?"

I look up at the stars, unsure what the honest answer is. "Who knows," I say. "All I know is my sister's struggling, my dad is sick, and I went hitless after I attacked Minnesota's greatest living legend." I laugh at my own words. "So I'm here. I guess that doesn't make much sense, does it?"

"Make sense to me," Oz says. "I mean there's no better place in the whole wide world than a baseball field, is there? If I could, I'd live here all the time." He points toward the dugout with a big grin on his face as he imagines his perfect world. "I'd bring a sleeping bag and a pillow and curl up in a corner of the dugout where there's not too much tobacco spit. And I'd buy all my food from the concession stand and eat hotdogs and crackerjacks and drink Pepsi. And I'd watch every single baseball game I wasn't playing in. But I'd play in every one they let me."

I like the kid's style. It's definitely a nice picture, but certainly one that could only come from the mind of a child. "You mean you would be a bum."

"Yeah," Oz says, laughing. "A baseball bum."

"Tell you what," I say. "If you ever become a real baseball bum you let me know. I'll stop by sometime with my baseball card collection and we can stay up all night looking at the stats of our favorite players. We'll break into the concession stand and eat all the popcorn. If you don't tell your parents I might even let you have a sip of my beer."

Oz's face lights up like I just told him I'd take him to Disney World. "Can I get drunk?"

"What?" I nudge him a little harder than the last time. "What kind of question is that? I take it back. No beer for you. Geez."

Our laughter echoes through the ballpark, mingling with the chirping of the crickets.

• • •

The next morning, I sit in my dad's recliner eating a bowl of oatmeal and watching SportsCenter. Something about the highlights make me feel isolated. In the past, I've always known that if I made an especially spectacular play that day, there was a chance it might run on SportsCenter.

I never made it myself, but a couple of my old teammates did. And, of course, Hudson White was a nightly fixture, especially once he was brought up. He made the American League All-Star team for the third time last season, and the media seems to have appointed him the face of the Twins organization. It's not always easy to admit, but Hudson has achieved everything I've always wished for myself. Success, fame, and fortune.

On the TV, a rookie for the Padres hits a single up the middle in his first major league at-bat. Then the screen cuts to a shot of him after the game, up in the stands, hugging an older man that is probably his father. The fire in my chest reminds me of how desperately I want that for myself. Without thinking, I slam my fist down on the remote control and the television flicks off.

"Morning," my father's voice calls from the kitchen. He limps into the three-season porch with a cup of coffee, the bags under his eyes looking especially dark. "Didn't like what was on?"

"Just not feeling like watching TV, I guess," I say.

My dad eases into the chair beside me. "Want to talk about the game last night?"

I stuff a bite of oatmeal into my mouth. What can I possibly say? That my stats matter more than they should because I'm worried about what Pippin will think of me if I don't play well? Or maybe I should go all the way and explain that my mother's leaving created an irrational anxiety that I need to make the Major Leagues to guarantee my father's love. "Not really," I say instead. "I'm pretty embarrassed about it, I guess."

"Well that's good," my father says lightheartedly. "If you weren't, that would be a problem." After a few moments during which I can't figure out how to respond, he says, "Not off to the start you were hoping for around here, are you?"

It's not an attack, simply an observation. I fought with a baseball legend and walked out on my team. Anything other than acknowledgement that things haven't started well would be disingenuous.

"It won't happen again, dad. I promise. None of it."

He nods, as if the word of his son is all he needs to be satisfied.

I study my father. His eyes are sallow and his skin is almost yellow. It looks like his hair has thinned since last night, even though he's not on chemo.

Can I get you anything?" I say. "I could make an omelet."

"No. I'm okay."

"You sure? Want me to run out and get something decent?"

"No, no. I just need to rest."

I get up and adjust the pillows behind his head. Then I pull the television closer to the chair. "Is that all right? Can you see it okay?"

"Fine, Charlie. It's fine."

"Okay," I say. I rack my brain for anything else I can do for him, but I come up empty. "I'm going to hit the shower then. Get some ice on my knees."

My father nods, but he's already mostly asleep. I make a decision to stop by the pharmacy after I get cleaned up. See if I can get some pain killers for him. Or maybe it's better to take him to the doctor? I just wish I knew knew what I'm supposed to do. I should probably figure that out. Make more of a plan for how to care for him.

I shower quickly and make plans to work out later. I throw on some sweat pants and a sweatshirt and scrub my hair dry, then rejoin my father on the three-season porch. SportsCenter is back on and my father is awake, but not paying it any attention. He softly touches the screen of his cell phone as if ending a call, then sets it down, looking perplexed.

"Who was that?" I ask.

"On the phone?"

"Yeah." It's such a strange expression on his face. Something along the lines of bewilderment.

"Bud Crawford," he says.

For a long moment, I can't move a muscle. Bud Crawford? If Crawford wasn't an old man, I'd think he was calling to set up some sort of a duel. *Meet me out back in ten minutes and we'll settle this like men.* And thinking back on what he said at the ballpark—to me and to Pippin—I just might accept.

"It surprised me, too," my father says. "Don't think I've ever talked to him. Never had a conversation, anyway. Of course, I know him, like everyone. Saw him play when I was a boy. I've still never seen anyone hit a baseball like that man."

"What did he want?" I ask. I try to keep the bitterness out of my voice, but fail miserably.

My father stares at me like he's seeing me for the first time. "He says he wanted to help you hit better."

$$\bullet \qquad \bullet \qquad \bullet$$

Bud Crawford wants to help me hit better.

The Sweetwater legend, the former Major Leaguer, the man I attacked, wants to help me? I wonder what I'll walk into if I actually go to Bud Crawford's house. Maybe an array of booby-traps? Or will the old man sabotage my hitting by telling me a bunch of things he knows will backfire? Either way, I have no intention of finding out.

"Are you going to meet him?" my father asks, as if reading my mind.

"You do remember what happened, right? At the ballpark? I don't think Bud Crawford's a big fan of mine, and I'm certainly no fan of his. If he called and told you he wants to help me, something's up."

"Oh, I don't know," my father says. "Maybe he just wants to help. People can forgive, you know."

There's a twinge in my chest at the look he gives me. I don't know if he's saying I need to forgive or be forgiven. Personally, I think it's the former. "I'll think about it," I say. "But right now, I have to run. Anything you want?"

"What, you're going to grant an old man his dying wish?"

"No," I say. "A living wish. You're not dying."

"Dead? No," my father says. He covers my hand with his. "But dying? We both know that's true."

I give a reluctant smile. "Fine. So what's your wish."

"I've got two."

"What? You get one. What kind of dying wish do you think this is?" I enjoy the crinkled smile that reaches his eyes. Something about bantering with him makes him seem healthy, if only momentarily. Or at least alive. "Fine. Two wishes. Name them."

"Good," my father says, sitting up a bit straighter. "One. Meet with Bud Crawford. I heard what he said to Pippin and I didn't like it either. But he's been through a lot in his life. And he's an old man, he's not going to kill you. Besides, if he really does want to help you?" His expression tells me everything I need to know. If *the* Bud Crawford is actually offering help, I'd have to be a special kind of idiot to turn it down.

"Fine," I say. "And number two?"

"Take Emily Conroy out sometime."

"Seriously? What is it with you and that girl? I haven't seen her since we were kids. And besides, she hates me more than Bud Crawford does."

"She doesn't hate you. She feels strongly about you."

"Exactly. She hates me."

"That's not what I said. And here's your chance."

I hear footsteps behind us and smell Emily's perfume. I'm assuming my elevated heart rate is due to anticipation of an argument. Certainly not something else.

"Sorry to barge in," she says. "But I've been knocking for a while." She looks right at me and says, "Bud asked me to bring you over."

"How did you know I was going to see Bud?" I ask. "I didn't even know until ten seconds ago." When Emily doesn't answer, I throw my hands up. "Fine. But you two are freaking me out, you know that?"

I kiss the top of my father's head, but then feel a bit self-conscious about it, realizing Emily is here. Emily's gaze lingers on the spot I kissed my father, looking slightly confused.

"Mr. Fightmaster," she finally says. "How are you feeling?"

My father looks from me to Emily and he smiles. "A bit tired today," he says, and it pains me to see how much effort it takes to make the words. "Do you know what Bud Crawford wants to tell Charlie?"

"In theory," Emily says, looking uncomfortable. "But he didn't want me to say anything. He's kind of protective of his ideas."

"Well, you two kids go have fun. I'll be here if you need me."

"Sure, dad," I say. "If we need someone to get a ball out of the tree or maybe help moving the couch, we'll come for you."

"You do that."

I kiss his head again and lead Emily out into the sunshine, giving her plenty of space. As we walk toward Bud's house, I try to figure out how to act. Before returning home, it had been years since I'd seen Emily Conroy, and if the way she looks at me is any indication, she hasn't exactly missed me. But I'd like to be back on better terms with her and not just because of my father's wish. Also not just because she turned out to be stunningly beautiful — well, I don't think it's just because of that.

"I'm sorry about my little fit last night," I say, unable to look at her. "About the error."

She lets the apology linger for a while before nodding, but her voice is tight. "Apology accepted."

"Wow," I say. "Not exactly a warm response." It felt like a big concession to say that, and her answer was along the lines of, *Whatever.*

"What do you want me to say, Charlie?" she says, with more anger in her voice than I expected. "That I'm still mad at you after a full decade? Fine. I know it's silly and trivial and not very forgiving of me, but I'm still mad at you. Maybe I always will be. You really hurt me, you know."

I swallow hard. "For what it's worth, I'm sorry about everything."

I'm really hoping she'll recognize how genuine my apology is. Maybe she'll show a little understanding. When I'm met with silence, I shake my head in frustration. "Why are you here? If you hate me so much, why are you escorting me to Bud Crawford's?"

"Bud and I are friends. And he asked me to." After a long pause, she seems reluctant when she says, "And I don't hate you, Charlie."

I wait for eye contact, but it doesn't come. "So, what? We'll just have a strictly business relationship?"

Something sparks in Emily's eyes, as if the thought hurts her. I hate how everything I do seems to make her sad. It's a depressing thought and I want to do something about it, especially considering I promised my dad I'd ask her out. But what can I do? After the way I broke up with her as teenagers—insensitively stating that she wasn't good enough for me—what could possibly change things between us?

I decide the best I can do is be myself—as I am now, not how I was at eighteen. I'll try to enjoy her company, and hope it rubs off on her.

"Look, I really am sorry about everything. After ten years, it's pretty easy to see the error of my ways. Get it? The 'error' of my—"

"I get it."

I'm treated to one of Emily's now-familiar glares, but after a moment her expression softens. She even cracks a smile. That's one thing I always used to be able to do—make her laugh.

I figure it's as good a time as any to tackle my father's second wish. "Maybe after we meet with Bud, we could grab a coffee or something," I say. "Catch up a little bit." At Emily's incredulous look, I raise my hands in surrender. "Business only, I swear."

I can still see her face the day I left her, just a sixteen year-old kid. She was so innocent. So young. So hurt. I push the shame aside and smile at her for the first time in more than a decade. The look on her face is guarded, and I'm probably about to be shot down again. But finally, a small crack appears in her stoic expression.

"Business only," she says.

Hidden Ball Trick

Baseball has always been a game of deception. One of the most famous methods of deception, if one of the least used, is the Hidden Ball Trick. One common hidden ball trick occurs with a runner on first base. The pitcher attempts a pick-off and while the runner is brushing off the dirt from his uniform, the first baseman fakes a return throw to the pitcher. While the pitcher pretends to prepare for the next pitch, the base runner takes his lead. The first basemen, who still has the ball, then tags him out.

As with any deception, the basis of the Hidden Ball Trick is the withholding of information.

Chapter 6

I seriously can't believe I'm walking up to Bud Crawford's door. After what he said — and what I did — it's like I'm walking into the lion's den. But even if I could put aside our initial meeting — which I can't — why would a baseball legend like Crawford want to help me anyway? It doesn't make sense.

When Emily knocks on the door of a beat-up ranch-style house, I can't help it. I position myself slightly behind her. Pathetic or not, I don't want to give Bud Crawford a clear shot at me. It sounds like Bud and Emily are friends. Surely he wouldn't go through her to get to me.

Instead of opening the door, Crawford's craggy voice rattles through the cracks in the frame. "It's unlocked," he says.

Emily twists the chipped doorknob and pushes through the entrance with a loud creak. I'm pretty sure this is a terrible idea, but I take a deep breath and follow a step behind.

The place is unusually dark for the middle of the day. The rooms — kitchen, dining area, living room, and a hallway — are small and compartmentalized and whatever natural light might have entered is blocked by thick curtains, which are pulled together tightly. Apparently, the legendary Bud Crawford is a hermit.

Emily flips on a lamp, which casts a yellow glow over the rooms. Bud Crawford sits at a flimsy table in the dining area, stuffing the last of a rolled up piece of lefse into his mouth. He glares at me as he tips back a glass of milk, chews, and swallows loudly.

"So?" he says, staring at me with those fiery eyes of his. I sure wouldn't have wanted to be a pitcher having to face that scowl. The guy looks half-psycho.

I fight the urge to hide behind Emily again. "So…what?" I say, trying not to feel intimidated. The guy's fifty years older than me, but he still has broad shoulders and wiry muscles in his forearms. And that stare…his eyes are the size of apples, and I swear he hasn't blinked since I got here.

"You wanted to see me," Bud says. "To apologize for being such an ass, I assume."

"Bud," Emily says.

"What?" I say. "You're the one that wanted to see me. You called my dad."

"Because I heard you wanted me to teach you how to hit, as if you could ever learn. And out of respect for Emily—"

"Okay, guys," Emily says, putting her hands up as if trying to calm things down. "It doesn't matter how we got here, we're here right? We might as well make the best of it."

I thought I was pretty brave for coming here, but if Emily flat-out lied to convince us to get in the same room with each other, she's the one with real guts. And yet, here we are. One look at Bud and I can see we're both realizing we've been played. A feeling something like sympathy seems to pass between us, despite the fact that we hate each other.

"Sit," Crawford says. "If I know this woman at all then I know we're going to do this whether we want to or not."

"Thank you," Emily says.

She motions to a chair opposite Bud and I sit cautiously. As Emily takes the chair next to me, I feel Bud's glare like a heated laser and look out the window to avoid it. The old man's voice comes out rough and accusatory, but I'm surprised by the words.

"I was an ass," he says. When I'm too shocked to think of an answer, Bud continues. "The way I acted at the ballpark. And especially what I said to your sister. She didn't deserve that. But I don't deal with people much." Bud nods as if satisfied with his logic.

"Thank you," I say. "I'm sorry I attacked you."

"If you think that was an attack, I should teach you about fighting, not batting."

After a long, awkward silence in which I have no idea what to say, Emily leans forward. "So, Charlie. Are you ready to learn about the secret to hitting?"

I chuckle under my breath because the whole idea of a secret to hitting is ridiculous. To think there's a secret to hitting a baseball that's only been discovered by one person out of the millions who have played the game? Ludicrous. "Look," I say. "If you've got some things that worked well for you, I'm happy to hear about them. But a secret to hitting?"

I let my obvious implication linger.

"Oh, there's a secret to hitting," Bud says, glaring at me again. "There's a secret to hitting as sure as there's tobacco spit on a dugout floor. And it has nothing to do with launch angles or leg kicks or whatever these ballplayers today are doing."

Emily leans forward in her chair, but I slouch back. I'm not going to buy into this mystic drivel without some convincing. "Okay then, let's hear it."

When Bud shoots me another of his legendary glares, Emily puts her hand on Bud's forearm, which seems to calm him immediately. He leans forward in the same way Emily had.

"Perfect harmony," he says. "That's the secret to hitting a baseball."

Bud pauses, as if just uttering those words is sacred. As if anyone who hears them should bow down and pray. It looks like he's having a religious experience and I'd probably break out in laughter if Emily wasn't sitting right beside me, apparently eating this whole thing up.

"Perfect harmony," I say. I don't mean to sound so mocking, but they can't be serious. The old man is claiming there's a secret to hitting — which is the first ludicrous thing of the day — and that the secret has nothing to do with body mechanics or pitch selection or anything else that might actually make sense. No, the secret is "perfect harmony." He might as well have said "feeling the spirt of the baseball within your heart."

Bud's apparently having no trouble reading my thoughts because he looks barely able to stop himself from attacking me on the spot.

"That's right," Bud says. "Perfect harmony. Only someone like you will never find it. You'll stay a Triple-A player for the rest of your career. Or more likely, you'll never again leave Sweetwater."

"You don't know what you're talking about," I say. "I got the call. I could be a Major League baseball player right now, if I wanted to."

"Of course you could," Bud says, obviously not believing a word of it. "And yet here you are. In a tiny town. Playing amateur ball. Makes perfect sense."

"Boys," Emily says, butting in before I can retaliate. "This isn't going to work if you two keep fighting like little kids on the playground."

"It isn't going to work if he doesn't believe it," Bud says.

The air conditioner hums and Bud stuffs another piece of lefse into his mouth, looking like he doesn't much care what happens next.

"All right, fine," I say. "Look, I know all about you, all right? Making it to the big leagues, playing in the All-Star game as a rookie, the arm injury, the amateur ball home run record. Fifty in a season, five-hundred-eight in your career. You're Mr. 500. I get it. It's just that it's hard to be told you're doing something wrong when you've been doing it successfully your whole life."

"That so? You've experienced every bit of success you've ever dreamed of? Couldn't get any better? Then what the hell are you doing in my house?"

"Bud," Emily says again, and raises her eyebrows at him. That's all it takes for the old man to back down. I don't understand where it comes from, but she has some sort of power over Bud, that's for sure. Like she's some kind of sorceress. Of course, I know a thing or two about her sorcery.

"Okay," I say.

Bud sips his tar-black coffee. "Okay what? What exactly are you okay with?"

"I'm saying I'm in."

"No more sarcasm?"

"No more sarcasm."

"And the search for perfect harmony? You done laughing at it?"

"Completely," I say. "Just tell me how to do it, and I'll listen."

Bud shifts in his chair and pulls again from his coffee. "Not *how,*" he says. "Not right away. First, *what.*"

"What?"

"What." Bud leans onto his elbows. "Do you know what hitting is like when you find perfect harmony?"

I shrug. "I figure it's when you're seeing the ball well."

Bud puts his coffee mug down hard. "No, that happens to every schmuck now and again. That's just baseball. But perfect harmony? That's different. It's like an entire world opens up to you. The pitches slow down. The seams tell you exactly how the ball will break, without even having to think about it. You know if it's going to be a ball or a strike as soon as it leaves the pitcher's hand. Your swing happens totally on its own. When you're rounding third base and jogging home, you don't even remember how you got there. When you achieve perfect harmony, the game is easy."

"So it's like being in the zone."

"Being in the zone is part of it. But there's more."

"Look, I've been in the zone," I say. "In double-A ball I once had twelve straight hits, five of them home runs. Trust me, there's nothing more than being in the zone."

Bud shifts his weight, as if trying to think of how he can put it into words. "When you're in the zone, everything works out perfectly, without even trying, right? But with perfect harmony, you get all of that—all the success and the ease and the calm—but you also have that one thing that's so elusive. That one thing every one of us wants, every one of us searches for whether we realize it or not."

Bud closes his eyes and gets that look again—like he's having a religious experience. I let him sit quietly for a long moment before I say," What is it? What do we all want?"

"Peace," Bud says.

"What do you mean?"

Bud glances at Emily, who nods her encouragement. "When you find perfect harmony, you're overwhelmed by the sense that everything is right in the world," Bud says. "That you are who you were meant to be. That you're living the life you were made to live. You can call it Zen or enlightenment or straight-up magic, but the moment you achieve perfect harmony, you're almost a god. You actually touch the divine." He shakes his head, as if still in disbelief. "It's more beautiful than anything you've ever experienced before. Including being in the zone."

"That sounds great," I say. It actually sounds crazier than ever, but I promised to have an open mind." How do I get it?"

"It requires three things," Bud says. "Three steps. You can't skip one and you can't pretend. Today, you'll learn the first. If you master it, I'll tell you the second. If you ever perfect that, maybe you'll hear the third."

"Why don't you just tell me all of them so I can get to work on them?" I hope Bud doesn't pick up on the insolence of my tone.

He stares me down like I'm an opposing pitcher. "Because I'm not convinced you're ready for it. Last thing I need is some punk spreading the secret to hitting around like it's a joke. You could ruin the game for a thousand miles in every direction."

I try really hard to keep my skepticism in check. "Fine," I say. "What's the first one?"

As if on cue, a cloud covers the sun. The rays that had been weakly struggling through the blinds turn nearly dark. Bud takes a deep breath and looks to the ceiling.

"When I was eighteen, this new franchise called the Minnesota Twins offered me a contract. The biggest contract ever put in front of a kid my age. I was the best. I knew it, they knew it, everyone I played against knew it. Soon, the world would know it." A flash crosses Bud's face. Maybe regret, or disappointment. He swallows it with a swig of his coffee. "Before my first minor league game, they announced my name and I got a standing ovation. Thousands of fans had come out to see me. Not the club—they hadn't been getting more than a couple hundred fans per game. No, they came to see me.

"I went hitless in five at-bats. Each worse than the last."

I can't help but think of my first game as a Stallion and again feel a connection to Bud. "You needed confidence," I say. "You lost your swagger after the first at-bat and then you were screwed. That's the first secret, isn't it? Confidence."

"No," Bud says. "It's the opposite of confidence."

Bud stares at me challengingly, as if he's waiting to see if I'll pass the first test. But apparently I'm failing.

"That doesn't make any sense," I say. "Without confidence and swagger and convincing yourself you're better, how can you possibly be successful? How…"

My voice trails off and Bud stays silent. It's like he's waiting for me. But waiting for what? He's here to teach me, not the other way around.

After a few odd, silent moments, I realize he's waiting for me to ask the right question. He wants to make sure I'm listening. That I actually am open to his ideas.

"What's the opposite of confidence?" I finally ask.

Bud nods his approval, like I passed the test. He stares at me again, but not with his angry, intimidating glare. This time, it's a quiet intensity. His voice comes out as a whisper.

"Vulnerability," he says. Then he stands up and leaves the room.

•   •   •

As I leave the dark living room, I mull over Bud's words, hoping repetition will help me understand. But how can vulnerability lead to any kind of success? I've been coached to be confident, to exude a swagger that will intimidate opponents and convince myself of my own superiority. Kind of a fake-it-'till-you-make-it thing. That's what leads to success. Not vulnerability.

Does Bud Crawford think I should tell opposing pitchers that I don't like the ball low and away? That I have a tendency to chase sliders in the dirt when I'm down in the count? The more I think about vulnerability in a baseball player, the more I think Bud Crawford is losing it.

But I agreed to keep an open mind. To give the whole search for "perfect harmony" thing a shot. I just hope I'm not sabotaging my career in the process.

I close the door of Bud's house behind me and follow Emily to the sidewalk. She turns to me and we stand in awkward silence for a moment.

"That was…interesting," I say. We start walking slowly down the sidewalk. "So, how do you know Bud? Did you volunteer at the mental hospital or something?"

"Very funny. He helped me once. And if you let him, he'll help you too."

"To find perfect harmony? Yeah, Bud Crawford just oozes harmony, don't you think?"

"Don't be such a jerk. He's a lot smarter than you know."

"Look at you. You've really bought into this stuff, haven't you? You think there actually is some sort of perfect harmony out there and that we can attain it. What, do we have to stand on our heads and chant to the gods of Mars or something?"

"Don't mock me."

"I'm not mocking you," I say, wondering why I feel such a strong need to resist the ideas so vehemently. "I'm mocking Bud Crawford's apparent insanity."

"Same thing."

"What are you talking about?"

Emily looks straight ahead as she speaks, as if talking to herself. "I know about the search for perfect harmony because I learned it from Bud," Emily says. "Because I was lost. I was depressed. I was borderline suicidal at one point in my life."

"What?" I had no idea Emily ever went through such hard times. Of course, how could I? I've been gone for a decade. "When? Why?"

"When I was sixteen. Because this boy I once knew took my virginity before I was ready, and then told me I wasn't good enough for him and left me with a broken heart."

Oh. I'm pretty sure I know who the boy was.

"I could barely function," Emily says. "I was still a kid, I thought my world was ending, and I had no one to talk to."

"I get it, okay?" I say. "I ruined your life. I'm sorry. What do you want me to do?"

"I don't think you want me to answer that question, Charlie." After we walk several steps, during which I can't find a single thing to say, Emily continues. "Anyway, Bud helped me. Perfect harmony isn't just about hitting a baseball, you know."

As if on cue, the crack of a baseball bat echoes from Sweetwater Ballpark, three blocks away. My gaze lingers on the field while I imagine the high school kids taking batting practice. "So you understand the 'vulnerability 'mumbo-jumbo?"

Emily heaves a deep sigh and, catching myself, I touch her shoulder with as much sincerity as I can. "I'm sorry. It's a habit. I didn't mean it." Emily glares at me out of the corner of her eye, but doesn't scold me this time, so I continue. "I just meant that you know what he's talking about. Because you've talked about it with him before."

She seems to gather her thoughts for several moments. "Vulnerability is about freeing yourself from the fear of failure," she says finally. "When we embrace vulnerability we realize we aren't perfect, that no one is perfect, which means there's no longer any pressure to be perfect. So we can relax and live our lives—or have an at-bat—without having to be perfect, and that takes us one step closer to harmony.

"But you can't fake this, Charlie. It has to be real. That knowledge—that you are vulnerable, that you are able to be defeated, that you are not perfect—has to be real. And if it is, it will transform your swing more than any amount of work on the tee or in the cage ever could. Because you'll be free to fail. The paradox is that the freedom to fail will lead to success."

We walk silently for a long time. Me deep in my thoughts about what Bud and Emily have said. And Emily deep in her own thoughts, although I don't have a clue what they might be. Eventually, we end up walking into a Starbucks, where I order a black coffee and Emily some multi-syllabic exotic-sounding drink I've never heard of. Before I can make fun of her she says, "Don't even think of insulting my coffee. We are not at that level yet."

I hold up my hands in surrender, because she doesn't seem like she's kidding, and back out of the café, coffee in hand. She follows and we walk down to the river.

I know I agreed to "Business only," but I hope Emily might accept a bit more than that. We were friends, after all, once upon a time.

Before ruining things by becoming more than friends. "I heard you finished school," I say, tentatively.

"Three times actually." I'm sure I look pretty confused, so she says, "Since I've seen you last I finished high school, college, and law school."

"Law school? What's a lawyer doing in Sweetwater?"

Emily hides behind her coffee cup, then mumbles something into her drink.

"What was that?" I say, laughing.

She turns on me with a challenging glare. "I said the Stallions. My dad thinks this team could actually do it this year. I know he's just the assistant coach, but that stupid team is still the most important thing in his life."

"Seriously? You stayed in town to keep book for the Stallions?"

"It's been forty-nine years," Emily says. "The last Sweetwater team to win the state title was back in—"

"Bud Crawford's day," I say. "I know. Everybody knows about the woeful Stallions of Sweetwater." Judging from Emily's expression, she doesn't see the humor.

"The team means a lot to the whole town. It's not like the people here have a lot of other things going on."

"All right," I say. "I get it. But seriously, you have a law degree. You can't stay in Sweetwater forever."

Emily kicks at a rock on the sidewalk and watches it roll away. "I know. But I want to be there for my dad. Just for the summer. And actually..."

"What?"

Emily seems more uncomfortable than I've seen her since arriving in Sweetwater. "Well, it's because of your dad too."

"*My* dad?"

"I've known him for a long time," Emily says. "You and I grew up together and he was around. He was always good to me, even after you left. Actually, especially after you left. He's coached the team for a long time now and it would mean a lot to him to win a state championship. He doesn't have much time left and I want to be there for him while I can. Just like you do."

"Yeah but…" I don't know how to say what I'm thinking without sounding insensitive. But it's not her dad. How many people would give up the beginning of a career for a man who was nothing more than her high school boyfriend's father?

Hoping to avoid more conflict, I let it go. "So you'll leave after the state tournament? The end of August or something?"

"Probably."

"Probably? Why the uncertainty? The baseball season will be over. The Stallions of course will be state champions once again, returning to their proper glory." My attempt at humor drifts into the summer air as I say, "And I think it's pretty obvious my dad will be gone by then."

The words jab like an unexpected blow to the stomach. The force of it is surprising, but I try not to let Emily know. I'm still not convinced about the whole vulnerability theory and anyway, I'm not on the baseball field.

"I don't know," Emily says. "It's complicated. Things have changed since you knew me. Things have happened."

"Like what? What could've happened to change a smart, pretty girl into someone who would give up her career for a life in Sweetwater?"

Emily sips her drink so long I wonder if she's ignoring me. Finally, looking into the distance, she says, "I have a son."

"My dad told me," I say. "It surprised me, I have to admit."

"Why? Did you think I wouldn't be able to find a man? Or did you think once the Almighty Charlie Fightmaster had been with a woman she'd never again be tempted by anyone else?"

I try to wrap my mind around it. Emily Conroy, with a kid. I'm on auto pilot. I can't think of anything but standard questions. "How old is he?"

"A couple years younger than Pippin. He turns ten next month."

A bit of vertigo hits me and I put my arms out to steady myself. "I'm not that great at math," I say. "But…correct me if I'm wrong…that couldn't have been long after…"

I'm not going to vocalize my thoughts. But no matter how slowly I speak she's not bailing me out. Finally she raises her eyebrows up-and-down twice and says, "You asked what happened to me? Well, you happened, Charlie. Just before you left town, if you remember."

There's no misinterpreting her meaning, which is completely insane. "Oh no," I say.

"Oh no? Are you serious? I tell you you have a son and all you can say is 'oh no'?"

My mind is scrambling for traction. There are so many things I want to ask. "What's his name?"

"His name is Eli. But when he was a baby, when I had just delivered him and was still head-over-heels in love with a boy named Charlie, who had used me and cut me loose, I gave him a nickname that I thought that boy would like. That's what he goes by."

I knew the boy's eyes looked too familiar to be coincidental. But what I hadn't allowed myself to consider under the darkened lights of the baseball stadium now refuses to be denied.

"It started out as The Wizard," Emily says. "After Ozzie Smith. But for years now he's been known as Oz."

• • •

Oz is my son.

I have a kid.

I'm a father.

I have been for years and I've never known it.

Thoughts bombard me as I struggle to wrap my mind around what Emily just said. She looks at me cautiously, as if she planned out how and when to tell me but didn't know how it would go.

"Do you need some time?" she asks, studying me as if I might explode, or maybe melt down.

"Yeah," I say. "Just, give me a moment."

I sit on a bench facing the river and watch the ripples in the slowly drifting current. I sip coffee and try to imagine myself as a father. My father as a grandfather. All this time...

"Does my dad know?"

"He does." Emily's voice is tentative, unsure. Her anger is gone, for the moment.

My thoughts continue to swarm. This explains my father's strange desire for me to take Emily out. And her presence around the house. "And he never told me? You never told me?"

"I was going to tell you, Charlie."

"When?"

"What, you want the exact date?"

"Yeah, if you were really going to tell me, it would probably be pretty memorable, wouldn't it?"

"Oh, it was memorable all right."

"Fine," I say. I'm not sure why I keep challenging her. Maybe I just want to get some of the blame off myself. "Then when was it? When were you going to tell me I'm a father?"

She turns and looks me squarely in the eye. "Friday, May 14th."

I recoil, stunned. Suddenly, it all makes sense. The reason she didn't tell me she was pregnant. Her enduring anger at me. Now I get it.

"See?" she says, watching my reaction. "That dress I spent all my babysitting money on. The roses I bought for you. It wasn't going to be just another birthday for you. I was going to tell you that night. Until…"

Her voice fades and she puts her hand out, palm up. Not an invitation for me to take her hand; an invitation for me to finish her thought.

"Until I broke up with you," I say.

"Yeah. Great timing. I certainly wasn't going to tell some guy who didn't think I was good enough for him that he was stuck with me for the rest of his life."

"I'm sorry I said you weren't good enough for me. I was young and stupid and arrogant. But how was I supposed to know you were pregnant? I was a high school kid breaking up with his girlfriend, that's all. It doesn't exactly make me evil, you know."

Emily heaves a long, deep sigh. "I know. It just…it just sucked, Charlie. The whole thing just sucked."

"You still could have told me."

"Yeah, and then you'd get to decide between staying with a girl you didn't want to be with even before you knocked her up – getting more resentful every day because I kept you from your dream – or going to play baseball and having to feel guilty the whole time about leaving your pregnant girlfriend. Ex-girlfriend, actually, since you'd already broken up with me. Not exactly great options." She takes a deep breath, as if consciously pulling away from her anger. "When I put it like that to your dad, he agreed not to tell you."

"When was that? How long has he known?"

Emily stares at the river. "Since before Oz was born."

I breathe out a giant sigh and rub my face hard. "So that's why you've stayed," I say. "This is a lot, Emily. I mean this...I have a son."

"I know. And I'm sorry. But he's an amazing kid, Charlie. You're going to love him so much."

I think back to the only night I've spent any time with my son, on the scoreboard after my first game as a Sweetwater Stallion. I felt comfortable around Oz — inexplicably so. And we laughed. We connected right away.

"Does Oz know?"

"No," Emily says. "For a long time, he didn't seem to care that much. He had me, he had my dad, and he had your dad, although he still doesn't know your dad is his grandpa. It just was what it was. But recently, he's been asking questions."

"I bet he has." I lean my elbows onto my knees and stare at the river running by. "How should we tell him?"

"Tell who?"

"Oz. We obviously need to tell him I'm his father, but how should we—"

"I don't think that's obvious at all," Emily says. "In fact, I don't think we should tell him. Not until he's ready."

"But you just said he's been asking questions."

"He has."

After a long pause, it becomes clear Emily isn't going to expand on her answer. "And you just told me the truth. Why would you tell me and then make me keep it a secret?"

"I don't know, okay Charlie! I've never done this before. I just thought you were adult enough to know the truth, and you had a right to know."

"Seems like Oz does, too."

"Of course he does. When he's ready. Charlie, you don't get to come in and start making decisions like this. You haven't been parenting him for the past ten years."

"That's because I didn't even know he existed!"

I take a deep breath to calm myself. So many thoughts bombard my mind. As I play the situation out, I realize Emily might be right not to tell Oz. What would happen when I leave town again? Then I'll really be a dead-beat dad. I take a deep breath and continue in a softer tone. "What am I supposed to do here? What's your plan?"

"I don't have a plan, Charlie. I don't know the right thing to do either. But like I said, Oz is asking questions. Or maybe it's more accurate to say he's not accepting my vague answers anymore." She tosses her hands in surrender. "I'm dealing with this in the moment, just like you are. I'm just telling you, that's all."

I definitely need some time to digest the news — both that I have a son and that I'm not allowed to reveal myself to him. While I'm trying to wrap my mind around the idea, another question comes to mind.

"I don't get it," I say. "If I have a son here, then even if we're not together you'd want me to stay around and be a father to him — after I'm allowed to tell him, anyway. Right?"

"I suppose," Emily says.

"So what's up with the Bud Crawford stuff? Why would you want me to learn this secret to perfect harmony or whatever, if it might help me get back into pro ball? That would mean leaving again, you know that right? So why try to help me?"

Emily just shrugs. "I have my reasons."

"Okay." I stare at the river a while longer, searching for answers that don't come. I'm starting to realize I might have to learn to live without answers to all my questions. "Okay," I repeat.

"Come on," Emily says, standing from the bench. "We'd better tell your dad that you know."

•   •   •

My dad isn't in his normal spot. Rather than watching a Twins game or highlights on SportsCenter, we find him outside the house, pulling weeds from a patch of raspberries. But instead of bending over or kneeling, his weakness has relegated him to lying on his side in the dirt, pulling thistles and dropping them into a bucket set up next to him. When he sees Emily and me approach, he sits up — slowly and painfully, I notice — and studies my expression more closely than normal. "Looks like something's up."

I resist the temptation to help him up, knowing that doing so would hurt his sense of independence. "You're looking at your new shortstop. That's what's up." When my father struggles to stand, I can't watch anymore — I rush forward and help him.

My father smiles, but cocks his head sideways. "I thought you already were my shortstop. When you weren't too busy picking fights or walking out on your team."

The words are harsh, but they're said with crinkles at the sides of his eyes. I wipe some dirt off his shirt. "I was expecting something more along the lines of, 'That's amazing and we'll set up a fundraiser so we can give you the signing bonus you deserve, 'but I guess what you said works too."

The crinkles in my father's eyes turn into a full-fledged smile and he hugs me, getting dirt on my pants and shirt. "So you'll stay?" he says, as if suddenly afraid he misunderstood. "Until the end of the summer, at least?"

"That's the plan," I say. I glance at Emily, whose expression I would interpret as happiness, if I didn't know better. "I'll have to talk to the Twins and figure out what to do at that point, but for now, I'm here to play ball, for the Stallions."

My father pats my shoulder, as if he can't get enough physical contact. "That's great, Charlie. Really great. What made you change your mind?"

I shrug, like nothing on my list is of great importance. "You're here I guess, with this cancer thing going on. And Pippin wants me to make some sort of super-bat with her, she's been on me about staying. Then there's Bud Crawford, of all people, wanting to teach me some mystic crap about perfect harmony." My father watches me closely, as if trying to decipher if there might be one more reason to stay. "Oh yeah," I say. "And my son lives here. There's that little detail."

Emily shakes her head. "Of all the ways to tell him," she says. But even she's struggling to hold back a grin.

Until that moment, I figured there was a remote possibility that Emily was playing a joke on me. Maybe trying to get back at me, in some messed up way, for what I did to her all those years ago. But when I see the color in my father's face return, I know it's no joke.

"This has been one interesting day," I say.

Bench Coach

In addition to the manager, pitching coach, and hitting coach, many teams have a bench coach. Responsibilities include assisting with decision-making, communication, and scouting.

But maybe more than anything else, it's the responsibility of a bench coach to foster a positive attitude in the dugout.

Chapter 7

Shortly after talking to my father, I lean against the front desk at the lumberyard, filling out an application. I'm not sure how much help I'll be at making Pippin's bat, but she says the things that would make her feel the best are to make this bat and to win the science fair, and neither of those can happen if I don't figure out a way to pay for that wood.

I've never really thought about it before, but I have no work history, except for professional baseball, which doesn't translate very well into the real world. So I apply for an entry-level job, taking in shipments of wood, operating a forklift, and organizing the wood in the giant back room.

When Mr. Edmond arrives and sees me handing the application to the woman behind the desk, he clasps my shoulder and says, "You're needing a job?"

"Yeah. Looks like I'm sticking around for a bit and Pippin really wants that slab of quebracho, which means I need to make some money."

"Well," Mr. Edmond says. "I've got good news on two fronts. First, the job is open, no one in town seems to want it, and I have no doubt that someone who can make it to Triple-A baseball has good work ethic. So if you want it, you're hired."

"That's great," I say. "I'll take it."

"And the second one is even more exciting," Mr. Edmond says. "When I saw how disappointed your kid sister was when she found out how much quebracho costs, I did some digging. Turns out there's an outfit down south that grows it for construction. They're willing to ship it up here at a fraction of the cost, since it's domestic."

"That's amazing. I can't wait to tell Pippin."

"And I tell you what. If you'd like, I'll give you an advance on your first paycheck and get an order filled so you two can start working on that bat of hers."

I don't know what to say. I stammer a thank you and hope Mr. Edmond can tell how sincere it is.

Mr. Edmond glances at his watch. "It's almost two o'clock. Would you like to start working right now, or wait until Monday?"

The Stallions have a game starting at seven, but I figure I can get a few hours' work in before batting practice. Every dollar makes a difference "Now is great," I say.

Mr. Edmond takes me to the large warehouse area in back and points at various stacks of lumber that need organizing. "It's backbreaking work," Mr. Edmond says. "But it will give you strength. You'll be hitting longer home runs than you've ever dreamed of. It'll be like you're on steroids." He laughs at his own joke, slaps my shoulder, and lets me get to work.

I lift two long slabs of maple from a pile and realize immediately how true Mr. Edmond's words were. My only concern is whether I'll have any energy left after a day of work to play baseball.

The job is monotonous and repetitive, but I don't mind at all. As I execute each motion, each repetition of lifting, carrying, and distributing the slabs of wood, I think about Oz. The reality that I have a son couldn't be crazier. But the more I think about it—and the more I think about Oz—the more I see it as a good kind of crazy.

After what feels like no more than an hour, Mr. Edmond pokes his head into the warehouse and nods his approval.

"Good work," he says, studying my efforts. "It's five o'clock, and I know you have a game tonight, so you can clock out. Oh," he says, as an afterthought. "And you have a visitor."

I walk out of the lumberyard and into the front office, where Pippin waits for me with a paper bag. "I wasn't sure if you'd have time to go home," she says. "So I brought you dinner."

We sit outside in the shade of a maple tree and I peer into the paper bag. I remove a sandwich and take a bite, but it's not the peanut butter and jelly I was expecting.

"What is this?"

"Hummus and Swiss, with tomato and sprouts," she says.

Truth be told, I've never heard of such a thing. I grew up mostly on macaroni and cheese, microwave dinners, and spaghetti. Hamburgers on the grill were my delicacy. But I have to admit, whatever it is Pippin said she made, it's delicious. It makes me realize again how much my little sister has grown.

"There's Brie with the apple slices if you want some," Pippin says, and I just nod rather than admit I have no idea what Brie is.

I'm famished from the hard work and scarf my food down in minutes. Pippin takes her time, savoring every bite, sometimes even with her eyes closed. It hits me how much I enjoy having her around. She doesn't feel like a charity case. Right now, she doesn't even feel like the reason I came back home. She just feels like Pippin.

"You know what," I say. "Why don't you come to the field with me when I go?"

Pippin hesitates longer than I expected. "What would I do?"

"Watch practice. Get to know the players. You could hang out with Oz, he's the batboy." I'm hit with the desire to announce my relationship with Oz, but force myself to keep my mouth shut. "And during the games, maybe you can be an assistant coach, keep pitch-count and stuff." I lean back on my hands. "Actually, I'm surprised you've never joined dad in the dugout before, as big of a fan as you are."

Pippin purses her lips together. "Dad asked once, and I always wanted to, but it's kind of scary. I mean, all those people, and they're all so good at baseball. It's intimidating."

I want to challenge her assessment of some of the players' talents, but I'm sure it would come off as arrogant. My sister, after all, does love the Stallions. "But I'll be there now," I say. "It'll be different."

Pippin's quiet for a moment, scratching her chin and staring blankly at the trunk of the tree. "Do you think dad and Coach Mack would let me?" she asks.

It's a good question. Both men take the team seriously—too seriously, in my opinion. I'm not sure either will be excited to listen to a twelve year-old assistant coach if it's about in-game decisions like whether to change pitchers or send up a pinch-hitter. But if she sits near Emily at the end of the dugout and just keeps track of the pitch count, I can't see any reason why she shouldn't be allowed. Besides, as the team's best player, I have plenty of influence.

"I'm sure I can convince them," I say.

Pippin stares into space, as if visualizing herself in a Stallions uniform. A wide smile spreads across her face, showing her crooked front teeth. She seems energized by the thought, which gives me a surprising jolt of energy too. As if we're connected somehow. Her joy is my joy.

Pippin puts her sandwich down and covers her mouth with her hands, distorting her voice. "And introducing the coaching staff of your Sweetwater Stallions. Assistant Coach, Pitch-Count-Keeper and Expert Bat-Maker, Pippin Fightmaster!"

She dances around like she's just hit a game-winning home run while I cross my ankles, lean back on my elbows, and soak in my sister's joy.

·   ·   ·

A few days later, I finally feel settled in Sweetwater. The leisurely flow of the Stallions' schedule — only three or four games per week — allows plenty of time for my body to recover. And I bounce back from my terrible first game, driving a long home run in each of the next two. My defense, which has always been solid, continues to be strong and it becomes obvious that my teammates look up to me. My father's on the bench — or more accurately, in his recliner. Now, even my little sister is with me in the dugout. When you consider Oz is the bat boy and Emily keeps the scorebook, I don't know whether to love the fact that this is a family affair, or hate that it shows how small-town it all is.

As has become our routine, Pippin and I are eating lunch under the maple tree — more foods I can't pronounce but wholeheartedly approve of — when a delivery truck screeches to a halt in front of the lumberyard and a young man dressed all in blue hops out. As he opens the back of the truck and removes a long, thin package, Pippin's breath catches and she grabs my forearm.

"Pip?" I say, looking down at the death-grip she has on me. "I think you're cutting off circulation."

"Shhh," she says. She stares at the man walking through the front door like she's trying to see through the cardboard casing. A few moments later, the delivery man exits empty-handed and right behind him, Mr. Edmond waves toward us.

Pippin hops up from our spot beneath the tree and bolts to the entrance and through the door. I make a valiant attempt to keep up, but by the time I get inside, Pippin has already torn through the cardboard box and is caressing a large block of deep red wood. Even from a few feet away I catch the drifting scent. It's nutty, with a hint of cocoa.

"It's even more beautiful than I imagined," she says reverently. "Mr. Edmond, can Charlie and I go in back and start on our bat right now?"

I glance at Mr. Edmond, embarrassed for my sister. Her excitement, while certainly cute, leaves a little to be desired in the social-awareness realm. "We should probably take that back home, Pip. We'll have to see if we can find a lathe at the hardware store. And all those other tools you mentioned."

"Everything we need is already here," Pippin says. "Why can't we just make it back in the shop area?"

I cringe and lower my voice, hoping Mr. Edmond won't overhear. "It's not our stuff. We can't just use other people's equipment."

Mr. Edmond, who's watching us with a broad smile, speaks loudly. "Pippin's right," he says. "I don't see why you can't use the equipment here."

"That's very nice of you," I say. "But you don't have to let—."

"Yes, it's really, really nice of you!" Pippin says. "Thank you so much!"

I want to clarify that it's a generous but unnecessary gesture. But before I can get a word in Mr. Edmond says, "You wouldn't be able to work on it until after Charlie's shifts are over, of course."

"That's understandable," Pippin says.

"And of course Charlie has to get back to work soon and there's a game this evening, so you wouldn't be able to start just now."

"Of course," Pippin says, seriously. "Definitely not just now."

"But I think I can trust you two with a key to the place," Mr. Edmond says.

"You sure can!"

I'm completely helpless to do anything about their plans. So finally, I give up. "We really do appreciate it. We'll be sure to lock up on the way out every time."

"Please do," Mr. Edmond says.

Pippin pumps her fist and under her breath I barely hear her say, "Yes!"

Mr. Edmond holds his shoulders back, his good deed done for the day. He pats Pippin on the shoulder. "Well you better let this guy get back to work now. We don't want him getting in trouble with the boss."

"Right," Pippin says. "I'll just put this in back so it's ready for us." She grabs the quebracho and heaves it one step at a time into the warehouse.

"She's quite a kid," Mr. Edmond says when Pippin is out of earshot.

The quebracho log thumps with every step Pippin takes. "You have no idea," I say.

·   ·   ·

That night, things really start to come together for me on the baseball field. I hit two home runs to go along with a single and the Stallions win by seven runs. With my multi-home run game, I'm on pace for one-per-game. There's no way I'll ever approach Bud Crawford's career mark of 500 — I won't be around anywhere near long enough. But even though we're only a few games in, I'm on pace to match his "untouchable" record of 50 home runs in a season.

I can't help but fantasize about it. The pitchers in this league are surprisingly good for amateur ball, but they're nothing compared to what I saw in Triple-A. If I continue seeing the ball well, I have a chance to hit a lot of home runs throughout the course of the summer.

Enough that at the end of the Stallions season—with Pippin feeling more confident and on a better track—I'll get my spot back on the Twins Triple-A team. Maybe even be in position to get another call-up—which I'll definitely accept this time. Who knows, maybe my father will live several more months. If I'm a September call-up, he could even watch me tip my cap from a Major League stadium.

But there are a whole lot of maybe's involved.

The morning after my two-home-run-game, I walk with Pippin and my father to Sweetwater High School, all three of us huddled under a large umbrella. Rain pours down in sheets and thunder cracks right over our heads. The forecast is calling for clearing later, but if this rain keeps up there won't be any baseball today.

The low, brick building of the high school brings back a wave of memories, both good and bad. The actual events I recall don't seem momentous now, but each one is still imbibed with a strength of feeling I've never felt since. There's something about being seventeen that's unlike anything else.

"When can we start working on our bat, Charlie?" Pippin asks as we approach the entrance. "We need to get started on it if it's going to be ready to use this summer."

I study the rain clouds, which look like they're going to stick around for a while. I know how excited Pippin is to start on the bat, and her energy is contagious. I really want to see what this idea of hers turns into. But the rainy day also provides an opportunity I can't pass up.

"There's something I have to do later today," I say. "But I promise we can start tomorrow, okay? It's an early game, so we can do it afterwards."

Pippin looks less than enthusiastic about having to wait another day to start on her quebracho bat, but she manages a small nod.

"Thanks for understanding, Pip," I say, squeezing her shoulder.

We enter the unlocked front doors to the school and shake raindrops from the umbrella. My father looks stronger, a flush painting his cheeks in a way that almost makes me forget his disease, for the moment anyway.

I follow Pippin and my father through the halls and down a flight of old, cracking stairs. When we arrive at a heavy metal door in the depths of the building, my father fishes a keychain out of his pocket. It clinks with a mixture of silver and bronze and I watch my father flip through them. "Always the last one, isn't it," he says, his eyes twinkling as if the fact that he had a hard time finding the key is a funny little joke. He's having a good day, and I enjoy a rare wave of relief.

I watch him closely. His lips turn up slightly into a smile. He has dexterity in his fingers, which so often eludes him these days. And that twinkle. I study it all, trying to sear every detail into my memory.

The door opens with a screeching creak, and only after my dad pushes his shoulder into it twice. A stale smell of old sweat and rusted metal hits us and I follow Pippin and my father into the weight room.

"I know it's probably not what you're used to," my father says. "It's in pretty rough shape, I'm afraid. I don't think anyone uses it anymore. Probably haven't since you were here. But it's all we've got."

"As long as the weights are heavy," I say. I find two rows of dumbbells and lift a fifty pounder from the rack. The rust coats my palms, chalky and red.

"Can we stay and watch?" Pippin says.

"It won't be much to see," I say. "I'll probably just get a quick cardio workout. Maybe throw a few weights around, but with the new job, I don't need much more."

"That's okay," Pippin says. She smacks her palm against an old medicine ball, sending plumes of dust into the air, then sits on it like a bean bag. "We need to talk to dad about my idea for the emblem."

Once again, Pippin is showing her ability to be cunning. "Watch out," I say to my father. "Before you know it she'll have you getting an advance on your paycheck for something or other."

Pippin rolls her eyes and my father winks at me. "What's this emblem all about?" he says.

"Every bat company needs an emblem," Pippin says. "Like, a trade mark. Louisville Slugger has theirs. Axe bats have theirs. And I have an idea for ours."

I hop on a stationary bike and start warming up. "Let's hear it."

My father leans heavily against a squat rack and I continue to watch him carefully. The ebbs and flows of cancer are hard to predict. Pippin starts talking animatedly, swinging her hands around and using her entire body to talk.

"Okay, so picture this. Two baseball bats crossing, and around the bats, a circle in the form of...wait for it...."

She spreads her hands out in front of her as if looking at a Broadway headline and closes her eyes. I lift an eyebrow at my father, who's laughing silently.

"We're waiting," I say when Pippin still hasn't finished her idea.

"Sorry," she says. "It's just too amazing to spoil. Okay. In the shape of...braids!"

"Braids?" I say, pedaling a bit harder on the bike to get my heart rate up.

"Yeah, braids. Like, a girl's hair, you know?"

"On a baseball bat?" I say.

"Oh, no," my father says. "Now you've done it."

Pippin stomps toward me and plants herself, hands on hips, directly in front of the stationary bike.

"You say that like braids shouldn't be on a bat because they're girly. Like you think girls shouldn't be involved in baseball."

"No," I say quickly. I'm pretty sure I've found a cure for her blinking issue—livid anger. "I'm just saying that...like...traditionally...not that everything has to be traditional but...I just mean that baseball bats have..." I cower my head and pedal harder, hoping she won't burn me with her stare. "Braids sound great, Pip. Awesome idea."

I feel her eyes on me for a moment longer before she spins on her heels and returns to her seat on the medicine ball. "I figure dad can design it and then take the drawing and make it into one of those branding things."

"Branding things?" I say.

"Do you really not understand any of the words I say? Yes. Branding things. Like you see in the movies for burning a symbol into a cow, which is super mean. But it's perfect to use on a bat." She shrugs. "The big companies do it with computers and lasers, but we can be old school. Mr. Edmond has a torch to heat it, then we press it to the bat. Voilá."

I hop off the bike and make my way to the pull-up bar, studying my father's reaction. Or lack thereof. But he must be calculating his odds of surviving long enough to see a finished bat. Not to mention the work it'll take to design an emblem that will meet Pippin's standards and put it on some sort of branding iron.

"What makes you think dad knows how to make a branding thing?" I ask.

Pippin shrugs like she's never considered it. "I don't know." She flicks her eyes to my father. "Maybe there's a store that does it. I'm just delegating responsibility. That's what leaders do."

My father grins, but there's a strain behind it. I wonder if it's because he's in physical pain or because he has no idea how he'll come through for his daughter.

"When we get home, we'll talk more about your design," my father says to Pippin. "And I'll see what I can do about figuring out how to get it on your bat."

His answer makes me uncomfortable. Why would he get Pippin's hopes up when he knows better than anyone he might not be able to come through? Maybe he thinks he's stronger than he actually is, or maybe he needs to assume he'll live long enough to finish the project for the sake of his own sanity. But the truth is, no one knows how long he'll live. Not me. Not him. Not even his doctor.

The smile on Pippin's face doesn't give me joy this time. Instead, it creates a sense of dread at the disappointment she'll feel if my father dies before our project is finished.

Have a Catch

Baseball has always been more than a game. Nothing is more indelible in the American psyche than a father and son playing catch. The act has appeared in literature, cinema, and countless real-life relationships. Since male gender roles have often prevented them from intimate verbal communication with each other, having a catch has become irreplaceable in the deepening of relationships between American fathers and sons, who have a long history of difficult relationships.

Chapter 8

The rain continues pouring down from a blanket of gray clouds so thick I think it might rain forever. But I don't mind at all. It's a perfect day — for some things.

In the minors, I learned a few things very well. To accept free food whenever it was offered. To stay away from any girl who seemed more interested in my Major League prospects than any other detail about me. And to make the very most of every off-day, because there aren't many in the long, professional season.

In amateur ball, the demands are nowhere near the level of pro ball. But I still can't let a weekend rain-day pass by without doing something to relax my mind, calm the nerves, and recharge my batteries. So after my workout in the dilapidated high school weight room, I shower, put on some old, hole-filled jeans, a ratty tee-shirt, and a rain jacket, and make my way to the garage.

The darkness inside feels musty and full, like a museum storage room. I flick a light switch and a single bulb hanging from the rafters pops on. My father's car sits in the middle, taking up most of the space, but every nook and cranny is packed with relics from my childhood.

My Little League bat is in a corner and I reach through thick cobwebs to pick it up. It's a metal Louisville Slugger — Pippin wouldn't approve — with the label and emblem completely bald from use. Something about the fact that the barrel is beaten and battered while the rest of the bat still looks relatively new gives me an odd sense of satisfaction.

Part of me wants to wade through the entire garage, looking and touching and remembering. The plastic sleds, nearly torn apart from winter use, sit propped against a wall. Above, hanging high in the rafters, a dismantled ping-pong table reminds me of the endless hours my dad and I played, before baseball came calling and changed my life. I look around for a few more moments before remembering I'm in the garage for a reason. I go straight to the far corner where they've always been — the fishing poles.

Old fishing line tangles two poles together, with bobbers and hooks dangling in odd positions. I carefully take the poles by their handles, grab the rusted metal tackle box and hand-held shovel from the ground, and leave the garage with a bounce in my step.

Three minutes later, I'm knocking on Emily's door.

Oz's groggy face appears from behind the door as he opens it. His hair sticks straight up, his eyes are half-closed, and his mouth is full of scrambled eggs. But when he sees me, he perks up, chews as fast as his mouth can move, and swallows hard.

"Charlie Fightmaster!" he says. "What are you doing here?"

I hold the fishing poles high in front of me. "It's raining, which means the Crappies will be biting. Want to come with?"

"Heck yeah," Oz says, and he bolts down the hallway, yelling for his mom. I step into the entry way and close the door behind me. A moment later Emily appears around a corner, warming her hands with a cup of coffee and wearing a full-length bath robe. I can't help wondering what — if anything — she's wearing underneath.

If her reaction is any indication, the answer is "not much." Emily nearly drops her coffee mug in an attempt to make sure the robe is sufficiently closed. She stops in her tracks as if trying to keep the most possible distance between us.

"What are you doing here?" she asks, echoing Oz's question.

I hold up the fishing poles again. "I thought I'd take Oz to the creek. As long as you don't mind."

For a moment, Emily seems flustered, then annoyed. She looks back toward where Oz disappeared. "Well, it looks like he already thinks he's going."

I'm not sure if that's permission or not so I stand silently, feeling awkward.

"Next time, Charlie, run it by me before you show up on the doorstep, okay? What if I had plans for him this morning?" she asks. "You come by, get his hopes up, and then I have to be the bad guy and say he can't go?"

I hadn't even considered that scenario. I was simply trying to take my son out fishing. What could be wrong with that? "I'm sorry," I say.

Emily sighs and pulls her robe tighter. "It's fine. Just don't keep him out too long."

She turns and walks away. An invitation for me to follow is noticeably absent, so I set the poles against the wall and wait for Oz. It doesn't take long. A minute later, I hear rumbling on a staircase and Oz bolts into the entry way wearing old clothes under a rain jacket and a faded Stallions baseball cap.

"Where are we going?" he asks.

Judging by the gleam in his eyes, I could say The Moon and he'd follow me. "First stop, your back yard."

Oz's face crinkles in confusion, but I lead him out the front door, into the rain, and around to the back yard.

A small garden is organized in rows of tiny green sprouts. I go to a corner of the garden where I won't disturb anything that's been planted, and drop to my knees. When Oz does the same, I hand him the shovel.

"Let's get in there and find some bait."

Oz looks at me quizzically for a moment, but then he digs into the dirt and flips a shovel-full onto the grass nearby. I reach into the small hole and pull out two worms, which I put in a container in the tackle box, along with some wet dirt from the garden.

"The Crappies are going to love these," I say, and relish Oz's laughter.

We spend a few more minutes shoveling and picking out worms, the pitter-patter of the rain on our waterproof jackets holding steady the entire time. When the small container is full, I show Oz how to replace the dirt, then lead the way out of the yard and toward the creek.

"You had a really good game yesterday," Oz says.

"Thanks." I've never experienced a physical response to a compliment before, but at the words from my son, my chest definitely expands. Something washes through me, giving me energy and lightening my mood.

"Do you think you'll break Bud Crawford's record?" Oz asks.

"Which one? Season or career?"

"Start with season."

Fifty home runs in fifty games. It's probably impossible. But I've been thinking more about it and I've come to the conclusion that I might actually have a chance. It's not that I'm the best baseball player in the world, by any means. But I do have three things going for me. First, the 95 mile-per-hour fastballs I was seeing just a month ago are now 85 miles-per-hour and without the movement of Triple-A pitches. Second, most of the ballparks I'll be playing in — including Sweetwater Ballpark — are cracker boxes in comparison to professional fields, meaning a harmless fly ball to right field in past years might be a three-run home run this summer. And lastly, amateur ballplayers are here to play ball. Sure, they'll be as careful with me as possible, but when push comes to shove, I'll get something to hit. These kids have nothing to lose, so they'll take their chances, hoping to be able to lay claim to having struck out Charlie Fightmaster.

Putting all that together could equal a lot of round-trippers this summer.

"I'm learning some stuff from Bud Crawford and Pippin says she's making the best bat ever, so who knows? I might just have a chance."

Oz giggles and I lead the way through town. The rain turns into a soft mist and the clouds seem to lower and thicken. We walk several blocks, through a few neighborhoods, past Sweetwater Ballpark, and into a small wooded area.

My father showed me the spot and we fished it for years before I left town. As I lead Oz through a clearing, I'm happy to see the fishing hole hasn't changed a bit. Maybe the trees around the creek are a bit taller, but it only enhances the secluded feeling I've always loved about this spot.

"Here we go," I say. "You can grab a Coke out of the cooler while I try to get these poles untangled."

Oz does as I asked, cracking open a can and plopping down on the tall, wet grass near the riverbed. As I unwrap the tangled line, I sneak glances at my son. He's a kid in the woods, fog hanging low in the trees, enjoying a day with his dad. I want desperately to tell him the truth, but I know it's not my place. Not until Emily gives me the green light. Until then, I'll just have to be a friend to my son. An admired baseball star. But not a father.

When I finally manage to detangle the fishing line, I put a worm on each of the hooks and hand one pole to Oz. We cast into the same eddy and sit in the hazy light, watching our bobbers shoulder-to-shoulder.

"How far do you think you can hit a baseball?" Oz says, still studying his bobber.

I can't help but enjoy the sense of awe in Oz's voice. I wonder if he'd believe it if I were to say six-hundred feet, or even a thousand. "Hard to say. Since I haven't made the majors yet, my home runs have never been measured. Not with StatCast, anyway."

"Yeah, but what do you think? Like, if someone threw a hundred mile-an-hour fastball and you timed it just right and crushed it as hard as you've ever crushed it before. How far would it go?"

I think hard about it, staring as my bobber rides the small ripples of the water. "If everything was just perfect? I bet I could hit one five hundred feet. Maybe five-twenty-five. But that's if all the stars were aligned."

Oz looks up to the sky, as if imagining a baseball sailing overhead. "I wish I was a good baseball player," he says.

It's painful to see Oz's posture slump. Obviously, being able to hit a baseball is important to him. "Don't worry, you will someday. It's in your genes."

As soon as I say it, my throat tightens. I try to figure out a way to take it back, but my mind is suddenly blank. In the several moments of silence that follow, I search my mind frantically for some way to change the subject, but can't focus on anything but what I said. I'm just praying Oz will let it go. Or that he doesn't catch my slip up.

"What do you mean?" Oz finally asks, and my vision wavers in panic. "Mom was never good at anything athletic. She's told me that a million times."

"I bet she was good at some sports." I silently plead with Oz to move on, but it's not in the cards.

"No she wasn't," Oz says. He stares at his bobber so hard I can feel the gears turning as he puts two and two together. "Do you know who my dad is?"

I swear under my breath. I have no idea how to answer. Not coming out and telling Oz the identity of his father is one thing, but he's asking me a direct question. Am I supposed to blatantly lie to him? Before I can figure out how to respond, Oz is back on the offense.

"You do, don't you? I know you and my mom went to high school together. So you would know who she was dating when she had me."

"Look," I say, buying time. "I'm not sure it's my place to talk about this."

Oz stands up and glares at me. "You do know! I knew it! You have to tell me."

"You mom doesn't think you're ready—"

"It's my dad, not hers. I get to decide when I'm ready. And I say I'm ready now."

"I can't just…"

My voice fades and I can't figure out what to say. Oz challenges me with a direct stare. He's done making his case and apparently thinks he's won the argument. As much as I want to disagree, I can't. It's not fair to keep that knowledge from Oz.

But I want to tell him in a different way. A better way. I envisioned surprising him, with Emily by my side, at the ballpark. After a game winning home run or maybe even after a state championship.

But the more I think about it, the better this moment feels. Oz and I are fishing, just the two of us, in the place where my dad and I used to fish. The weather has a cozy feel to it. The summer rain is warm and the fog lends an ephemeral feel to the moment that will definitely be memorable. When Oz looks back on the moment he found out who his dad is, the memory will be clear. He'll have a place he can visit often to remember the moment.

So I set my fishing pole down, slowly stand, and put my hands on Oz's shoulders. I smile, and when Oz realizes I'm going to tell him, his excitement bubbles over in laughter. Before I know it, I'm laughing too. I want to hold the moment, extend it. A father about to reveal himself to a son who already likes him, even admires him.

I finally get my laughter under control and take a deep breath. "Okay, Oz. I'm happy to tell you — to finally get to tell you — that your dad…is me."

I study Oz's eyes, waiting for the excitement, the joy. I'm having a hard time figuring out what's happening in Oz's mind as he remains silent for several long moments. No more than a few seconds pass, but it's long enough to know something's wrong.

"What?" Oz says. His voice is soft and confused. He won't look me in the eye.

"I'm your dad," I say. I squeeze his shoulders like I'm trying to wake him from a trance. "I'm the one your mom was dating in high school."

"But…"

"That's how I know you'll be good at baseball," I say. "That's how I know it's in your genes. Because you're my son."

Oz still won't look at me. The crinkle in his brow deepens and his posture becomes stiff. "But you left."

My heartbeat quickens and I swear it gets louder. This isn't the response I expected. Where are the tears of joy? The making of a memory that will last a lifetime? "Yes, but…well, that's complicated."

I have no idea what to say. Should I tell Oz that I've only just found out about our relationship myself? Or would that be throwing Emily under the bus? If I tell Oz the truth and he takes it out on Emily, she'll never forgive me. Suddenly, a wave of panic tightens my throat as I imagine Emily's reaction to what I've already done. She left no doubt about what I was allowed — or more specifically not allowed — to tell Oz.

"How can it be complicated?" Oz says, his voice rising steadily. "You're my dad, but you never even bothered to get to know me. I never even met you until now. You weren't even here. For anything."

"Oz, you have to understand…" I can't finish the thought. I have no idea what I'm supposed to say. What I've already said has caused more harm than I ever intended.

"I do understand," Oz says. "You got my mom pregnant and then left. You never cared about her at all. You never cared about either of us."

Oz throws his fishing pole at me. I fumble with it and drop it to the wet grass. "Oz, please. It wasn't like that."

But he has already stormed past me and is stomping through the grass, back toward the neighborhoods. I try one last time to call him back, but a loud clap of thunder covers my voice entirely.

•   •   •

I watch Oz go, wondering how things turned on me so badly. I realize now, immediately after telling him, that I still had other options, even after I'd put my foot in my mouth about his genes. I could have said his grandpa—Mack—was a baseball player. It would have been believable. I can't help but wonder, did I actually not think about that until now? Or was some part of me using my slip-up as an excuse to do what I wanted?

Either way, I regret it now.

Several minutes after Oz is out of sight, I gather myself enough to pick up the fishing poles and start walking through the rain toward my house. I consider dropping the poles in my garage, then calling Emily, but I've always hated having something hanging over my head. When difficult situations arise, it's better to face them right away. However painful it might be, I'd rather get it over quickly. Rip the band-aid off the wound.

So minutes later, I'm knocking on Emily's door, unsure if I hope Oz will answer, or Emily, or no one at all. But when the door opens and I see Emily's expression, I wish I'd procrastinated after all. Her eyes squint slightly, but whether from anger or confusion, I can't tell. Neither is any good.

"What happened?" she says.

I shuffle my feet, wishing I could be anywhere but here. "What do you know?"

"What do I know? What kind of question is that? I know that Oz was excited to go fishing with you and that he came back crying, ran up to his room, and won't unlock it for me. Is he okay?"

I have no idea how to answer that question. And I don't know how to explain what happened, either. I slump my shoulders and decide to rip off the band-aid.

"I told him."

Emily's eyes bulge and her shoulders set back. "Told him what, Charlie? And you better not say what I think you're going to say."

Her tone contains even more fury than her words and it takes all the will power I can muster to continue. "I told him I'm his father. I didn't mean to, I swear."

Emily curses under her breath and her gaze turns inward. Her body is perfectly still for several long moments before she speaks through a clinched jaw. "How could you not mean to? Did the words form themselves and jump out of your mouth on their own?"

I try to explain the accidental comment about genes, but before I can finish a sentence, Emily cuts me off. "Forget it. I don't want to know."

She looks up the stairs, where Oz is locked in his bedroom, and sighs deeply. It hurts to see her in such pain, but part of me can't help but prefer it to her wrath. "We're going to have to sit down and talk about this," she says. "All three of us. But not today. I don't know when, but not today. Today, just stay away from us. Okay?"

Before I have a chance to answer, the door closes hard in my face.

•　　•　　•

The rest of the day is brutal. The only good thing is that the weather clears and the sun begins drying the ballpark. Mack calls to say the Stallions game is still on, just delayed an hour to get the field ready.

The first pitch can't come soon enough. For my whole life, whenever something hard has happened, baseball has been my only shelter. Now, I just want to take batting practice, or field a hundred ground balls. But unlike pro ball, there's no one I can call. No assistant coach or close teammate who will help me dive into baseball as an escape.

So I spend the day trying to divert my attention in other ways — with television, music, even books. But all I can think about is the anger in Oz's eyes, and the betrayal in Emily's. I want to talk to my dad about it, but I'm embarrassed to admit what I did. So I spend most of the day away from the house, simply driving around wasting time until finally, it's close enough to game time that I can go to the ballpark.

On the way there, my cell phone rings. It's my father, desperately wanting to go to the game but physically unable to walk to his car. Another punch to the gut. I tell him to hold tight and I swing the car back toward home. Ten minutes later, I pull into the driveway, fighting back tears. I wonder if this day could possibly get any worse.

After two deep breaths to compose myself, I jog into the house and find my dad in the den, struggling to put his shoes on. I help him tie his shoes, trying to ignore the gurgling sound his heavy breaths make, then I drape his arm around my shoulders. Slowly, we make our way wordlessly to the car. I open the creaky door and set my father inside.

"Used to be the other way around," he says. "Back when you were a bit smaller."

I don't know what to say, so I smile and walk around to the driver's side, trying not to focus on how light he has become.

When we arrive at the field, I again virtually carry my father from the car to the dugout and set him in the recliner. I find a line-up card and pencil, and give it to him. I'm about to ask if he needs anything, but a couple players walk into the dugout just then and I don't want to make him feel helpless. He still needs to manage the team, which means he needs them to think he's capable of it — mentally and physically.

Emily is in the corner of the dugout, in her normal spot, pointedly avoiding looking in my direction. I lace up my spikes, grab my glove, and see Oz enter the dugout, carrying a long bag full of bats.

"Hey Oz," I say.

Oz sets the bats down, pulls his hat low over his eyes, and brushes past me. He glares at Emily too, then walks onto the field, where he joins a couple guys playing Pepper behind home plate.

I want desperately to fix the situation, but at the moment, there's nothing I can do or say that won't make things worse. So I turn my attention to baseball and start my pre-game routine.

An hour later, just as infield practice ends and Mack strolls to home plate for the pregame meeting with the umpire and the other team's coach, Pippin jogs into the dugout out of breath. She says hello to me—at least someone is still talking to me—while she pulls a Stallions cap down low. She sees Emily at the end of the dugout and bounces down onto the bench next to her.

Pippin pulls a notepad and pen out of the back pocket of her jeans, and stares out at the field as if the job she's about to do is the most important thing in the world. I'd forgotten about her new job as "assistant coach" and I'm relieved to see Emily put her arm around her and give her a little squeeze. It shouldn't surprise me that Emily's anger toward me wouldn't extend to Pippin, but it still eases some of the ache in my chest.

When game time arrives, I smack my fist into the the palm of my glove and sprint onto the field with the rest of the Stallions.

I still carry the weight of Oz's rejection and Emily's anger, but my position at shortstop has always felt like a sanctuary. And the game goes well enough. Although I'm certainly not going to stake a claim to perfect harmony, I do shoot a single to right field in my first at-bat and hit two other balls hard, although right at the center fielder. I make four routine plays at shortstop and a diving play to end the top of the eighth.

But any good feelings are short-lived.

Duane starts the bottom of the eighth with a bloop down the line that turns into a cheap double. The next batter singles up the middle and Duane sprints around third and scores. The entire bench hops out of the dugout, with me and Pippin last in line to greet Duane. Only Emily remains seated, marking the run in the scorebook. And my dad, too weak to do anything but clap three slow times.

Duane struts along the line of players, giving high-fives to each. But when he gets to me, he slams his hand against mine hard enough to hurt. Personally, I couldn't care less.

But when Duane gets to Pippin he quickly pulls his hand away, just as Pippin swings hers forward. She misses and hits nothing but air. No one else notices since they're all stepping back into the dugout. But I see the shock on Pippin's face turn to embarrassment as she scans the other players 'faces, making sure no one witnessed her humiliation.

I'm so furious my vision blurs. I take a step toward Duane, unable to believe someone would be so low as to intentionally hurt a twelve year-old girl as a way to get back at her older brother. In that moment, I have every intention of tearing Duane's arms off.

But Pippin grabs my wrist before I can reach him. "Don't Charlie," she says. "It's not a big deal, really. Besides, he's not worth it."

When I notice Oz near the bat rack, watching silently but intently, I take a deep breath and put my arm around Pippin. "Okay, Pip. You're right." I take a moment to get my breathing under control. "It's a good thing I have you around," I say.

"Good thing for who? You or Duane?"

"Both."

"But mostly Duane," Pippin says, and her bird-song giggle diffuses the rest of my anger.

I spend the rest of the inning, as well as the top of the ninth, trying not to dwell on what Duane did to Pippin. When we get the third out, I jog back to the dugout, scheduled to bat fourth in the inning, with the Stallions down by two runs.

Normally, Oz would greet me with my batting helmet, batting gloves, and bat. Instead, he sits pointedly on the bench, staring out at the field in defiance. I want to apologize again. To explain that I didn't leave him at all — that I never would have left him, if I'd just known. But I know it wouldn't do any good.

I'm not even sure if it's true.

I force my attention back to the game. I study the pitcher, trying to get a bead on his release point and looking for any tendencies that might give me a clue to what pitch he likes to throw on certain counts.

The first batter of the inning walks, the second flies to center, and I start swinging a weighted bat to loosen up near the on-deck circle. I try to focus on my next at-bat, but it's impossible. Too many thoughts — too many emotions — continue to pummel my mind:

Oz and his rejection. Emily and her anger. Pippin, and the look of shame on her face when Duane ignored her high-five attempt. And my father. Too sick to even stand from the recliner and take part. Full of cancer and knowing he'll die, sooner rather than later.

Lastly, I think about the Major Leagues, all I'm missing, and my promise to stay in Sweetwater through the summer. My chance at realizing my dreams are slipping away while I play on an amateur team in the middle of baseball purgatory.

My first reaction is to grip the bat tightly, strangling it with frustration. My shoulders tense and my breath becomes choppy. But then I remember something else. Bud Crawford, and his unexpected advice: Embrace vulnerability.

My life isn't perfect. My problems aren't just going to go away. But I decide, just this once, to embrace it. To open to the vulnerability of the helplessness I'm feeling. To the acknowledgement that I'm not perfect.

Surprisingly, it doesn't hurt as much as I thought it would. In fact, it doesn't hurt at all. If I don't have to worry about what people will think if I get out, I don't have to worry about getting out. Suddenly, unexpectedly, I'm free to play the game the way I played as a boy — for fun.

Three minutes later, with Stallions on first and second base, I blast a walk-off home run over the centerfield wall.

The Shake-Off

Before each pitch, the catcher signals to the pitcher which pitch he'd like thrown by putting down a certain number of fingers, or a sequence of fingers. Sometimes, the two players disagree about which pitch should be thrown. Rarely, it can even lead to an extended disagreement, with the catcher emphatically calling for a pitch, and the pitcher repeatedly shaking him off.

In the end, the decision lies with the pitcher, as he's the one who will actually throw the pitch. The catcher has no choice but to accept it.

Chapter 9

The next day I get up early. I have to be at work by 9am, have an early game at 5pm, and I promised Pippin we'd start work on the quebracho afterwards. But first, I have an important stop to make. So I get dressed and head straight to Bud Crawford's house with a bounce in my step.

I've hit hundreds of home runs in my baseball playing days, from high school all they way through the minor leagues. But I'd never hit a walk-off home run before. And I owe it all to Bud Crawford's crazy theory.

The only thing that could have made it better was if I'd rounded third base to see my son circling the plate, jumping up and down, part of the mob awaiting my arrival. Unfortunately, that didn't happened. Oz remained on the bench, refusing to even acknowledge me when the chaos subsided. I have to figure out a way to reconcile with him, but for the moment, I have no idea how.

I'm sure I'll continue to obsess about it until it figure it out, but there's nothing I can do now. So I turn my attention back to Bud Crawford. I still have two more secrets to learn.

I climb the concrete steps and knock on Bud's door, tentatively at first, but when no one comes to the door, I increase the force until I'm almost pounding. When Bud still doesn't answer the door, I walk around to the side of the house and peer into a window. There, at the dining room table, Bud sits, perfectly unconcerned, as if no one has been knocking on the door at all.

I consider leaving him alone, but when I remember the way I felt last night—embracing vulnerability and then driving the ball out of the park—I find myself tapping my knuckles against the window pane. I desperately need secret number two.

Slowly, Bud lifts his head, until his fiery eyes meet mine. Part of me—a very large and sane part—wants to turn, run, and never come back. But I force my feet to stand firm while Bud pushes himself up from his chair and walks to the window with a deep scowl.

The old man unlocks the window and lifts it half-way open. He stands several feet above me and looks down with obvious contempt.

"A man doesn't open his door, it means he doesn't want to be bothered," Bud says, his voice extra gravelly.

I notice darker bags than normal under Bud's eyes, and his shirt has stains down the front as if it's been a long time since it was last washed. "I'm sorry," I say. "But I need to hear the other two secrets to perfect harmony. Last night—"

"Last night you hit a walk-off home run. I heard."

"Because I embraced vulnerability. Just like you said I should."

"Well whoop-dee-do," Bud says. "I couldn't be happier for you. Now get the hell out of here and don't come back."

The window slams closed in my face and a drape is pulled tight. Hard footsteps stomp away, leaving me alone at the side of Bud's house, wondering what happened to make the old man so angry.

With no other option, I make my way to the lumber yard, where I put in a full day's work. The entire time, my mind bounces from wondering why Bud was so rude to scheming how to learn the two remaining secrets.

I could try Emily, since she's the only other person who knows Bud's crazy philosophies. But considering my last interaction with her, I'm sure I'd have no better luck than I had at Bud's house.

So I finish work, clock out, and go to the ballpark. But my distracted mind won't allow me to focus. Every time I see Duane, I fume at the memory of the hurt and embarrassment on Pippin's face when he pulled his hand away from hers. Every time something goes wrong, I blame Bud for kicking me off his property without sharing the second secret.

I go 0-4 without hitting a single ball hard and the Stallions lose 3-2 to a team that had no business beating us. It's my worst game as a

Stallion—even worse than the opener—and makes me even more desperate to talk to Bud.

It's been a long, useless day and I just want to go home, curl up in bed, and hope tomorrow is better. But the game only took two hours, and I promised Pippin we'd work on our bat. So while the players are filing out of the dugout, Pippin hops in my car and directs me to the lumberyard. Too tired to argue, I do as I'm told. Once there, Pippin leads me to the corner, where Mr. Edmond has allowed us to set up tools to make the bat.

"Three-eighths of an inch," Pippin says is if stating the meaning of life.

She waits for me until I dutifully say, "Three eighths-of-an-inch what?"

"That's the magic number. Most bats start with two inches of width at the knob and taper down to around three-quarters of an inch at the handle, and stay that way until the barrel begins, then get up to two-and-thee-quarters inches in width at the widest. With our quebracho, instead of stopping at three-quarters of an inch, we can taper that down to three-eighths of an inch in the area between the handle and the barrel. It'll lighten the bat so even with this super-strong wood, you can still swing your thirty-three-thirty-two."

"How did you know what size bat I use?" I ask.

"You think I'm an idiot?" Pippin says. "Thirty-two inch bats are easy to recognize because players have less plate coverage, unless the hitter's able to let the ball get really deep like Derek Jeter. And players I've seen using a thirty-four typically don't get the barrel through very fast."

"Wait a second," I say. "Are you telling me you figured out what size bat I use just by watching my swing?"

"It's not that complicated, if you just think about it."

I stare at my little sister, trying to see the resemblance to me. "You're unbelievable, you know that?" The sparkle in Pippin's eye eases some of the burden of my 0-4.

"Well, what are we waiting for?" Pippin says. "The bat isn't going to make itself."

She spreads out a large sheet of paper with instructions outlining each step of the process. She's even included hand-drawn diagrams. I get to work cutting a manageable piece off the large slab of wood so we can begin whittling it into the shape of a bat, using the lathe.

The wood is unlike anything I've seen or held in my hands. It's smooth, even without being sanded. And when I wrap my hand around the slab, I swear I can sense its power. It feels like granite. Unfortunately, it's nearly as heavy. I hope Pippin's calculations are correct, but I'm pretty skeptical.

I slide the wood through a circular saw, giving it more pressure than I expected it would need. Slowly, the wood gives and the blade slices its way through one ring after another. Just as I get to the end of the board, the saw jerks through and a small chunk of wood flies through the air toward Pippin.

I yell out to her and feel my heart surge with adrenaline. Fortunately, she's not where I thought she was and the small chunk of wood smacks against the wall and falls harmlessly to the floor. It bounces to my feet, where a jagged edge glares up at me.

"Okay," I say. "No more of that until we both get safety goggles."

Pippin nods her agreement and I find several pairs of plastic glasses on a nearby work desk. I grab two, put one on myself, and give the other to Pippin.

"When are you going back to Bud Crawford's?" she asks, sliding the safety glasses over her eyes.

My short chortle is without humor. "I tried today. It didn't exactly go well. He wouldn't even see me."

Pippin just shrugs. "Maybe he was trying to reinforce the idea of vulnerability. Of course, he does have his demons. When will you try again?"

"I'm sure whenever it is will be way too soon—for either of us."

"That's not true. You guys got over your baggage. The first meeting went well."

"Oh yeah? And how do you know that juicy bit of gossip?"

She shrugs and says, "Emily told me."

"Of course," I say. "The secrets that woman decides to tell, and those she keeps..."

"I happen to like her," Pippin says. "Not in the same way you do, of course."

I start to deny it. To protest such an obvious lie. But the words won't escape my mouth. Pippin wears a very self-satisfied look and turns her focus back to the bat. "You can't give up. Think of it like baseball. You have to persist. Bud still has things to teach you. He'll be expecting you soon," she says.

I set the wood into the lathe and turn the knob. "Yeah, probably with a shotgun pressed to his shoulder."

"We both know that's not true."

"How do you know it's not true? Did Emily tell you that, too?"

"No. I know because fighting with you isn't what he wants."

"Now you know what Bud Crawford wants?"

"Of course," Pippin says. "It's simple, if you just—"

"If you just think about it," I finish with her. I shake my head at my little sister. "All right, Einstein. What does Bud Crawford want?"

"He wants to coach baseball. He wants to be around the game. It's the only thing he knows. He still loves it, but, well, he has issues."

"You finally got one thing right," I say.

Pippin shakes her head hard. "No, you don't understand. But that's not important. The important part is that you realize that he wants to help you achieve your dream. He wants to help you make the Major Leagues. Not because he likes you-"

"Again, you nailed that part."

"—but because it's what he needs to do. He's a baseball guy. He knows the game better than anybody I've ever met."

I smirk at the idea that my twelve-year-old sister thinks her experience has been so vast.

"Bud Crawford's like a scientist," Pippin says. "But for baseball. Especially the mental part of the game."

"You might have to explain that one."

"No duh. I have to explain everything for you." Pippin heaves a giant sigh and continues. "Bud knows that if he dies without passing on his knowledge, all that knowledge dies with him. And that would hurt the game he loves. Hence, he wants to pass it on."

"Hence?" I say.

"It means—"

"I know what it means. Okay, you might be right that he wants to pass on his knowledge to somebody, but I'm sure he'd prefer to pass it on to someone else if Emily hadn't convinced him to tell me."

"You're so dense sometimes," Pippin says, and I wonder how offended I should be. "There's nobody else that can do it. Nobody else has your talent, and nobody else screws it up with their brain as much as you do. He might not like you, but you're the perfect candidate."

I'm not sure how to answer so I grab a piece of sandpaper and begin whittling the bat above the handle.

"Careful with that," Pippin says. "And promise me you'll go back to Bud's house."

"Fine. I promise I'll go back to Bud's house."

"As soon as we're done here," Pippin says. "Otherwise you might not do it."

"You think I'd break my promise?" I say with as much drama as I can.

Pippin shrugs. "I don't know. You've been gone a long time. You'll have to prove to me that you're a man of your word."

"What about dinner?" I say, grasping at straws. "Who's going to make you and dad dinner?"

"Yeah, like you're the responsible one here. Besides, it's eight o'clock. Dad's probably already eaten, and I think I can manage to make some mac-n-cheese, thank you very much."

"Okay." I throw my hands in the air. "I'll do it. As soon as we're done." I wonder when Pippin became so exasperating. I watch her work for a long time, not daring to interrupt her concentration.

•   •   •

I stand at Bud's door, without Emily again and feeling just as defenseless as the last time. I've already decided, if Bud doesn't answer the door this time, I'll have to beg and plead for Emily's help. I'm definitely not going to knock on his window again.

Standing on Bud's doorstep, I think I've procrastinated as long as possible. But still I don't knock on the door. I see Oz a few houses down, mowing the final strip of a lawn under a streetlight that has just turned on. Oz seems to always be mowing lawns these days, when he isn't in the Stallions dugout. I wonder if it's a way to avoid me and Emily. If, in addition to wanting nothing to do with his biological father, Oz still hasn't forgiven his mother for keeping the secret for so long…and then getting stuck with me as his father.

As Oz finishes the final strip, I watch closely, hoping he might look up so I can wave. But his gaze focuses on the lawnmower in front of him. It's like he knows I'm here and is intentionally keeping his gaze down. With a deep sigh, I finally knock on Bud's door.

"It's not locked," comes Bud's gravelly voice.

I push the door open and see Bud eating again. It's almost nine at night, but I'm less confused by Bud's eating schedule than his diet. Just like before, he chews on a rolled-up piece of lefse, with a tall glass of white milk in front of him.

"Bud, I apologize for earlier. But I was wondering—well, my little sister was wondering too—if you're free to tell me the second secret now." I surprise myself at how deferential I'm being. I came here without a plan. But rapping on the window had only made me feel like a pushy jerk and I don't want to feel like that again. It hadn't worked anyway. "If I had known you were eating, I would've come later," I say.

Bud waves it off and motions for me to join him at the table. I take the same chair as last time. "You said earlier that even though I embraced vulnerability two games ago and hit a home run that it wasn't perfect harmony. What did you mean?"

"Just getting right into it, huh? Probably best. So you had a good game." Bud whips his head back and forth. "You felt a little vulnerable and then hit a home run. You've been hitting plenty of home runs. It's not the same thing as perfect harmony. Not even close."

Bud stares at my hands—I'm fidgeting with my shirt for some reason. His lips purse in a way that could be understanding or annoyance. But then his voice softens. "You've made progress. But perfect harmony requires a lot more."

"That's what I'm here for," I say. "The second secret. I mean, I get the whole vulnerability thing. I still have some work to do, but I understand it." I look Bud straight in the eye—which is super uncomfortable. I'm hoping he'll read it as focus and determination, not as a challenge. I know how that story goes. "I need to know the second secret," I say.

Bud sniffs and stares out the window for a long moment. Finally, he nods slowly. I sit in the chair opposite him and wait as patiently as I can. After what feels like a full minute of silence, Bud finally speaks.

"The second secret to perfect harmony," he says dramatically, "is acceptance."

I wait for more, but apparently there is no more. I try not to feel let down, but acceptance doesn't seem like a very big thing for anyone who's played more than a little baseball in his life.

"You went hitless in four at-bats earlier tonight, right? Good."

"Good? How could a hitless game ever be good?"

"You have to understand that you will make mistakes and be okay with that," Bud says.

"I thought that was vulnerability."

"Yes, but acceptance is how you react to what happens. Don't just understand that you will make mistakes, but when you do, you must learn to accept it and move on."

I wait, expecting more, hoping for more. "That's it?"

"No," Bud says. "The trick is that you must accept when you have success in exactly the same way."

"That part I'm pretty sure I can do," I say. "I mean, why would it be hard to accept success? That's a piece of cake."

"In exactly the same way that you accept your failures?"

"But how—"

"Even keel. Even keel! No highs, no lows. Trust the process and accept everything in exactly the same way."

As Bud gets more and more animated, I shrink into myself, trying to understand. Staying at an even keel is like gospel in professional ball. With so many games, anyone who gets too high or too low inevitably runs themselves into the ground, emotionally. But to see success and failure as the same? That makes no sense at all.

Bud leans forward onto his elbows. "If you hit a home run or strike out, you must accept them equally. If you make a diving play or have a ball go through your legs, you must feel the exact same way about them. Do you understand?"

"I think so," I say, even though I have no idea how it could be possible. Bud slams his fist against the table, rattling our glasses.

"It's not that hard if you just think about it!" He glares at me and shakes his head. "Let me break it down for you. First, when you screw up—you have to learn from that. Learn but don't dwell. The moment you learn the lesson before you, you must forget the mistake was ever made. You must approach the next at bat, the next ground ball, with no recollection whatsoever of having ever made a mistake in the past. But with the knowledge you learned from those mistakes still present in your mind."

I feel my eyes squint in thought. "But how can something be both present in your mind and completely forgotten at the same time?"

"Ha," Bud says, leaning back in his chair. "Now we're getting somewhere."

I struggle with the idea, really gnawing on it, trying to understand. Apparently sensing that I'm close to making the necessary connections, Bud leans forward, putting his elbows on his knees. "And when you succeed—notice it. Accept it. Then let it go. But keep the feeling."

"Let it go, but keep it? It's..."

"This will help," Bud says. "Every moment you're on the baseball field, approach it as if you've never been there before. Because you haven't."

This just keeps getting more bizarre. I shake my head—not in disagreement, but in an attempt to clear some room for these crazy thoughts. "I've literally spent thousands of hours on baseball fields."

"Yes, but never on the field that you're on, in the moment you're on it. That only happens once, and then it's gone forever. Since you've never been there before, and you'll never be there again, you can accept whatever comes. Good or bad. Success or failure."

"Accept whatever comes," I repeat. "And how do I do that again?"

"It's simple, if you just—"

" —if I just think about it. So you've said. You know, between you and Pippin, I'm surrounded by the two most predictable people I've ever met."

"Well," Bud says, smiling for the first time and showing me to the door. "I guess I'm in good company."

Triple Play

The triple play—when all three outs of a half-inning are recorded on the same play—is very rare in baseball. With thousands of major league games played each year, there are only an average of five triple plays per season.

Due to the unique nature of the play and the momentum shift it can cause, the turning of a triple play can completely change the direction of a game.

Chapter 10

Over the next few weeks, I get back on track at the plate. I'm able to keep my home run pace going, although it would be nice to have a higher batting average. Every game, it seems like I'm either really on or really off. I guess it's good practice for Bud's acceptance thing.

Fortunately, when I'm on, the long balls seem to come easy. Before I know it, I've moved into second place on the Stallions all-time single-season home run list, with twenty-six. Unfortunately, every time my teammates line up at the plate to congratulate me, Oz stays in the dugout and refuses to even look at me.

As a distraction, Pippin and I spend most of our free time in the workshop trying to perfect the quebracho bat. I've never seen such focus and determination, and I wonder where Pippin's work ethic comes from. Sure, I've given everything in my baseball career, but the level of intensity with which Pippin works on the bat seems beyond anything I've ever done.

Somewhere along the line, Pippin took over most of the craftsmanship. She whittles and sands and weighs the bat to check her progress. And anytime I move to touch it she slaps my hand away.

Once I see the writing on the wall, I try staying in the background and giving some pointers, but that doesn't go over well, either. Pippin has apparently decided she's the expert, and when she attempts to explain the physics behind vibrational frequency, I don't have any idea how to argue. So yeah, I guess she's the expert.

But she has become cranky and distracted lately. Each time she makes a small adjustment to the bat, she seems dissatisfied. Each time I comment on how beautiful the bat is — and it is, without a doubt, the most beautiful baseball bat I've ever seen—she snaps at me about inefficient energy transfer or necessary improvements to aerodynamics.

It's a Friday, and the Stallions have an off day. That gives me and Pippin plenty of time after my shift to make progress on the bat. I peer over Pippin's shoulder as she takes measurements I don't understand. It looks so sleek, so light, and so strong, that I can't wait to use it in a game, or at least during batting practice. I want it so badly that I finally chance a tap on Pippin's shoulder. She turns her head slowly and glares at me. I back up a few inches to create a safe zone.

"It's a pretty bat. Are you close to being done?" I jump back at her stabbing eyes and hold my hands up in defense. "It's fine if you're not, perfection takes time, you're the one in charge here."

My over-the-top fear cracks through her frustration and she smiles that smile I love so much. The one that's unrestrained, unconcerned with the strangely placed dimples on her chin or the crooked state of her teeth. The smile only I see, when no one else is around.

"It's so close," she says. "But for the life of me, I can't figure out the exact vibrational frequency of quebracho of this size and shape."

I know before I say anything that I'm way out of my league, but I ask anyway. "Why do you need to know that?"

"To create the largest sweet zone," Pippin says."

"You mean sweet *spot*. Come on, Pip-squeak, you know that."

"No. I mean what I said. The sweet spot baseball players talk about is actually made of two different spots—the one that feels the best on your hands when you make contact and the one where the ball comes off the bat the fastest. Everyone thinks they're the same spot, but they're not. They're close, but they're not exact."

"Why does that matter?" I ask, genuinely curious now.

"Think about it. If there's a spot on the bat that feels the best to you as a hitter, what are you going to try to do?"

"Hit it there, I suppose."

"Exactly. Because you'll assume that if it feels the best, it'll go the farthest. But that's not true. So hitters all over the world are trying to hit the ball in a place on the bat that is almost—but not quite—the spot that will make the ball go farthest. Obviously, that's counter-productive."

"Obviously," I say, just happy to be following her train of thought.

"So if I can figure out how to make those two different types of sweet spots into one sweet zone, in which the ball will have the fastest acceleration off the bat from anywhere within that zone, *and* feel the best to the hitter, then this bat will be better than any bat ever made."

"Cool," I say. "And how do you do that?"

"I already told you that."

"Um, remind me."

Pippin shifts, opening her shoulders so I can see past her as she points to various parts of the bat. "If I can find the exact vibrational frequency, I can configure the design to create the least amount of vibration throughout the entire sweet zone."

"Not having vibration sounds good," I say. "Then my hands won't hurt if I get it off the handle."

"For wimps, I suppose that's a big deal. More importantly, when you hit the sweet zone, less energy will be lost through the transfer into vibrational waves, meaning more energy will go into creating acceleration of the ball off the bat."

I try to think of something smart to say in answer to her expression, which is obviously questioning my comprehension. "Like I said, it's a pretty bat."

Pippin flashes me her smile again and returns her attention to the bat. I pick up a few baseballs and start juggling, then swing a random piece of wood like a baseball bat, and finally decide to plop down on a hard wooden chair and wait until Pippin gets tired and is ready to go home—assuming that will actually happen before I have to clock in on Monday morning.

Just as I'm trying to decide on a strategy for interrupting Pippin to tell her we have to go home to bed, I hear a little squeal of delight. Pippin stands in front of me, holding the bat in her hands like she's offering a sword.

"Don't mess with me, kid," I say, and Pippin's smile widens. "Are you for real?"

In answer, Pippin grabs the bat by the barrel and extends the handle. The moment the wood touches my hand, I know it's a special bat. I set the barrel on my shoulder and make a little half swing. It's enough to feel that the weight distribution is perfect. The barrel of this thing will rip through the zone.

"How does it do that?" I ask.

I was talking rhetorically to myself, but Pippin takes the bat back and slides her fingers along the thin portion between the handle and the barrel. "Look," she says. "This space divides the two parts of the bat. But it doesn't separate them, it unifies them. It makes the entire thing more...I don't know. Harmonious, somehow."

"Perfect harmony," I whisper.

"Okay," Pippin says. "Maybe a little hyperbolic. But okay."

I gaze at the bat like it's a newborn baby. It truly is an amazing piece of engineering. But the question remains, will it swing well when a baseball is being thrown at me? And just as importantly, will the thin part of the bat cause it to break more easily, despite the hardness of the wood? And then all that vibrational frequency stuff Pippin has been talking about. How will that work out? I take the bat back and whip off a few more half swings, unable to hide my excitement.

"Let's go to the ballpark," I say.

•   •   •

Once Pippin and I are in the car—the quebracho held delicately in Pippin's lap—I call my dad. I can't wait to see the look on his face when he sees the bat we made. The elegant lines. The interesting angles. The taper and the rapid widening toward the barrel. But the phone goes to voicemail. I think about leaving a message or sending a text, but if my father is sleeping, it's probably best to let him rest.

Still, it feels like a momentous occasion: we're going to test the bat Pippin has been so passionate about, the one that she's hoping will win her a first-place ribbon at the state science fair next month. If my dad can't be there, maybe my son should be. So as I pull the Escort out of the lumber yard parking lot, I pick up my cell phone and dial Emily's number, wondering if she'll pick up.

"Emily," I say when she does. "Thanks for answering." I feel stupid when she doesn't reply, but force myself to plow forward. "Pippin finished her bat. We're going to try it out. I thought you and Oz might want to join us." There's a long silence on the other end, and I can't tell what she's thinking. "Please. This is important to Pippin."

After another long pause, Emily sighs into the phone. "I'll have to ask Oz. I can't make any promises."

"Thanks, Em," I say, hoping she'll be okay with me calling her what I used to call her, back in high school. "I hope to see you there."

In fact, Emily and Oz beat us there. When I pull my car into the parking lot of Sweetwater Ballpark, the lights are already on and I see Oz through the fence, playing catch with Emily along the right field line. I watch them, rubbing my left shoulder where an ache has just arisen.

I pull a bucket of baseballs from the trunk while Pippin carries the bat like it's a treasure, both priceless and fragile. As we enter through the dugout, I see that Oz has a pretty decent arm. I feel like I shouldn't be proud. Like it's not my right. But I still am.

"There they are!" I say to break the ice.

Oz smacks his fist into his glove silently, pointedly not looking at me, as Emily strolls toward us. "You finished it, huh?" she says, going straight to Pippin and giving her a hug. "Congratulations." When she straightens up, we exchange an uncomfortable bout of avoiding eye contact.

"Thanks for coming," I say, and Emily finally looks at me and nods wordlessly.

"Do you like my quebracho bat?" Pippin asks, holding it out proudly.

"Excuse me?" I say. "Who paid for it?"

"Fine. Our quebracho bat. Happy?"

"Yes. Thank you."

"But I did most of the work," Pippin says just loud enough to be heard.

Pippin holds the bat out toward Emily, who accepts it and holds it flat in both hands, as if weighing it. "Interesting," she says. "The taper. I've never seen anything like it."

"That's because it's never been done," Pippin says.

"Does it swing well?"

I take the bat by the thin taper. "That's what we're here to find out. Hey Oz!" I call out toward the mound. "What do you think about throwing a little BP?"

Oz still won't speak to me, but he straightens his cap in response. I step up to the batter's box and dig my left foot into the dirt. "Please don't break on the first swing," I whisper to the bat. "For Pippin's sake."

"Hang on, guys," Pippin says, fiddling with her phone. "I need to record this for my science fair project." Her fingers dash around the face of the phone and she says, "Okay, action!"

Oz leans forward onto his front leg, as if staring in for a sign from a catcher. Then he goes to the set position, kicks his left leg high, and fires a straight fastball, surprisingly fast for a ten-year-old kid. Still, he's throwing from the entire distance of sixty feet, six inches, so the ball loops its way toward the plate and I have to force my weight to stay back. When the ball finally arrives, I hitch my hands in a small circle, explode my hips open, and throw my hands toward the ball.

Something immediately feels wrong. My hands are so light it's as if the barrel isn't trailing behind. As if there's no barrel at all. Obviously, Pippin made a mistake in her final weight distribution calculation.

But I continue the swing. With a whooshing sound, the barrel zips through the strike zone at a speed I'm unprepared for. It's too fast. And even though I extend my hands far toward centerfield, keeping the barrel in the strike zone as long as possible, my swing eventually forces the barrel to begin its track over my shoulder. But since the barrel has gone through the zone more quickly than I anticipated, the ball hits the very end of the bat.

With every bat I've ever used, it's a sure recipe for the handle to split in exactly the spot where Pippin removed the strength of the bat by narrowing it. I cringe and wait for the telltale snapping sound of wood.

Fortunately, it doesn't come. While it certainly isn't a pure crack of the bat, the sound reassures me the bat survived. The ball sails over the first base dugout and bounces high off the blacktop of the parking lot, missing my car by mere feet.

"My fault, Oz," I call out. "Still getting used to the feel of this thing. Can you give me another one?"

"Come on, Charlie," Pippin says, her face hidden behind her phone as she continues recording. "We need something big here."

Oz straightens his cap again and flourishes it this time with a confident spit onto the dirt. He goes through the same routine and grunts a little as he releases another fastball. This one has a little more velocity and I know to wait back even longer than before. The result is nothing short of astonishing.

The barrel of the bat whips through the zone again but this time I make solid contact. It's a sweet spot like I've never felt—or a sweet zone, as Pippin says. The deafening crack of bat-against-ball is the only sign I made contact. My hands feel nothing as they whip through the strike zone.

Despite the pitch being only about fifty miles-per-hour, the ball sails easily over the maple trees in right-center field. A moment later, it smacks against the roof of a house on the other side of the street.

Oz, Emily, and I all stare at the spot where the ball disappeared from view. Only Pippin isn't still transfixed. After finishing her recording, she lifts her hands above her head, then starts dancing in circles and singing a song I've never heard.

"Wow," I say under my breath. I bring the barrel of the bat onto my palms to study the grains. Not a nick. Not even a mark. "Can we do another?" I say. It was the single most fluid and easy swing of my life, but it was only one swing. The question remains, can it be duplicated?

The answer becomes clear very quickly. Oz throws five more pitches: two are out of the strike zone and I don't swing. But I hit the other three as hard as I can remember hitting a baseball. Two fly well over the outfield fence, one of them to the opposite field, where I've never had much power. The fifth raps against the wooden outfield wall after three crisp bounces, causing a hollow boom to echo throughout Sweetwater Ballpark.

After the final swing, Duane walks into the dugout and says, "Jesus, Fightmaster! Do you think my homeowner's insurance is going to cover that?"

I gaze toward the maple trees where the first home run disappeared. "That hit your house?" I say, stifling a laugh.

Rather than answering, Duane points at the bat. "What is that? Looks like some sort of space-age softball bat or something."

"No," Pippin says, still dancing. "It's legal."

Duane stares, transfixed, his eyes bouncing from home plate to his house in the distance and back again. "Well then, how can I get one?"

Everyone laughs except me. Pippin's embarrassed, hurt face comes to mind again and I scowl at Duane. "You can't," I say. "Pippin designed and constructed this thing. It's not for you."

"Whatever, man," Duane says. He waves me off and leaves the field. I wait for him to get into the parking lot before trotting after him. I don't want Pippin or Oz witnessing this.

"Hey Duane," I say when I catch up.

When Duane turns and sees that it's me, his eyes flash like he's thrown into fight-or-flight mode. I'm sure he expects me to sucker-punch him here and now. Instead, I lower my voice threateningly.

"I'm serious about that bat not being for you. You gave up the right to use it when you insulted Pippin."

"You're crazy, man. I never insulted —"

"You know exactly what you did." I stare at Duane for a long moment until something close to guilt flashes in his eyes and he looks away. "If I ever see you touch one of Pippin's bats," I say with as much menace as I can muster, "I'll kick your ass."

I know I'm being a jerk. But when I think again about the hurt on Pippin's face, I can't manage to feel bad about it.

I stare long enough to make sure Duane understands perfectly, then head back to the dugout while Duane yells, "I don't want to use it, anyway."

In the dugout, Emily gives me a questioning look, but I ignore it.

"I'd say it swings just fine," Emily says, letting her questions go for the moment. She gives me a small smile I can almost convince myself holds pride. At least it doesn't seem to hold anger, which is a big step in the right direction.

She offers her hands again and I replace the bat like it's a display case. We all stare like it's a museum artifact.

"So Pip-squeak," I say. "If I swing this thing in a game like I did here, we might have quite a few people wanting one of their own. What do you think?"

Pippin seems to give the question considerable thought. "On one hand," she says, "it could ruin everything. What if a terrible hitter uses it? No bat in the world can turn someone who can't hit into a hitter." I can't help but agree. A quebracho bat in the hands of some of the guys on the team would be like putting a ninety-year-old grandmother in the driver's seat of a Ferrari. "On the other hand," Pippin continues. "Several of the guys on the team struggle because they can't generate enough bat speed, so finding the sweet zone is like a needle in a haystack. And those guys might be helped by quebracho." She taps her finger against the front of her chin for several moments. "I think we should give it a try."

"All right," I say. "Then we should get started on another one as soon as we can. If all goes well, we'll have to be able to make more of them fast. But to do that, we might need help." I make eye contact with Oz who, I'm happy to see, is actually looking at me. "And I think I know of just the right person." When I'm met with silence I say, "What about Oz? Do you guys like each other?"

They both erupt at once. "Ooh," Oz says.

Pippin objects with a firm, "No!"

I hold up my hands to calm them. "Not like that." I wonder if they've figured out their strange biological relationship—that Pippin is Oz's aunt. I don't think Pippin has even heard about me and Oz yet. "I mean, are you guys friends?"

They seem suddenly allergic to the site of one another. "I guess," Pippin finally says.

"Great. Then you won't mind working together. Maybe Pip can share some secrets of the bat. All that math and physics stuff I don't understand."

Pippin finally looks at Oz and studies his qualities as if she's looking through a microscope. "I guess I could do that," she says. "If he's interested."

Oz glances at his mother, but Emily just raises her eyebrows questioningly. There's a long moment in which I'm relatively sure Oz is weighing his excitement of helping make a bat with the torture of having to be in the same space as his newfound father. Finally, Oz bounces his head in a quick nod.

"It's settled then," I say. "We'll start tomorrow morning. If it's okay with you," I say to Emily.

Even if I didn't think this was a wonderful thing for my sister — which I do. Even if I wasn't excited about the fact that my son is at least acknowledging me again — which I am. Even if there was no other reason to be happy about the agreement, I'd still lose hours of sleep over the look of gratitude on Emily's face. And she's pointing that look right at me.

Bloop and a Blast

Unlike many sports, baseball has no time clock. This means a team can never be saved by the clock hitting zero. One way or another, all twenty-seven outs must be recorded.

Over the history of the sport, this truth has led to countless improbable comebacks, and nearly as many sayings related to comebacks. One such saying is "Bloop and a blast."

When a team is down by one run in the last inning, with no runners on, two outs, and two strikes on the batter, only two pitches are needed — resulting in a "bloop and a blast" — to turn a loss into a win.

Chapter 11

At the breakfast table the following morning, the excitement is palpable. I barely taste my bacon and eggs as I shove them in my mouth between excited retellings of the story. I repeat, over and over, how smoothly the bat whipped through the zone, how the sound it made was more pure, more complex, and of a different pitch than I've ever heard from a bat—from any player at any level. And the way it jumped off the bat and soared over the fence…

My father asks questions any time he's able to get a word in, and Pippin simply eats her breakfast in silence, a satisfied grin never leaving her lips.

"We're headed over to the lumber yard right after breakfast to start a new one, right Pip?" I say, shoveling the last strip of bacon into my mouth.

"Just don't get so caught up in the bat that you miss the game," my father says. "It's Cold Spring today, and we'll need all hands on deck."

"Don't worry," Pippin says. "I'll keep him on track." She plays it off like the whole thing is my passion instead of hers, but when I stand, she jolts up so quickly she knocks her knees into the table, causing the coffee mug in front of my father to slosh and spill. "See you at the stadium, dad," she says, then grabs my hand and pulls me toward the door.

I resist for just a moment. "You're okay?" I ask my dad. I've heard that cancer patients can have peaks and valleys in how they feel, and my father seems no different. One day, he'll look so sallow, so effervescent that his skin is almost transparent, his energy level lethargic. Then, without explanation, he'll be like this morning—

looking nearly like his normal, pre-cancer self. I never know what to expect or, if I'm honest, how to respond to the rollercoaster.

My father waves me off, as if the answer is obvious. "Just be ready for Cold Spring," he says. "I'll be just fine if we win."

He says it half-jokingly, but I've seen the truth behind it. Baseball, and the Stallions in particular, seem to be one of the few things that can give my father energy. I don't think it's a coincidence that so many of his" good days" coincide so perfectly with the Stallions schedule.

I try to focus on the health and vitality coaching baseball seems to give him, but I know there's another side to that coin. The baseball season won't last forever. And when the season ends and the cold winds of another Minnesota winter start to blow, what will keep my father going then?

I allow Pippin to drag me to the car. On the way out of the neighborhood, I swing into the Conroy's driveway and Oz, sitting on the front step in his Stallions bat-boy uniform, bounds toward us and jumps in the back seat, settling in and avoiding the rear-view mirror.

"What's up, Oz?" I say.

Oz's response is to look out the window and pull the brim of his baseball hat lower. He sneaks a quick glance at the rear-view, but as soon as he notices me looking at him, his eyes dart away. I heave a big sigh. Apparently, Oz agreeing to work on the bat doesn't mean he's forgiven me.

When we get to the lumber yard, we head straight toward the back. Pippin grabs Oz's sleeve and pulls him to the slab of quebracho, which the two of them instantly begin drawing on, marking their cuts and talking over the details of the bat in terms I still don't understand, and probably never will.

"You two just be careful with those tools, okay?" I find the same chair as last time, kick my feet up, and flip open the Sports Illustrated I brought along.

They work for hours, and the bat's form slowly begins to take shape, more quickly this time, since Pippin has already done it once. But eventually I have to interrupt them so we won't be late. So much for Pippin keeping me on track.

As they hop back into the car, Oz's little voice says to no one in particular, "That bat is going to be so cool."

At the stadium, my dad sits in his recliner in the dugout while Mack throws batting practice—another reminder of the cancer that prevents my father from doing so many of the things he used to love. But to give up throwing BP was particularly difficult.

"What's up, old man?" I say, sliding in next to him and nudging him softly with my shoulder.

"Can't decide on the seven spot," my father says, tapping the eraser side of a pencil against his chin.

"According to Pippin, it doesn't matter. Just the fact that quebracho exits means we'll put up runs no matter what."

I'm kidding, but from the first batter of the game, it seems to be true. The whole line-up comes out swinging. Home runs, singles, doubles...everyone seems to be squaring up the baseball on each swing.

Everyone except for two people. Duane, I'm not sad to say, hasn't hit anything all day. After each at-bat, when he comes back to the dugout, I see him trying not to look at the quebracho bat everyone else is using so successfully. But he fails every time, and I see in that quick glance his desire to use the bat. My guess is, he won't be doing anything to hurt Pippin again any time soon.

The other one to struggle is, of all people, me.

The quebracho bat feels good in my hands. Great, actually. But the weight distribution is just different enough from what I'm used to that I haven't been able to time the ball right.

I think about Bud again, and his advice. I embrace the vulnerability about my father's declining health and my failure to get a hit in my first three at-bats. And I try to accept my pop-up to first base in exactly the same way I accept my diving stop in the third inning.

Finally, in the ninth, I have my final at-bat. The Stallions have a comfortable lead. I step to the plate and take a moment to close my eyes and remember Bud Crawford's words. I let everything fade away and think about the game so far. The pop-up, the strikeout in the sixth, the diving play. I take a step back in my mind and try to look at all of them in the same, neutral way. Just noticing them.

When I do that, something amazing happens. It all fades away. The good, the bad, and everything neutral in the middle. And all that's left is this at-bat. This moment—where I've never been—as I face this pitcher. The only thing on my mind is the baseball that's about to be thrown toward home plate.

I step into the box, focusing on the feeling of acceptance, letting everything else fall away. When the pitch comes, I see it with perfect clarity. My swing is effortless. Contact is pure. My follow-through stretches long and flawless.

I hit it square and know it's the hardest I've ever hit a baseball. But no one could anticipate what happens next.

As the small crowd stands, the ball smashes into the old, wooden wall in right field—and continues. It blows straight through, putting a baseball-sized hole in the wall. A jagged sliver of wood drops onto the warning track as the right fielder stares through the hole, having no idea how to react.

·   ·   ·

Long after the game ends, the ballpark remains full. Fans linger, discussing what happened. Players from both teams jog out to inspect the hole in the wall and speculation runs rampant. The wall is old and weak, some say. Even a softly hit ball would have gone through that particular spot.

Others claim I must be taking steroids, meaning the whole episode should be forgotten or deemed illegitimate. An argument breaks out about whether even the great Bud Crawford ever hit a ball so hard.

I know I should soak up the moment and enjoy all the attention. The local newspaperman who covers most Stallions games won't leave me alone, demanding answers for how I hit the ball so hard and what my thoughts are. But there's only one person whose attention I crave, and he's unwilling to give it.

Oz watches closely from the dugout, as if he wants to be out here taking part in the rare moment—with his father, no less. But something holds him back. What it is, I'm not sure. Pride? No. Nothing so trivial. What Oz is having such a hard time getting over is his feeling of hurt and betrayal. And it makes sense.

As Oz and Emily pack up their things and head for the exit, a tall, lanky man ducks his head as he enters the dugout. Oz stiffens and grabs a baseball and a Sharpie from the bench, then offers them to the man, who takes them graciously, scribbles an autograph, then gives them back to Oz with a pat on the head.

I chuckle as a dozen fans, realizing who it is, rush onto the field — something that can't happen at a Major League ballpark. The man patiently signs autographs for all of them, then finally makes his way out through the infield dirt, heading toward the cluster of players still gathered around the hole in the right field wall.

I approach the man and extend my hand. "Look at these people. It's like you're famous or something."

He slaps my hand away and squeezes me in a strong embrace. Then he holds me at arm's length like he's studying me. "Just as skinny as you were in A-ball. How do you even hit a baseball?"

I hear several Stallions players talk excitedly behind me, trying unsuccessfully to keep their voices from being heard. But they're fans just like anyone else.

Is that Hudson White?

That guy's made the All-Star team three years in a row!

Don't the Twins play today?

No, they're off, then start a home stand tomorrow.

I see Hudson's eyes flick toward the goggling cluster of people, so I lead him toward the dugout, which is now empty.

"A swarm of fans wherever you go, huh?" I try not to be jealous, but Hudson has everything I've ever dreamed of. A successful Major League baseball career. Fans, money, fame. It's depressing to let myself imagine what his life is like, so I do my best not to dwell on it.

"You wouldn't even believe it, man," Hudson says. "It's like everyone in the world thinks they know me. And I can't get enough, Fighter. I eat it up."

"What's Janel think about it all?"

Hudson shakes his head slowly. "I don't talk about it much, but Janel isn't around anymore, man."

"What happened?" It's strange that Hudson breaking up with his wife would be such a blow to me, but it is. Janel was with Hudson when he arrived in A-ball. She was warm and kind, and completely over the moon about Hudson White. I never had any doubt they'd be together forever.

"Stardom and family life?" Hudson says. He shakes his head firmly. "They don't mix. Simple as that."

"What about Ayesha? How's she handling everything."

"She's good," Hudson says, but his gaze turns inward for a moment. "I don't get to see her very often, but she's still my little girl."

For a moment, I feel bad for Hudson. But then I remember his life. The stardom, the success. He's literally living the dream. It's tough to feel bad for that.

"Hell of a game tonight," Hudson says. "You looked different than when we played together."

"How's that?"

"It's hard to put a finger on. But let's face it, you used to be overly aggressive. Hot-headed. Now...well, it's like you're, I don't know, worldly or something. More mature out there. You had a couple rough at-bats, but stayed focused."

"I guess," I say, thinking of Bud Crawford. "But I really was a mess today until that last at-bat."

Hudson nods his agreement. "But that last at-bat?" He whistles and glances back at the right field wall meaningfully. "Don't see that every day."

I let myself enjoy the comment — from Hudson White, no less. Sure, he's the same guy I spent countless hours with back in A-ball, playing cards on the long bus rides, staying up late at night talking about hitting. But Hudson's career path was always different. He's a "bonus baby" who the team invested so much money in, they needed him to pan out. He would have gotten as many shots as it took, not that he needed more than one. Since his first call-up, Hudson White has been a superstar.

"Where's this kid you always talked about?" Hudson asks. "I gotta meet her."

Until he says "her," I thought he might be talking about Oz. But that wouldn't be possible. I've never talked about Oz with Hudson. Until just a few weeks ago, I hadn't even known about the existence of Oz.

As we reach the dugout, I see it isn't empty after all. Pippin is in the far corner, sweeping sunflower seed shells and shaking her head.

"Speak of the devil," I say. "Hey Pip-squeak, you got a second?"

Pippin's voice is stern. "In a minute. Your filthy teammates make a mess of this place and just leave it. What do they think will happen to the shells? That they'll just decompose before tomorrow's game? Geesh."

Hudson gives a look as if to say, *You weren't kidding about her, were you?*

"Don't you know who this is, Pip?"

"Of course, I know." Pippin continues sweeping the last of the shells into a dustpan, which she empties into a trash can at the edge of the dugout, then finally approaches us and extends her hand to Hudson.

"Hudson Jamal White. Centerfielder, Minnesota Twins. Lifetime .304 average, two-hundred sixteen career home runs, three-time All-Star, including the All-Star game MVP two years ago. It's nice to meet you."

Hudson's grin is wide as he shakes Pippin's hand. "You didn't list my greatest accomplishment," he says. Pippin's brow curls as she racks her memory for what she missed. "Two years of putting up with this guy's BS," he says, nodding toward me. "So how do you think he pulled off that little trick in his last at-bat?"

"That's easy," Pippin says. "Quebracho."

Hudson cocks his head to the side. "That some kind of supplement?"

Pippin giggles. "No, it's a kind of wood. We made a bat that's better than any bat ever made."

"That so?" Hudson says, turning his question to me.

"It's for real," I say. "It swings smoother than anything I've ever swung before."

Pippin runs to the end of the dugout, pulls the quebracho from the bat rack, and brings it back to Hudson. The All-Star takes the bat, looks it over curiously, then steps out of the dugout to take a couple swings. He sticks out his lower lip and nods. "Not bad. It looks a little funky, but the barrel—"

"—Really gets through the zone," I say, finishing the sentence in unison with him. "Seriously Hudson, it's pretty much the perfect bat."

Next to me, Pippin cringes. "It's true that I'm satisfied with the coefficient of restitution, but—"

Hudson puts his hands up to stop her. "Whoa, there, girl. Slow down for the rest of us. Coefficient of who?"

"Not of who, of what. It's just the ratio of incoming velocity to outgoing velocity. Basic stuff."

"Obviously," I say. I look at Hudson like I understand every word, which makes him nearly double over in laughter.

"But the ideal weight, now that's the question," Pippin says.

"I like to swing a 34-31," Hudson says. "You got any of those?"

Pippin shrugs. "That's about what our first one is. And I mean, I guess that's probably the safe play, considering the physical weakness of baseball players."

"Excuse me?" Hudson says. "Baseball players aren't weak. Look at me and your big brother."

"Sorry," Pippin says, standing her ground. "But if baseball players weren't weak, they'd all be using forty-one ounce bats."

I chuckle at the idea of trying to swing a bat so heavy. I've heard that Babe Ruth used a bat as heavy as fifty-two ounces early in his career and several other old-timers used heavy bats. But no one does anymore. Modern day pitchers throw too hard. I know for a fact that Barry Bonds used a thirty-two ounce bat in 2001, when he hit a record 73 home runs—and he was using steroids. "Why would anyone use a forty-one ounce bat?" I ask.

"I don't know," Pippin says sarcastically. "Ask Ty Cobb or Joe DiMaggio. They both swung forty-two ounces."

"Ouch," Hudson says. "That stings, doesn't it Fighter?"

"Are you going to answer my question?" I ask my sister.

"Fine. Because according to research, forty-one ounces is the optimum weight for a baseball bat to create the most acceleration of a ball. But that assumes the hitter can control it, which he can't, because again, they're too weak. Fortunately, if you have to pick, it's more efficient to swing faster than to swing a heavier bat."

"And why is that, again?" I ask.

"It's obvious. Even though both heavier bats and faster bat speed create more acceleration, the research says that if you can't have both, increased bat speed results in 45% more acceleration than a heavier bat would."

Hudson and I stare at her with no idea what she's talking about. She seems to understand this and waves her hand like she's shooing a fly. "It's fine. Somewhere between twenty-nine and thirty-one ounces is what most hitters can swing, so that's what we'll make. It'll still be better than any other bat."

"Good," I say.

"But not as good as if baseball players were strong enough to handle a forty-one ounce bat."

"The kid's got us there, Fighter."

"As for this one," Pippin says, holding the quebracho up to Hudson, "you can keep it."

I nearly fall over from shock. The bat is for her science fair project, which is coming up soon. And I just hit a ball through the wall with it. Not to mention, I know how much a state championship means to her, so how could she possibly consider giving the bat away?

As if reading my mind, Pippin says, "Oz and I are almost done with the one we're working on. The Stallions can use it when it's done. And you can use this one," she says, motioning to the bat in Hudson's hands.

Hudson smiles wide, but he's obviously uncomfortable. And I know why. A guy as successful as Hudson What isn't about to mess with his recipe for success. Sure, the quebracho swings smoothly, and Pippin sounds ridiculously smart when she talks about it. But what if it changes Hudson's swing, even the slightest bit? In Sweetwater, I can get away with that and still hit mammoth home runs. At the big league level, it could ruin everything Hudson has worked so hard for. And the stakes aren't an amateur baseball state championship, they're his livelihood.

But Hudson graciously accepts the gift, thanking Pippin over and over for her thoughtfulness. He promises to use it in batting practice some day in the off-season, and he'll be sure to let her know what he thinks. At first Pippin looks deflated, but after a moment she seems satisfied.

"It was great to finally meet the girl Charlie always talked about so much," Hudson says, shaking Pippin's hand again. "But do you mind if I steal your brother for a minute? We need to talk shop for a bit."

"No problem," Pippin says. "I rode my bike." And with that, she bounds out of the dugout.

"That kid's got a bright future," Hudson says, watching Pippin go.

"I sure hope so."

"Why wouldn't she? She's obviously smart as a whip, and she seems pretty fearless."

I realize I didn't notice Pippin's eyelids flicker when she talked to Hudson. It seems backwards — the time she talks to a person who makes everyone else nervous, she wasn't intimidated? But then I understand — she was in her element. It was her dugout. Talking about her bat. I feel an unnatural fondness for the baseball bat beyond how it feels as it tears through the strike zone.

As Pippin pedals away, Hudson slaps my shoulder. "Speaking of bright futures, what about you?"

I scratch my temple, trying to figure out how I'm supposed to explain to a Major League All-Star about the importance of an amateur baseball state championship. Or about my meetings with Bud Crawford. Or my hopes for a relationship with Emily. Or my need to make sure Pippin will be okay. Or my struggle to make my son accept me. My life in Sweetwater has become so much more than I expected.

"I don't really know. I guess I'm just playing ball. Living the dream, you know?"

I say the last part with a smile, a throw-away comment to diffuse any tension. But Hudson looks serious.

"The club heard about what you're doing here, man. This league ain't bad. I mean, it's not Triple-A ball, but averaging a home run a game down here? Man, that's something."

"What are you getting at?"

"I'm getting at the fact that the big club wanted to take a look. Get some eyes on you to see if you're still swinging it like you were a couple months ago. Maybe see how much to offer to get you to accept this time."

"How much to offer? Did they send a scout or something?"

Hudson laughs. "Or something. They were going to, but first they asked what I knew about you, since we go way back. I found out they wanted to take a look and offered to come down myself. That way I could see you again and finally get you to pay up on that dinner you've owed me for eight years."

I can't believe what I'm hearing. Sure, the home run chase has been fun, but it's only about the Stallions, and catching Bud Crawford, and Sweetwater. I never expected my performance here to lead to anything bigger than getting my Triple-A spot back. I didn't expect them to keep tabs on me. The scouts left weeks ago, with Raimel.

"What are you going to tell them?"

"What am I going to tell them?" Hudson's laughter booms through the dugout. "I'm going to tell them you hit a baseball straight through the right-field wall, that's what I'm going to tell them!"

I try to slow my heart rate, but there's no stopping the adrenaline that's coursing through my veins. Pippin seems like she's been doing better recently. My dad's stable. Maybe now's the time. "You don't think they'd give me more than the league minimum, do you?"

Hudson looks out to where the gathering of players are split between studying the hole in the wall and watching Hudson White in the dugout. "Look, no one in the farm system is tearing it up right now and this is the Twins, not the Yankees. We can't just go buy the best free agent in the league. You're a local kid, good PR. And the higher-ups think we can win the pennant this year if we can shore up a few holes."

"What are you saying?" I ask.

Hudson smacks my shoulder again and looks at me meaningfully.

"I'm saying if you keep hitting balls through walls, you could end up a multi-millionaire before the season's out."

•   •   •

I can't even pretend I'm not on cloud nine after talking with Hudson. Hudson White. *The* Hudson White. Not that I've ever seen him the way all his adoring fans do: as the superstar center fielder whose only controversy is about whether Mike Trout or Willie Mays is the more appropriate comparison. But even though I don't see him that way, others do. Which means Hudson has influence. The kind of pull that only comes with superstar status. The kind of status that makes people listen.

And he's going to tell the Twins they should give me a big contract offer.

Hudson and I go out for a beer after the game but even in Sweetwater, the swarm of autograph seekers makes it difficult to hang out. After less than an hour Hudson says he'd better get back to Minneapolis. He's religious about his routine and a late night out isn't in the cards. So I go home early, too. But instead of sleeping, I spend the majority of the night staring at the ceiling, dreaming of signing a million dollar contract.

The next morning is Sunday and I have no plans other than daydreaming as much as possible and waiting for the phone to ring. But Pippin bounces down the stairs with other things in mind.

"I'm headed to the lumberyard," she says, red pigtails bouncing as she skips toward the door.

"Okay, but let me grab some breakfast first," I say.

"No, you don't understand." Pippin strokes her pigtails nervously. It's true, I don't understand the look she gives me. The sideways glance is unlike her. She looks to her shoes and says, "You're not invited."

"I'm not...what?"

"I'm sorry, Charlie. It's just, Oz says he doesn't feel comfortable with you around. I don't know why he's so weird about it, but he says he wanted to work on the bat, just the two of us."

Pippin may not know, but I understand perfectly well why Oz is so weird about it. "Okay," I say, trying not to sound as deflated as I feel. "I'll talk to you later then."

Pippin heads toward the lumberyard and all I can do is watch her go, fighting what feels like an eruption in my chest. After a few minutes of feeling sorry for myself, I recover enough to call Emily. She answers after three rings.

"I think it's time we talked," I say. "Can I pick you up in an hour?"

· · ·

Uncertainty gnaws at me as I drive my car toward the batting cages in town, Emily in the passenger seat. I've been so wrapped up in what Hudson said to me and the latest rejection from Oz that I haven't planned what to say to Emily. How can I apologize for breaking my promise not to tell Oz about us in a way that will make her forgive me? In the end, I'm opting for the comfort of the cages and hoping they'll make talking easier.

Summer air drifts through the car, thick and humid and fragrant, and the mother of my child lifts her chin into the sunlight next to me. The thought is still too unreal to wrap my mind around.

"Batting cages, huh?" Emily says as I pull the car into the parking lot. She sticks out her bottom lip and nods. Not exactly a ringing endorsement of my decision to bring her here, but it certainly could have been worse. I make a mental note to make reservations at a nice restaurant the next time we get together. Make it more of a date, if Emily is willing.

Thinking about whether she might be willing feels a lot like trying to decipher trigonometry. She definitely gave me a look when I invited Oz to help us make bats. And the look was definitely meaningful. But did it mean *We're good now*, or even *I like you*, or simply *Thank you*?

I wish there was a way to figure it out without having to ask. To just know, somehow. But that's not how it is with women. For some reason the male species has never been able to figure out, it's always more complicated than that.

We hop out of the car and I pay for a handful of tokens at the automatic kiosk. When I go to pick out a bat, I stare dubiously at the selection of beat-up, metal poles. "Not exactly quebracho," I say.

"Speaking of which," Emily says, taking one of the bats from its holder. "What's up with you and Duane?" Her smile is smaller now and she squints at me.

"Nothing. What do you mean?"

"I noticed he's the only one on the team not using quebracho. That's interesting."

"You heard him. He doesn't want to use it."

"Really?" Emily says. "You're going with immaturity? Are you sure that's the route you want to take here?" When I don't respond, she continues. "My dad says Duane's not going to be in the line-up next game. He's been benched, Charlie. He lost his spot because of you. Again. And just like Pippin and Oz and both our dads, the Stallions mean a lot to him."

I don't personally care what the Stallions mean to Duane, or that he's getting benched. We've never been friends and in my mind, the fault is entirely his. "Why do you care that Duane's getting benched? He's a jerk. Always has been, always will be."

Emily taps the metal bat softly against the cement, watching it the whole time. "I don't think you know anything about Duane."

"What's that supposed to mean? You're on his side? You know what he did to Pippin? How he rejected her high-five?"

Emily hesitates and I realize she probably didn't know about that. But she recovers quickly. "Did you know that Duane's older brother died in Afghanistan?" she says.

In truth, I didn't even know Duane had an older brother. He would have graduated from high school before I got there. But hearing that Duane's brother died in service to the country shuts me up long enough for Emily to continue.

"And did you know that he was getting letters from colleges about potential scholarships when he was in high school, until he lost his spot to you and spent his senior year wasting away in right field? He didn't end up getting any offers and his family couldn't afford to send him to college. So now he doesn't have a degree, he's perpetually in and out of employment—"

"And it's all my fault," I say, feeling defensive.

"That's not what I said, Charlie. But you can see why he might blame you." She takes a deep breath, like she's tired of the conversation, but she doesn't stop. "Besides, think about the example you're setting for Oz and Pippin. Is that really what you want to teach them? That vengeance and getting even are more important than taking the high road?"

I can't figure out what to think. It's true, I didn't know anything about Duane's personal life. Not the loss of his brother or the loss of his scholarship opportunities. I have to admit, it does make me feel bad for him. But when I remember Pippin's face when he rejected her, I can't imagine ever letting him use the quebracho bat.

"I don't know," I say. "I just...don't know."

"Well, think about it," Emily says.

She twirls the bat around a few times before resting it on her shoulder and striding into the batting cage. "In the meantime, get ready to take some notes." She closes the gate behind her, latches it, and says, "Set it to the fastest speed, Fightmaster."

"Seriously?" I ask.

"How dare you doubt my abilities?"

"Suit yourself."

I set the machine to 85-miles-per-hour and, shaking my head, push the start button. "Be careful in there."

Emily smacks the bat against the outline of a home plate painted on the blacktop and wiggles her butt. I wonder if she knows how sexy it is, or if she's one of those cluelessly beautiful girls. Probably the former. I'm not convinced the latter exists.

The mechanical arm of the pitching machine rotates backward and a ball slides into place just before the arm swings forward with a loud rattle. The ball sizzles out of the machine and darts toward home plate. Emily screeches, turns away from the ball, and ducks her head. When she manages to peek from beneath her forearm, which is draped over her brow, her eyes are so full of terror I can't even laugh. She quickly unlatches the gate and jumps out of the cage, squealing again as the next pitch smacks into the fence behind her as if in chase.

"You take it," she says, extending the bat toward me. "That was the single scariest moment of my life."

I accept the bat with a laugh and step up to the plate. I hit each pitch squarely, having more fun than I expected. When the last ball I hit slams against the metal facing of the pitching machine and it stops working, I'm not sure if it's the end of the round or if I broke it.

"One more token," I say. "Then you can have another go."

"I'm not getting back in there," Emily says, pushing a token in and pressing the button. "You have to be crazy to go in there."

I spray the next ten pitches in every direction. I couldn't wipe the smile off my face if I tried. But I don't need to bore Emily by making her watch me take more batting practice, so I force myself to leave the cage.

"Not bad, Fightmaster," she says.

"Yeah, well, big league offers don't come around to just anyone."

Emily squints, but her gaze is inward. "What's that supposed to mean?"

I shrug and feel silly for bringing it up. "I guess I never told you, did I? I got the call. From the Twins."

"What? The Minnesota Twins?"

"No," I say, unable to hide a wide grin. "The Mankato Twins...of course the Minnesota Twins."

"But," she says, the inward gaze turning confused now. "But you're here."

"I am."

"Why?"

I shake my head a little, wondering the same thing. "A little piece of news I received on top of the scoreboard at Fenway." Emily's confusion grows, and I realize she has no idea what I'm talking about. "My dad," I say. "He told me Pippin was really struggling. So I came back."

Emily takes a deep breath, like she's struggling to fit this new information into her worldview. "I heard you say your Triple-A team was holding your spot, and I knew your dad was sick, but I didn't know...Charlie, that's amazing. That's...so selfless."

"You sound surprised," I say.

"Well, I am, to be honest."

I nod my understanding. It still baffles me sometimes. "There really wasn't another option," I say. "Pippin needed me. At least, that's what my dad said. Do you think it was true?"

"Definitely," she says, without hesitation. "It's been really hard to watch her struggle. But ever since you've been back—from the moment you got back—she's been a different kid."

"Good," I say.

Emily shakes her head slightly, still trying to frame this new reality. "How about some ice cream?"

She loops her arm around mine—a surprise which I'm more than happy with—and we stroll slowly toward the concession stand. "So, Charlie. What makes you happy?"

"What makes me happy?"

"Yeah. It's been years since we've spent any time together, and we do have a kid. It seems like maybe we should know each other a little better."

My original plan was to talk about the mistake I made in revealing myself to Oz. But Emily doesn't seem to be dwelling on it, so I figure I shouldn't either. "Fair enough," I say. "But you go first."

"Okay." Emily turns her head to the sun and closes her eyes. "Summer days, books that make me cry, the smell of babies and puppies—not necessarily in that order—and music that makes me feel right down to my soul. But mostly, my son." When she opens her eyes, they hold such joy that it's obvious she's been picturing each of her favorite things. "Our son, I mean." She seems momentarily uncomfortable and covers it by saying, "Your turn. Go."

"I'm pretty simple," I say. "Baseball makes me happy."

Emily scowls. "That's not what I mean."

"What are you talking about? You asked what makes me happy. I'm telling you."

"No, it's just, baseball's a game. And I get it, it's fun. It's...enjoyable. But I'm not talking about games and…and…pastimes. I'm asking a deeper question than than. I'm asking what makes you happy."

"You just don't get it."

"Then explain it to me."

I stop walking and look to the ground, trying to collect my thoughts. Trying to figure out how to explain what I mean. "Look, you're right. There are things like what you're talking about that give my life meaning. Pippin, for one. The look on her face when we finished the bat. Spending time with my dad. Seeing an old friend. The first rain of the spring makes me happy. But…"

"But what?"

I take her hand, wrap it in both of mine, and look at our fingers as I speak. "There's a moment, and it doesn't happen every day. Around dusk. And you realize you've been at the ballpark all day long, haven't had a break since lunch. And you haven't thought about the time even once. And all the sudden the world gets still. The sun has dropped behind the horizon, painting the sky — and the whole world is this incomprehensible shade of purple and blue. Smoke from someone's bar-b-que drifts over the field and you can almost taste the hamburgers on the grill. In the distance, someone starts up a lawn mower and the buzzing tells you that other people's lives are going on, but you know without a shadow of a doubt there's nowhere you'd rather be than right where you are. Evening birds start to flutter in the trees and the scent of the grass and the dirt of the entire day is on your skin. The humid air is full of leather and pine tar. And for the first time, you realize you're so tired from playing the game you love all day that you can hardly move a muscle. But you find just enough energy to play catch with a friend for just a few more minutes.

"The ball is mostly shadow now — a silhouette slapping into one glove, then the other, and pretty soon it's too dark to see the ball at all. As we gather our things, the first fireflies of the night start their dances on the other side of the right-field wall. All the mistakes I made, all the times I swung and missed, every error in the field — they're nothing but jokes to laugh off and tell stories about now. And all that's left is beauty. You look at the world around you and think, if God himself sent down a bolt of lightening and killed me where I stand right now, I'd die the happiest man in the world."

When I finish talking, I want to look at Emily and gauge her reaction. But I feel more vulnerable than I have in a long time—even more than on the baseball field. Surely, Emily will hear my words and think I'm silly and childish. I've let my guard down, I wasn't manly or macho or tough—or even a baseball star.

The thought terrifies me until I feel Emily's finger on my chin, forcing me to look at her. Her eyes shimmer as she leans toward me and kisses me for the first time in ten years.

The Beanball

No matter how much a player may deny it, the danger of a baseball is always in the far reaches of his mind. With pitchers throwing in excess of 100 miles-per-hour and batted balls flying even faster than that, every player knows the risks involved in stepping foot on the field.

The 1920 beaning of Cleveland Indians shortstop Ray Chapman led to his death 12 hours later and began the push for batting helmets.

But a pitched ball is only one of the dangers on the baseball field.

Chapter 12

As I step through the gates of Sweetwater Ballpark, I have no doubt it's the greatest place on earth. I stroll into the dugout, unzip my bag, and pull out the brand new quebracho Pippin and Oz finished last night. It's just as beautiful as the first one and I can't wait to break it in.

Behind home plate, Oz joins some players in a game of Pepper. I watch him play, unsure how to act around him. I want to keep trying to make things right between us, but something tells me I'm better off giving him space. Hopefully he'll come around soon.

Maybe it's nothing more than my new knowledge of our relationship, but everything Oz does, from his mannerisms to his facial expressions to the way he pronounces his vowels, reminds me of myself. Now that I know the truth, I can't understand how it's not obvious to everyone who sees us together.

On the other side of the dugout, the girls – Emily and Pippin – sit conspiring about whatever it is girls conspire about. But when Pippin sees me looking she jumps up and jogs over.

"You think the guys would let me play Pepper with them?" she says. "Just for a little bit until they start taking batting practice?"

"Wouldn't hurt to ask," I say.

I crack my knuckles as she approaches the group of guys. Pippin picks Oz as the one to approach, and I feel a little glow inside when Oz repositions himself to make room for her in the half circle.

"Where's Skip?" I ask the handful of players in the dugout. A couple guys shrug and the others say they don't know. And that's all it takes to get my heart racing. I try not to let panic take over, but it's unlike my father to be late to a game. My mind is bombarded with images of him at home, unable to stand. Or worse.

Finally, my dad's voice echoes outside the dugout as he yells a greeting to someone in the stands. But my relief is short lived. My dad rolls through the dugout entrance in a wheelchair, looking tired and beaten down everywhere but his eyes, which sparkle.

"What?" he says, and I realize I'm staring. But how can I not? I've never seen my father in a wheelchair, and the implication terrifies me. "It's just a chair with wheels," my father says. "I don't need it all the time, but it makes it easier to get around. Don't look too much into it."

I want to give him a hug and tell him I see through his words and know how tough it must have been to start using a wheelchair. How scary that decision must have been. How sorry I am I wasn't there to help him make it. But before I say anything, my father's voice rings through the dugout.

"The old man was slow getting going, boys. So starters only for BP today."

I wait until no one's watching, then reach under his arms and lift him from his wheelchair into the recliner. "Thank you," he says. When he sees the look on my face, he smiles and pats my hand. "I'm good," he says. "Really. I'm at the ballpark on a sunny summer day. I'm happy."

The words ease my mind a bit and I kiss him on the top of his head. With my father settled, I snag my glove from the bench, give the line-up card a perfunctory glance to verify I'm hitting third, and run out to shortstop. I keep an eye on the game of Pepper, and I'm happy to see enough of the bench players remain for the game to continue behind the batting cage while the starters take batting practice.

If the day is near-perfect, the condition of the field is its equal. Every hop is true. Every ball finds the pocket of my glove. Every throw explodes out of my hand and travels a straight line to the first baseman's chest.

The Stallions are twenty-seven and nine, and winners of our last eight in a row. In the thirty-six games, I've hit thirty-five home runs. And in the latest state-wide rankings, we've cracked the top ten for the first time in recent memory. The field is covered with the confidence and chatter that only comes from a winning streak.

I watch Duane near the batting cage as one of the starters walks past him and steps up to the plate. Duane stands over the new quebracho for a long time, looking down at it like he's trying to decide whether to pick it up. He looks out to my shortstop position but quickly looks away when he sees me watching him. He punches his fist into his glove and jogs into the outfield to shag fly balls.

When I peeked at the line-up card before jogging to my position, I noticed that Emily was right—Duane isn't in the line-up today. The way everyone has been hitting lately, it's the right move. But I also can't entirely fight a feeling of regret at my role in the fact that Duane has been left behind. The memory of Pippin's face when he rejected her high-five fights hard against that regret. Mostly, I'm unsure how I feel about Duane's benching.

Several others take their turns in the cage while I field balls at shortstop until Mack waves me in, last as always. When I get by the batting cage, I grab a weighted bat and begin swinging it around my head to loosen my shoulders. Then I pick up the quebracho, step into the cage, and take a couple practice swings.

The fluidity of the barrel through the zone amazes me all over again. I step up to the plate, Mack winds and throws, and I drive one pitch after another all over the park. The quebracho feels exactly the same as the first one did. I'm loose and confident and excited about the upcoming game. On my last swing, I pop the ball up—the only ball I didn't hit solidly the entire round. It doesn't matter. The sun feels warm against my cheeks.

A few of the bench players begin pushing the wheeled batting cage out of the way. They steer it toward the bullpen, where it will remain out of the way for the game. I walk toward the dugout, but can't get the last swing out of my mind. It's ridiculous—I hit every other ball hard. One bad swing can't take that away, and it shouldn't affect me.

But it does. The pitch had been low and in—right where I like it best. The fact that I didn't make solid contact with the pitch I usually hit hardest gnaws at me until I finally turn back to the pitcher's mound.

"Hey Mack, you mind throwing me one more?" I say. "I need to end on a good one." Mack stops dropping baseballs into the bucket next to him and waves me back to the plate. "Low and in, if you can," I say. "Just like that last one."

As Mack winds up and throws, I hear something behind me. A shuffling sound of some sort. But I'm focused. The pitch is exactly in the same spot — no one can argue that Mack doesn't throw a great BP — and I trigger my hands, then explode them toward the ball.

The contact is pure and I know the moment it leaves the bat that the ball will hit Duane's roof again. It shoots into the beautiful summer air.

I follow through long and strong, like I've been taught. My arms extend toward center field until I run out of length and the bat flies in a long arc toward my back.

The next split-second lasts an eternity. In the back of my mind, I remember the shuffling sound from before the swing. A rush of adrenaline shoots through me until I remember I'm taking batting practice, which means I'm isolated in the cage. But when I remember that the cage was removed and I'm standing out in the open, something makes me try to cut my back-swing short.

It's like I can see her coming, even though I'm facing the other way. Even though there's no reason for her to be near me. She's busy playing Pepper with the guys, not wandering around home plate. But somehow I know beyond a shadow of a doubt that the ball has rolled free, she assumed batting practice was done, and the shuffling I heard is the sound of her feet. Her eyes are focused solely on the ball she's chasing.

The bat's momentum is too great to stop, or even to slow very much. And when I feel the contact and hear the sickening crack, I know I've hit Pippin.

In the moment it takes to turn around, my mind explodes with possibilities. Maybe I hit her shoulder. Or maybe, since it made a cracking sound, she was carrying a bat and I hit that. Maybe it wasn't even her. But deep down, I know what I've done.

It's only confirmation when I see my sister's head, gashed and bleeding, fall hard to the ground behind me.

•   •   •

The chaos that ensues takes place outside my conscious mind. Somewhere at the edges of my understanding, every player on the Stallions club rushes to the home plate area. There are silent murmurs, open questions and speculation, even some loud wailing, which I soon realize is coming from me.

Emily is the first to reach Pippin—which is strange since I'm standing immediately over her. Emily covers the wound at Pippin's temple as if removing it from sight can steal its terrible power. With a stern but calm voice she instructs someone to call 9-1-1.

Later, I know at the edges of my consciousness, I held my sister in my arms, stroking her hair back from her face. I know I watched as some of my teammates lifted Pippin's unconscious body into the back seat of my car. I know Emily made the very short drive to the hospital next to the field and I rode along, asking questions to nobody in particular, seeking reassurance that Pippin was okay. But, although I know those things happened, as I sit in the hospital waiting room, I can't convince myself the events of the day are real.

Emily sits in the chair next to me, but I have no idea how long she's been here. Where did my teammates go? Is the world outside really moving on as if nothing happened?

"She'll be okay," Emily says.

But it gives me no comfort. Emily went to law school, not medical school. Her words, though well-intended, are as empty as the voice in my head, also clinging to false reassurance.

I have no idea how long we sit. Time no longer has meaning, not when every second feels like an hour. I don't know where my father is and the fact that he isn't here sends another pulse of panic through my temples. It's like I'm just waking from a dream, still too groggy to tell what's real and what's a terrible nightmare.

Inside the hospital waiting room there are no windows to the outside. It could be midnight or it could be noon when the doctor finally comes out from the back room, pulls his mask down, and says, "Charlie Fightmaster?"

I bolt out of my seat, Emily right by my side. "Is she okay?"

It was Emily's voice. Shouldn't I have been the one to ask about my sister? But my mind is so jumbled and confused I wasn't able to form words.

"She's stable," the doctor says. He's an aging man with gray at his temples and thin wisps of hair at the top of his head. He wears glasses, which he now removes, and rubs his eyes in fatigue. I wonder what he's been doing back there, and for how long.

"Pippin sustained a serious head injury," the doctor says. "In situations like this, these early hours are always the most important. We've done what we can for now."

"What is that?" I say, speaking for the first time. "You've done what you can for now. What does that mean? What did you do to her?"

The doctor shifts uncomfortably and seems to gauge the threat before him. He opts for addressing Emily.

"We had to drill into her skull to create space to relieve the pressure on her brain. She's in a medically-induced coma for now."

"How long?" Emily says as I struggle to comprehend what he's saying.

"That depends on how effective it is. Ideally, not long. But it's difficult to put a timetable on something like this. Each case is so different. Sometimes it works, sometimes it doesn't. But we have your information, obviously, and we'll let you know as soon as anything changes."

"I need to see her," I say.

The doctor nods as if it's expected. "She won't be awake, of course," he says. "And she's pretty bandaged up. Sometimes it's easiest to wait until after this initial period."

"She's this way?" I say, ignoring what he's saying and pointing to where he entered the room.

"Room 312," the doctor says.

I bolt through the doors and frantically scan the numbers until I come across 312. I stand at the threshold and look inside. Due to the layout of the room, Pippin's head is hidden around a corner wall. I only see her feet reaching halfway down the bed. Emily's hand appears on my shoulder and I take a slow step into the room. With every inch, more of Pippin's body is revealed around the corner. And suddenly, when I can see the nape of her neck, I freeze.

"Are you okay?" Emily asks.

I try to move. To go to Pippin's side. But my body won't obey my mind.

"I can't," I say. Then I turn away and run from the hospital room as fast as my legs will carry me.

.   .   .

I drive home, fighting the agony erupting in my chest, my throat, and behind my eyes. It's everywhere.

On auto pilot, I park in the driveway and enter the house. My father isn't in the recliner, so I go straight up to Pippin's room.

I haven't been in her room since returning to Sweetwater, which is strange. But then I realize why: it's because each and every morning, Pippin bounded downstairs as quickly as possible. To see me.

I sit on her bed, scanning the posters on the walls — one of Einstein and another of the Periodic Table of Elements. There are stuffed animals near her pillow and a well-used homework desk in the corner. On it, Pippin has been working on her science fair project. Knowing that everything I find might put me over the edge, I tentatively approach the desk and study her project.

It doesn't take long to realize it's brilliant. She has charts and diagrams, pictures and videos. I push a button on the laptop computer and watch the video of me testing the quebracho for the first time. I can't bear to see the beauty of that night, to hear the joy in her voice as she narrates.

Her research is exhaustive and well documented. From vibrational frequencies to coefficients of restitution, it's all here in front of me. I have no doubt, it's a project that can win the State Science Fair Competition.

I can't handle the guilt, seeing all Pippin has accomplished. And all I've taken from her. So I leave the room, closing the door softly behind me, and drive to the only place I might find comfort.

It's dark, although I still have no idea of the time. The lights at Sweetwater Ballpark are off, and the fact that they don't have a soft red glow illuminating from the bulbs means they haven't been on for some time. A poster board is duct taped to the entrance:

Due to a tragedy in the Stallions' family, tonight's game has been cancelled. We apologize for any inconvenience.

I climb over the chain linked fence and wander through the dugout. The field is empty, the night is dark. Everyone cleared out long ago. But here, lying on the bench, is the quebracho bat.

I stare at it for a long moment, curious. Why didn't anyone take it with them? Someone went to the trouble of picking it up from wherever it had been lying and bringing it to the bench, but they didn't bother to put it away? Or to take it with them and keep it safe?

A mosquito buzzes near my ear and I swat at it, feeling a rush of anger at my teammates. Don't they know how hard Pippin worked on this bat? How much thought and energy and time went into making it just perfect? And they just left it here, discarded.

I realize now, how small our circles really are. For each of us, there are only a handful of people who actually care—who would hurt in any real way if something happened to us. For everyone else, there would be shock and sadness and loss...but then it drifts away and their lives return to normal. Soon, it's as if the thing never happened at all. In a few years, when they're reminded that the person is gone, they're surprised, having banished the tragedy so thoroughly from their thoughts that they've forgotten it ever happened.

That's how fleeting our lives are. How meaningless.

I pick up the bat and cradle it in my hands, like it's a baby. As I stare out at the field where the accident happened, I fight to contain the boiling in my chest. I try to figure out where it should be directed — at my teammates for neglecting the bat? Or at myself for not being more careful? Eventually, my rage finds a home in the instrument that did the deed.

Before I know what I'm doing, I grip the handle of the quebracho and smash the barrel against the batting-helmet shelf. The quebracho slices through the wooden shelving like a sword. I find a large Gatorade cooler and unleash my fury on it, striking it so hard the lid flies high into the air while the rest of the cooler bounces out toward first base.

With nothing left to hit, I take a small leap to generate momentum and swing the bat as hard as I can against the concrete wall of the dugout. The shock reverberates through my hands and wrists and forearms, shooting a jolt of pain all the way to my shoulders.

But I can't stop. This is the bat that hurt my little sister. The one person in this world I'm supposed to protect. Over and over and over I smash the bat against the wall. Exhaustion nearly overtakes me, but still I don't stop.

Until Emily's now-familiar hand touches my shoulder.

"Charlie," she says simply.

And finally, I stop smashing the bat. I try to look at her but I'm surprised to realize I can't see anything through clouds of tears that blur my vision and streak down to my jaw.

I squeeze my eyes shut and force the tears to stop. When I'm finally able to control myself, a rush of panic sticks in my throat. I remember the science fair project.

I scan the bat for damage. The perfectly-crafted quebracho isn't just the thing that hit Pippin's head. It's my strongest connection to her. It's a bond we shared, a vision we created. It's the one thing of her I still have that can't be taken away.

In the darkness, I run my hand along the surface, praying I didn't damage it too badly. But it doesn't take long to find a large jagged crack right at the eighth-of-an-inch taper. I drop to my knees, cradling the bat once again. And through my agony and self-loathing I barely even hear Emily's attempts to comfort me.

•   •   •

Every minute that follows feels like a month. Each condolence from a well-meaning person is like a stab to the gut. Every "It's not your fault" and "I'm sure she'll pull through" cuts like a knife.

I've never felt so lost. So unsure of what to do and where to go. Everywhere in town seems to have a reminder of Pippin. I wander around for a minute. Or a year. It's impossible to tell.

There's nowhere in town that doesn't contain Pippin, so I eventually go to the place where, recently, she's become the most real—the lumberyard.

"Charlie," Mr. Edmond says when I arrive. He shakes his head and starts to speak, but nothing comes out. I don't know what to say either, so we just look at each other, then to the floor.

"Can I work?" I ask.

Mr. Edmond squints at me. "I don't think that's a very good idea, Charlie. The equipment back there takes a lot of focus. The last thing we need is another injury."

I toss my hands up in surrender. "I don't know what to do."

"Go home. Get some sleep. Or go visit Pippin. Anything but work."

I nod and slowly turn toward the door when Mr. Edmond's voice interrupts. "I know it's a terrible time to ask," he says. "But you don't know anything about the money in the till, do you?"

"The money?" It's as if I've heard of the concept of currency, but can't figure out why anyone would care about it. Or anything else.

"Yeah," he says. "There's been a bunch of extra cash in there recently. I don't know where it's coming from. But then when I do the books at the end of the night, everything adds up just right. It's strange."

"Yeah," I say. "Strange." And that's all I can muster.

Mr. Edmond squeezes his lips into a thin line. "I wouldn't even ask except, the only two people with keys to this place are me, you, and Pippin. And Pippin's...well..." His voice trails off, as if he doesn't know how to finish. "Like I said, I know it's a terrible time to ask."

"Sorry," I say, just wanting to escape to a place where I won't have to see anyone. "I don't know anything about it. But I'm sure Pippin wouldn't steal, if that's what you're worried about."

"No, of course not," Mr. Edmond says. "Like I said, the books add up. I just wish I knew what was happening."

I try to say goodbye, fail, and walk out of the lumberyard. Thinking about Pippin lying in the hospital bed, I realize that I, too, wish I knew what was happening.

.   .   .

There's nowhere else to go. Nothing else to do. I've put it off long enough.

It's time to go see Pippin.

The thought is terrifying. To see my little sister so helpless, when it had been my job as her big brother to protect her. Instead, I was the one that hurt her. But I have to go see her, if only to force myself to endure the torture I deserve.

I stop by the house to finally change out of my baseball uniform and I'm surprised to see my father. When I enter the three-season porch, he's sitting in his wheelchair, staring straight ahead, a dazed look in his eyes. I don't think I've ever seen him look so tired, or so frail.

"I must have dozed," he says when he sees me. He looks at his watch and shakes his head. "It was only going to be for a minute. Just to rest. But it's been hours. It's ten at night."

He seems panicked as he wheels himself to the front door and tries to grab his car keys from the hook. He leans forward and nearly falls out of his chair, barely catching himself against the wall as the key falls to the floor with a clang. I put my hand on his arm and help him back into the wheelchair. "I got it, dad. We can take my car."

I'm sure I see a flash of loathing in his eyes, but I don't know if it's directed at the disease that took his independence or at his son who took his daughter's health. A comforting hand on my back assures me it isn't the latter, but it does nothing to assuage the guilt.

"I've got something for you," he says. "Well, for Pippin actually. But since she's…" His voice drifts away, unable to finish the thought. He slowly wheels back into the three-season porch where he picks up a long metal bar with a flat square attached to the end. When he holds up the bottom of the square, I immediately recognize the image, despite being upside-down.

"The emblem."

"I hope she likes it," he says. "It took…well, it took just about everything I had to finish it."

"How did you do it? I mean, you've been so sick."

"I drew the design, that's all. It's all I had in me. Your boss put me in touch with a couple fellas down at the metal shop. They actually made it. Mr. Edmond has been driving me to the hospital and back, too, in his van. It's become a lot harder to get out of this damned chair." He shakes his head, trying to understand the random act of kindness from my boss.

I study the design for a long moment, holding back tears. My father's voice also wavers. "In case I don't make it long enough to see her wake up, you'll be sure to…"

He breaks down in earnest and buries his face in his hands. I lean down and hold my father tight, wanting nothing more than to make his cancer go away. The feeling of powerlessness is overwhelming. "Of course I will," I say. "And she'll love it. It's perfect."

My father pulls back and holds me at arm's length, where he studies me like he's never seen me before. He nods, and I swear I see approval in his eyes. "Okay then," he says. "Let's go see her."

• • •

In the car, with the wheelchair in the trunk and my father's frail body beside me, I drive toward the hospital. My father's voice is raspy from crying. "I can tell it's haunting you," he says. "Do you want to talk about it?"

I shake my head no, but then start talking anyway. "I just keep trying to figure out how it happened. Like if I can figure that out, I'll be able to go back and stop it."

"What did happen, Charlie?"

I squint at the road in front of me. Partly so I don't drive off the road, but also as protection from the power of that terrible memory. "I keep trying to come up with something. Something that would make sense, but not be my fault. But there's nothing. It was because I took the extra swing, after they'd moved the cage. It was my fault. The entire thing was my fault."

"It's not your fault, Charlie," my dad says. His voice is dry and gravelly and it seems to take more effort to speak than normal. "It was a terrible accident. No one meant for it to happen."

After a minute of driving in silence, I ask, "Did you see it? When..." It's so hard to force myself to say the words. "When I hit her?"

My father's head bobs up and down slowly, almost imperceptibly. "I tried to yell to her, but nothing came out. I just stuttered, like I couldn't decide what words to use." He heaves a deep sigh and turns his stare out the window, at the streetlights blurring past. "There was nothing I could do. Nothing anyone could do."

"Why didn't Mack see her coming?" I say, grasping at straws. "He was pitching, he should have seen her."

"You know how Mack is when he's throwing BP," my dad says. "He gets tunnel-vision. And Pippin snuck up there so fast..." His voice fades and neither of us says a word for the remainder of the drive.

When we arrive at the hospital, I park in a handicapped spot and remove the wheelchair from the trunk. I help my father from the passenger side and down into the chair. The lack of weight brings a sting to my throat. It feels like everyone I love is dying.

On the third floor, I take a deep breath before entering Pippin's hospital room. When I see her face, my throat starts to ache. Her innocent eyes are hidden by puffy lids and a bandage is wrapped around her head, hiding her entire forehead. A breathing tube snakes out of her mouth unnaturally, and several lines run from her body to a machine next to her bed.

I don't even notice the other man in the room until Bud Crawford stands from the chair he's in and motions for me to take it.

"Thanks," I mumble.

I sit in silence as my father and Bud talk about the latest word from the doctors and Pippin's prognosis moving forward, which sounds uncertain to say the least. It takes several minutes for me to register the oddity of Bud Crawford's presence.

"Do you know her?" I ask.

The wrinkle between Bud's eyes deepens. "Never met her," he says.

"Then why are you here?" I ask. I don't mean to be tactless, but I find the effort of civility takes more energy than I have.

"I had a boy," he says. He seems to want to say more, but doesn't.

"I'm sorry," I say. Pippin once mentioned that Bud has his demons. Until now, I never bothered to find out what they are.

"I don't know why I said that to her at the ballpark," Bud says. "Sometimes, I see kids my boy's age, and I can't hold back the anger."

Part of me thinks it's a betrayal to Pippin that I don't get upset about the memory of what Bud said to her that day. Another part of me knows I should feel empathy for Bud, for his loss. But the strongest part can't muster any feeling at all.

Bud turns his piercing eyes on me. "The search for perfect harmony? It's more important now than ever."

I laugh a short, humorless laugh. "No offense Bud, but baseball is about the last thing on my mind right now."

"I'm not talking about baseball," he says.

Before I can ask what he means, he pats my arm and leaves the room. My dad studies me from his wheelchair on the other side of Pippin. He seems to be trying to figure something out.

"What is it?" I ask.

"Baseball," he says. "The Stallions." He swallows hard, then continues with visible effort. "I know it doesn't seem to matter, with Pippin like this. But think about her. About how bad she wants that state championship. Think about how bad she'd feel if she knew she was the reason you didn't play, and the Stallions lost."

I shake my head, wondering how he can be thinking about such things at this moment. "I won't say the team hasn't been a big part of my life, Charlie. It's given me diversion and pleasure, more than makes sense, I admit. But I'm nearing the end of my own road, as we both know. Most days I don't think I'll even make it to the end of the season to see if the Stallions win or not. No," he says, shaking his head in defeat. "I can't honestly say it makes that much difference to me any more. Not after all this. But to Pippin...well, to Pippin it means the world. Right or wrong, it means the world."

My father puts his hand to his temple and closes his eyes, as if warding off an intense pain. "Excuse me," he says, and rolls the chair toward the bathroom. When the door closes, I kneel beside Pippin and gently take one of her hands.

The familiarity of her hand, mixed with the strange lack of animation, brings the knot back to my throat. Maybe I should tell her about what I did to the quebracho, but I can't do that to her. Not now. Not knowing how much it means to her.

"I'm so sorry, Pip. For everything." I rub my thumb over the back of her hand, thinking about what I destroyed. When I broke that bat, I broke two of her three dreams with it. There's only one that I have any control over now. Thinking of that last one, I say, "I'll do it. I'll do whatever it takes. I'll take extra batting practice, I'll show up early and stay late." I stand and kiss Pippin's forehead. "I'll make sure you get that state championship, Pipsqueak. I promise."

The Show

In 1869, the Cincinnati Red Stockings became the first professional baseball team. Today, Major League Baseball is where the best players in the world compete, with more than a quarter of the players foreign-born.

That supremacy has led to many nicknames. The Big Leagues, The Big Club, The Show.

It is still the dream of millions of boys—American and international—to one day play in the Major Leagues.

Chapter 13

The days stretch on, and still Pippin doesn't awaken. The prognosis is unclear. Traumatic head injuries are unpredictable, the doctors keep repeating. It's possible she could wake up any day and have a complete recovery. She could be the same kid she's always been, but with a story to tell.

But it's just as possible she may never wake up from the coma. That the damage the bat caused to her brain is too great for such a small, fragile child to overcome. The doctors try to prepare us for the worst, but I won't allow myself to consider anything other than my little sister exactly as I've always known her.

It takes an amazing amount of distraction to accomplish the feat. I find the distraction by pouring all my time, energy, and thoughts into one, all-consuming thing: baseball.

After a few days, it isn't as difficult as I feared. When I'm on the field, nothing exists beyond me, the ball, and the bat or glove. I field grounders until one coach or player can hit no more fungos, then convince someone else to keep them coming. I take batting practice until Mack can't lift his arm, then talk a fellow player into staying after practice and throwing until his arm is sore. I start calling in sick to work, going straight to the ballpark at 9am, and not leaving until after the game that night.

The hard work pays off. One late summer evening in the dugout before the start of a game with a rival from a nearby town, Emily tells me I'm leading the league in hitting with a .435 average, and in RBI with 67. And it surprises me to learn that my home run total, despite having no quebracho, has reached 45 in 46 games. It's an unheard of pace, already more than twenty home runs past the second-most ever hit by a Sweetwater Stallion.

Of course, my statistics mean nothing. I don't care if I break Bud's single-season home run record. I have no desire to stick around for twenty years and become the new Mr. 500. The only thing I want is to go back in time and accept the Twins offer. I'd be a Major Leaguer and, more importantly, I never would have come back to Sweetwater, meaning Pippin wouldn't be in a coma.

But it's too late now. Now, my only other option would be to go back to Triple-A. To go back to the long bus rides, minimum-wage pay, and no guarantee to ever make the big club. I should have taken the opportunity when I had the chance. Everyone would be so much better off.

For all the accomplishments I'm accumulating on the field, one place affords no such success. Late each night, after the last of the Stallions have cleared out of the dugout and gone home, I pull out my key, sneak into the lumberyard, and work into the early morning hours trying to duplicate the quebracho bat Pippin was so proud of. No matter what I try, I can't seem to get it right. I've placed the emblem my father made in the corner where I can see it, hoping it will give me inspiration. Instead, it just taunts me.

Emily and Bud continue to try to convince me to meet at Bud's house to complete my education on the search for perfect harmony. But the whole thing feels empty now. The idea of vulnerability seems impossible. How could I open myself in that way without being crushed by the weight of the guilt? And acceptance? Forgetting my mistake? That's no more likely than Oz forgiving me for leaving town before he was born.

So I ignore their insistence. I continue to go to the ballpark, and I continue to hit. It's all I know. It's all I can do.

In the second-to-last game of the regular season, I take out my frustrations on the baseball. I know my swings are so wild, so undisciplined, that I wouldn't even make contact if a decent pitcher was throwing. But this guy is tossing straight, 80 mile-an-hour fastballs right over the heart of the plate. I hit three home runs for the first time in my life—lifting my season total to 48 with one regular season game remaining, and as many as four games in the state tournament. I pack up my things at the end of the dugout not even feeling like I accomplished much.

As I sit on the bench, a wave of exhaustion makes it impossible to move. The entire team files through the exit and Emily touches my shoulder in silent understanding before following Oz out of the dugout. Oz still hasn't said a word to me.

My father's equally tired eyes look sadly at me. Sitting in his wheelchair, his head tilts slightly to the side, as if simply sitting upright is quickly becoming impossible. "Good game tonight, Charlie," he says. His voice is so weak, I wonder how much longer he'll be able to speak. It's yet another thought that terrifies me.

After studying me for a while, my father seems to understand my inability to move. "I'll catch a ride with Emily," he says, and he slowly spins his wheelchair around. The crunching of the dirt beneath the wheels is the saddest sound I've ever heard.

The summer is winding down. The state tournament is almost here, but so is another competition that breaks my heart to think about. The middle school State Summer Science Fair. Pippin's project sits in her bedroom, where it will continue to sit until she wakes up. If she never wakes up, I guess it'll sit there forever.

The fans are long gone and I think I'm alone at the ballpark until I hear a set of footsteps shuffle into the dugout. I close my eyes, hoping whoever it is will turn around and leave. But the person seems determined to get my attention. When, for several seconds, I sit with my eyes closed, a man's voice finally says, "You Charlie Fightmaster?"

Eyes still closed, I take a long, deep breath, hoping it will let the man know in no uncertain terms that I'd rather be alone. But whoever it is doesn't leave. He seems perfectly happy to wait me out.

"Yeah," I say, finally opening my eyes to see a middle-aged man wearing a Minnesota Twins hat. I don't look too deeply into the meaning of the hat, but when I notice the matching Twins logo on the man's Polo shirt, I sit up straight.

"My name's Dennis Bjork," the man says, extending his hand.

I've heard the name before but I'm thrown by the appearance of the man before me. I've always imagined Bjork as Scandinavianlooking. Tall with blond hair and fair skin. But the man before me is short and tanned, and although he's balding, the sides and back of his head are covered with thick, black hair. "The Twins scout?" I say.

"Head Twins scout," Bjork says. "That was quite a performance tonight."

I shrug. "That kid couldn't make the rotation on a decent high school team."

"True enough. But you've put up some pretty unbelievable numbers against much better pitching than that this summer. And your Triple-A numbers were solid, too. I think Hudson White talked to you about our belief in your ability to hit the baseball."

"He said I could be a multi-millionaire."

"We're not the richest franchise, you understand," Bjork says. "We're looking for value. We need a left handed power-hitting pinch-hitter in the late innings against righties. We want to see you trot like you did tonight."

My brain is working so slowly. From thoughts of Pippin laying in the hospital, to whether my father got home safely, to Oz, and back to what Bjork said. The Twins still want me?

Suddenly I shoot off the bench. I'm on my feet and searching Bjork's eyes for the meaning behind his words. Bjork, apparently accustomed to the varied reactions of hearing life-changing news, has a crooked smile.

"We need you, Charlie. But we need you now. We've been as supportive as we can, allowing you to stay here all summer, and we'll continue to support you, personally. But professionally, this is the last chance. It's now or never." He nods, as if satisfied with his ultimatum. "So, how does two years for two million sound?"

• • •

The drive home is a blur.

I drive so fast I pull in front of the house at the same time Emily is just returning to her car after helping my father inside. The silhouette of a baseball cap sits in the back seat of Emily's car. Emily, Oz, and my father are all here. Perfect.

Well, as perfect as possible with Pippin in the hospital.

I jump out of the car and slam the door behind me. As Emily walks to her car, I hold my hands out to stop her. "Grab Oz," I say. "I have big news you guys need to hear."

Emily responds to the excitement in my voice. Her posture straightens and her eyes brighten. She gives me a look of astonishment, as if she understands the implication, and rushes to get Oz from the car.

I can't wait to see Oz's reaction. How will it feel to hear that his dad is going to be a Major League baseball player? And for my dying father to learn that he'll see his own son on television, stepping to the plate in a Minnesota Twins uniform? With the money I'll make, I can buy Pippin all the quebracho she wants. It's nothing short of a dream come true.

I rush inside and find my father fully reclined in his chair, settling in for the night. "Dad," I say, gently shaking his shoulder. "I'm sorry to wake you, but you have to hear this."

Just then, Emily and Oz rush through the front door and join us in the three-season porch. Even Oz bounces on his toes, unable to contain his excitement for me. The Major Leaguer. I waste no time in starting in on the story.

"I was sitting in the dugout after the game, and the head Twins scout came in looking for me." I pause a second to give it some drama, but can't wait any longer. "He offered me a contract for two million dollars!" When a confused silence covers the room, I start laughing. I get it. It's too much for any of them to comprehend. "I'm getting a second chance. I'm going to be a Major League baseball player! The Twins have three more games in their home-stand, starting tomorrow. So I'll sleep here tonight, then head up to Minneapolis in the morning."

The silence stretches on, which I can't understand. Sure, it's a shock. But I used English words they all know. What's with the delayed celebration?

Emily is the first to break the silence. "Wait," she says. "You mean you're actually considering leaving? Now?"

"No," I say. "Not until the morning. It's a night game tomorrow so I'll have plenty of time to—"

"That's not what I mean, Charlie." Oz leans into her, burying his face in her shoulder. "I...," Emily says. "We thought this was about Pippin. We thought...you're saying you're actually going to leave Sweetwater while she's in a coma? Charlie, we don't even know if she's going to live!"

I can't follow what's going on. They thought I had news about Pippin? How would I have received news none of them have heard? And Emily is questioning my desire to go? She wants me to give up my lifelong dream for a second time, even when there's nothing I can do for Pippin here? Look what happened when I turned it down the first time.

In the silence that follows, Oz begins to cry. My father, noticeably silent, has an expression I can't interpret. Emily's voice, dripping with contempt, shakes with emotion.

"First, you told Oz you're his father, after I explicitly told you not to. And as if that wasn't enough, now you're going to leave us again?"

I can't believe what I'm hearing. Do my dreams mean nothing? Am I expected to sit on my butt and wait for word about Pippin, when there's nothing I can do to change it? I'm powerless here, don't they understand that? "I told you, I didn't mean to tell Oz like that," I say. "And he hasn't exactly embraced the idea. He won't even talk to me. But now I'm supposed to stay?"

"Yes, Charlie. That's how it works. You stay for the people you love, even if things are hard. You work it out. That's the right thing to do."

"The first time, you never even gave me a choice to stay. Was that the right thing to do?"

"Well you have a choice now, don't you?" Emily says. "So what's it going to be, Charlie? What's your choice this time?"

I wish Oz wasn't here. My father either. Because anger wells up within me—a righteous indignation that is certain I'm being wronged. After spending my entire life working toward being a big leaguer, I gave it up to come home for Pippin. But the truth is there's not a single thing I can do for her now. So how can Emily expect me to simply let this opportunity slip by? Baseball has been my entire life. It still is my entire life. When all this is done, it will be my entire livelihood. This is my second chance. There won't be a third.

It takes all my strength to prevent my eyes from looking to Oz. "They told me it's now or never," I say. I swallow hard but can't look any of them in the eye. "I'm sorry. But I choose baseball."

•   •   •

I go over the calculus again and again on the drive to Minneapolis. Pippin is in a coma. Oz won't talk to me. I can make my dad proud and give him the gift of seeing his son tip his cap from a Major League baseball stadium, and find financial security doing it. Not to mention, I'm a two-hour drive away from Sweetwater. At least, while the Twins are playing at home.

It makes sense. All of it. So I shake off the lingering pit in my stomach and finish the drive. I check into a cheap hotel and spend a sleepless night trying to turn my brain off.

The following morning, I text Hudson White to thank him for his hand in things, and to let him know I'm in town. The idea is to enter Target Field alongside the team's best player, rather than by myself. But Hudson doesn't reply right away. In fact, three hours later, he still hasn't replied. So I eat an early lunch of a greasy fast-food burger and fries, and head to the ballpark.

My welcome to the club doesn't go like I was hoping, either. I understand that I'm an unknown around here. I was never officially brought up from Triple-A and I wasn't traded from another big league roster. I spent a couple months on a Double-A team with three of the players, but that was years ago. Mostly, no one knows me. Except Hudson White, and he's nowhere to be seen.

The people I deal with are nice enough. Just indifferent, somehow. To me, it's the biggest day of my life. To them, it's just another day getting another rookie a uniform.

I'm given number 26, a number with no significance at all. It's the first time in my life I'm not allowed to choose my own number. They offer me new spikes and a new glove, both of which I decline. I want to use the gear I'm comfortable with. But it's still exciting to have so much stuff offered for free. It's all so…Big League.

But the excitement in my belly vanishes when they ask what kind of bat I want. I look over more makes and models than I knew existed, but I can only think of quebracho. Meaning I can only think of Pippin. I remind myself over and over that there's nothing I can do, and if she wakes up, I'll hear about it right away and head straight back to Sweetwater, Big League contract or no Big League contract.

In the end, I pick out four maple bats of a model I've used in the past and feel comfortable with. I curse myself for the thousandth time for breaking the quebracho. Then I suit up and step through the tunnel and onto the playing surface.

The sun is shining, the grass is green, and I run my hands down my Twins jersey in disbelief. The embroidered logo is perfectly pressed, perfectly smooth.

"You the new lefty bat?" a gruff voice says behind me.

I'm face-to-face with a stooped-over man with wisps of white hair sticking out from beneath his hat. I recognize the Twins manager from TV. "Yes, sir. Charlie Fightmaster."

We shake hands and the manager nods toward the playing surface. "Probably no need to take extra ground balls," he says. "We'll get you in there as a pinch hitter in the late innings, but we won't put you in the field. You're here for your bat."

"That sounds great," I say, pushing aside my annoyance at the manager's flippant attitude about my fielding. I've worked hard on my craft and have a lot of pride in my fielding prowess. I realize we're standing in awkward silence, so I stammer and say, "I was just hoping to take some extra BP before the game."

"That's all well and good," the manager says. "But there's no BP on the field until 5:30. Feel free to take some hacks in the cage off the clubhouse. I'll send someone to throw for you."

"Oh," I say, trying to hide my disappointment. "That sounds great. Thanks."

I wish I could think of something to say other than *That sounds great,* but my nerves have taken over like a marionette. I walk to the dimly lit batting cages under the grandstand and a minute later, an assistant coach I've never met shows up and wordlessly begins firing strike after strike.

I swing the bat well, hoping with each crack of the bat that the coach will spread the word about the new guy's abilities.

It not until just before game time that I finally see Hudson White. The All-Star strides into the clubhouse just a half-hour before the Twins take the field. The perks of being a star, I guess.

"My man," Hudson says, giving me a big hug and slapping my back hard. "Good to see you up where you belong."

I could cry. All my insecurities, my annoyance at Hudson for not returning my texts, all my feelings of being an outsider, melt away with Hudson's greeting.

"I heard about your sister," Hudson says. "I'm sorry. If there's anything I can do…"

I shake my head. "Thanks. I'll let you know."

Hudson lifts the bat he's carrying by his side and offers it to me. "I haven't been able to check this out yet," he says, and I realize it's the original quebracho. The one Pippin let Hudson take with him. "But maybe you can carry a little bit of Pippin with you when you get your first big league at-bat."

Not wanting to break down in front of the other players, I give Hudson a quick hug and rush toward my locker. Thanks to my friend's thoughtfulness, when the game starts, I sit on the bench almost feeling like a Twin.

The assistant coach who threw me batting practice walks past and drops a stack of papers on my lap. "Study these," he says.

I wonder why the coach is so short with me until I see him do the exact same thing to three other players who aren't in the starting line-up. I guess I'm being soft. Baseball is a business at this level. The coaches aren't here to coddle anyone. They're here to win. So I dive into the stack of papers, which turn out to be an in-depth scouting report on each of the Cleveland Indians right-handed relief pitchers.

I pour over the data, trying to memorize each arsenal of pitches, tendencies of when they throw them, and the recommended plan of attack. Before I know it, the game has entered the ninth inning with the Twins trailing by a run.

When the Indians make a pitching change, sending their right-handed closer to the mound, the manager, standing at his perch at the edge of the dugout, cranes his neck toward me and says, "Time to see what you can do, Fightmaster. You'll hit for Bautista."

I nearly have a heart attack. I'm about to get my moment. On one hand, I've worked toward this moment for my entire life. But on the other hand, it's come up on me so quickly I haven't had time to prepare. I glance at the giant, high-definition scoreboard in right-center field and see Bautista's name listed as the fourth hitter in the inning. I can't help but imagine a walk-off grand slam.

I struggle to control my breathing as on pull on my batting gloves. After a deep breath, I imagine what I'll do...

My name will be announced over the public address system. I'll step to the plate, holding Pippin's quebracho as prominently as possible. I'll dig my back foot in, knowing the television cameras will have the close-up shot from the side—the shot from the camera bay just past the first base dugout. And I'll look straight into the camera and tip my cap to my father.

Several of my new teammates slap my back as I walk to the rack and grab the quebracho and a newly polished helmet.

The leadoff hitter strikes out for the first out of the inning and I put one foot on the steps of the dugout. The first out makes me face a thought I haven't even considered—one batter needs to reach base if I'm going to get my chance. When the next hitter lines the first pitch to the gap in left-center, I breathe much easier. But the centerfielder is closing on the ball with unbelievable speed. Just as the ball is about to sail past him, he leaves his feet, sprawls out and snags it out of mid-air for the second out.

The pitcher tips his cap to the center fielder in acknowledgement of the amazing play. The Twins home crowd groans loudly, sensing that their best chance at a comeback has just been robbed. It was a Big League play, and I'm amazed yet again that I'm actually in the Big Leagues. But now there are two outs and I desperately need the hitter in front of me to reach base somehow.

It doesn't take long to realize my fate. After a first pitch fastball out of the zone, the hitter swings at the second pitch. It jams him badly and the broken barrel of the bat flies farther than the ball, which drops easily into the glove of the first baseman for the final out of the game.

I stare at the field. The Indians players calmly congratulate each other on the win. The Twins players quietly file out of the dugout and into the tunnel to the clubhouse. No one seems particularly excited or dejected. It's simply another game. Just one out of one-hundred-sixty-two.

But to me, the disappointment is crippling. I came so close to my Major League debut. I had my tribute to my father and the unveiling of quebracho all planned out. Everything was set up perfectly, if only one batter had reached base. Just one batter.

But nothing can be done about it now. I fight back tears, swat at a mosquito that buzzes near my ear, and stare out at the giant scoreboard. The final box score shines in bright lights, casting a glow on the rapidly emptying stadium. Since I was never officially announced as a pinch-hitter, the name Fightmaster is noticeably missing. It's like I was never even here.

I hear spikes clicking against cement behind me and feel Hudson White's presence. "Hey man," Hudson says. "Don't sweat it. Skipper showed he's not afraid to use you. You'll get your chance."

I know he's right. It was my first game, and I almost got an at-bat. I should be excited about the future. About tomorrow.

But I can't shake the nagging feeling that the on-deck circle I'm standing in is as close to a Big League baseball game as I'll ever get.

• • •

I really wanted my Major League debut to be at Target Field. Growing up in Minnesota, a Twins fan my entire life, how great would it be to follow in the footsteps of Kent Hrbek and Joe Mauer as hometown kids to play in front of a hometown crowd?

But it will have to wait. The last two games of the Indians series are started by Cleveland right-handers—with me on the bench, as expected—then dominated by lefties out of the bullpen. My late-inning pinch-hit against a righty never materializes. The Twins fall in both games to complete the three-game sweep and I never have another close call. Being in the dugout is exciting in itself. But it isn't why I'm here.

The disappointment is real and it's profound. But fortunately, it's also short-lived. After the game, I'm sitting at my locker in my perfectly clean home whites, when the Twins manager rambles over to me.

"We need to mix things up a bit," the old man says. "Some kind of kick in the pants. So we're going to start you at shortstop in Oakland tomorrow." After a moment in which I try not to choke on my tongue, the manager says, "It's a one-time thing, just so you understand. To wake Martinez out of his trance. But be ready. And enjoy it. You only get one big league debut," and he limps toward his office.

I immediately fish my phone out of my locker and text my father.
—STARTING LINE-UP TOMORROW!!!—

Moments later, my father's reply—a smiley-face emoji—is confusing. I expected a much bigger reaction. More excitement. But I chalk it up to the older generation's lack of understanding of texting. Surely, he's every bit as ecstatic as I am, but just doesn't know how to articulate it through text. After all, his son is about to start a big league ballgame, how could he not be over the moon?

Suddenly, I can't wait to pack. Debuting in Minnesota, or Oakland, or China for all I care—it doesn't matter anymore. I know I'm going to play.

I've never flown to a baseball game before—on any airplane, much less a team charter jet. And I won't even have to pack any of my baseball gear. I don't need to worry about cleaning my uniform, or making sure to have the right combination of jerseys and pants. I've been living out of my suitcase since leaving Sweetwater, so after I change out of my uniform, I'm ready to go.

Hudson White lifts his chin as I walk past his locker on my way out of the clubhouse. "Congrats on tomorrow's start, rookie," he says. "Save me a seat next to you on the bus to the airport. We'll be roomies again."

Things are falling into place so well I can almost—almost, but not quite—get a moment's peace from the guilt I feel for not being in Sweetwater with Pippin. But as soon as I step out of the clubhouse, I stop short and any peace I felt is shattered. It's Bud Crawford, in the flesh, waiting for me.

"Oh my God," I say. "Is Pippin okay?"

Bud looks confused for a moment, but recovers quickly. "She's the same. No change. That's not what I'm here about."

I look around, searching for a clue as to what Bud's doing here. "We need to talk," Bud says.

I cringe, hating those words in any situation. "I'm sorry, Bud, but I've got a plane to catch."

"I know you do. But this'll only take a minute. You won't miss your ride on account of me."

"Okay," I say. "Fine. So what's up?"

Bud shuffles his weight back and forth. "The third secret to perfect harmony. You need to know what it is. And you need to know before you get on that plane."

• • •

I follow at Bud's heels through the bowels of the stadium. The place is like a luxury hotel. Nothing like the dark, cement tunnels under the minor league stadiums where I've played for the past decade. This place has spacious, carpeted hallways. Even the walls are decorated with old Twins memorabilia.

Several of my new teammates hurry past us toward the idling bus that waits outside the stadium. One of them, a relief pitcher I haven't met, slaps my shoulder as he passes by.

"The earlier we get going, the earlier we get there and into bed, man."

Several others follow, also seemingly in a rush to get out of town. If they're in this big of a hurry to get out of town, I can't imagine how much of a rush they must be in when it's time to return home.

I pick up my pace, annoyed that Bud is moving slowly, now holding me back. But then, while turning to tell Bud to hurry up, I notice a series of old black and white photos. One in particular catches my attention. I crane my neck so I'm just inches from it. "Hey Bud, Is that you?"

Bud leans in and stares at the younger, healthier version of himself swinging a bat in the middle of a big, mostly empty stadium. He grunts something I can't make out.

"This is amazing." I step back and scan the pictures all around. "They've got every Twins All-Star in team history on this wall. I mean, I'd heard you made an All-Star team, but to see it like this…"

Bud grunts again, obviously uncomfortable with the picture, although I can't fathom why.

"Your rookie year even," I say. "You would have been amazing. I mean, you were amazing. But if you hadn't blown out your arm…"

Bud looks away from the picture, down to his feet on the carpeted floor, and heaves a long, deep sigh.

"Bud," I say, facing the old man. "I know I haven't shown it, but I've idolized you every bit as much as every other kid from Sweetwater. I mean, you're Bud Crawford. This should make you…" I gesture to the picture, trying to figure out what I'm trying to say. "I mean, you should be proud."

"I never had an arm injury," Bud blurs out.

I turn my head so fast I'm surprised I don't get whiplash. I study Bud's eyes for a long moment, searching for a sign that the old man is kidding, until Bud finally looks away. I'm too confused to even know what to ask.

Several more players stride past and I know I need to hurry. But what Bud just said makes no sense. Of course he had an arm injury. Everyone knows the story. He was a rookie phenom, he made the All-Star team, people were comparing him to the best ever and assuming his day in Cooperstown was just a matter of time. It was a foregone conclusion. Until he blew out his arm and had to retire from pro ball.

Eventually, Bud takes another deep breath. "I was a gambler," he says, speaking softly even though, at the moment, no one else is around. "It wasn't a big thing. I wasn't addicted. Just liked putting money on a game now and then. And once—just once—I put money on one of my own games. Just so happened someone found out. As I'm sure you know, since the 1919 World Series, gambling on your own game in baseball simply isn't allowed. No three strike rule. Not even a second chance. Didn't even matter that I bet on my team to win.

I was kicked out of professional baseball for the rest of my life, because of that one, stupid mistake made by a 22 year-old kid I can't even recognize anymore."

Bud shakes his head, looking afraid to see my reaction. I'm glad he doesn't look. I'm sure I'm not hiding my shock very well. "The league wasn't doing so hot at the time," Bud says. "Not like now-a-days. They didn't want bad publicity but they were also firm about the fact that I had to go. So they sent me out on the field the next day with direct orders. The first time the ball was hit to me, I was to throw the ball and collapse in a heap of pain. If I did that, I'd get the rest of that year's salary. If not, they'd sue me for every dime I had. Some clause in the contract I'd signed about not gambling on baseball."

Bud stares at the picture of himself mid-swing, squeezes a tear out of one eye, and wipes his nose. "It was that night, after I'd faked the injury and my career was over, that I realized something."

After a long pause, I finally gather my thoughts enough to ask, "What's that?"

"Something about perfect harmony. You see, ball players would be lucky to experience it, even for one moment. The way it makes you feel on the field is like nothing else. But the thing I didn't know until that day is that it doesn't do a thing for you if you don't take those same lessons with you when you step off the field and into the rest of your life."

Several employees push open a nearby door, guiding a wheeled cart full of baseball gear behind them. One of them looks at me and taps his watch.

"Soon as we get this all loaded, we're out of here," he says.

Bud and I watch until they're gone and the doors swing shut behind them. "I don't understand, Bud. Why are you telling me this?"

"Because you need to know the third secret to perfect harmony. The one I forgot, when I was a young kid." Bud's eyes flick to the old photo of him again, then down to his feet. He nods, as if accepting what happened, then turns his weathered eyes to me. "The third secret is to find your reason. You need to discover, what is your 'why'? See, I lost track of my reason, forgot my why, and the next thing I knew,

I'd blown it. It was over. Kaput. All because I forgot my reason for doing what I was doing."

I have no idea what to say. I have no idea what to think. "What was your reason?" I finally ask. "When you had it."

Bud once again looks back to the picture of him mid-swing, driving a baseball high into the air. "My love of the game," he says.

I nod hard, feeling validated. And feeling a closeness to Bud I haven't experience before. We're alike, Bud Crawford and I. Despite our differences. We're baseball men, through and through. We share a bond that very few people can understand. "Mine too," I say. "The reason I do it, my 'why' as you call it, is my love of the game. Just like you."

Bud jams a finger into my chest, hard enough to hurt. "That's a crock of shit," he says. "You and me are nothing alike."

"What are you talking about?" After a moment of shock, a flare of anger takes over. It's like I've been betrayed by a trusted friend. "Who are you to say what my reasons are? You don't know me that well, Bud."

"Apparently I know you better than you know yourself."

"You're crazy," I say, turning away. I have to get on the bus with the rest of the team, almost all of whom have loaded and are ready to head to the airport. The manager limps onto the steps, turns around, and waves at me to get on the bus. The last thing I need is to get on his bad side.

"Do you love the game?" Bud says, grabbing my arm. "Of course. Is it one of your favorite things to do? Sure. But it's not the reason you strive so hard. The game itself isn't what has motivated you for so long."

A rebuttal is on the tip of my tongue when I stop, feeling like I've been hit by a fastball to the ribs. What Bud is saying is true. My reason, my 'why,' has never been my love of the game. My love of baseball made it possible to continue climbing the minor league ladder. But there's always been something bigger at play.

"My father," I say, my voice coming out as barely a whisper.

"Fightmaster," the manager yells from the bus steps. "Let's go. Now!"

"Sorry, Bud. I have to go." I pick up my bags and start toward the bus. I'm starting in a Major League baseball game tomorrow. All of my dreams are about to come true.

"That's right," Bud says loudly from behind me. "You wanted to make your old man proud. It was about your dad. Your family. And now your family has grown."

I stop, still facing the bus, and my increasingly exasperated manger. But I can't move my feet. Behind me, Bud's gravelly voice continues.

"You have Oz now. You have Pippin. And your father is still alive. I know you think that playing in the big leagues will help them somehow. You think it's what they want. But it isn't. The fact that you're here and not in Sweetwater is proof that you've lost your reason, you've lost your 'why'. And I can promise you, that never ends well."

"Fightmaster, you've got ten seconds to get your ass on this bus or we're leaving you behind," the manager says.

Panicked, I sift through thoughts and emotions, trying furiously to figure out if Bud is right. If I fly to Oakland, start tomorrow's game, and even become a star, will it change how I'll feel if I lose Pippin? If Pippin wakes up and I'm not there, will she ever forgive me? If it really is just about baseball, I shouldn't need anything else. But when I think about my father, Pippin, Oz, and Emily, a realization becomes perfectly clear.

Bud is right. My reason for playing baseball isn't just my love of the game. I do it for my family. And right now, my family needs me at home.

"Three seconds, Fightmaster," the manager says. "I am not messing around."

I turn to face Bud. "I can't go to Oakland, can I?"

Bud shakes his head. "Not if you want to be able to sleep at night ever again. And you can trust me on that one."

The manager turns and disappears into the bus. The headlights flick to bright and back several times. I know what waits for me on that bus. A trip to my first Major League road trip. My first Major League at-bat. All of my boyhood dreams finally coming true.

I watch the silhouette of the manager lumber to the back of the bus and gesture wildly to another form of a person. That person makes his way to the front of the bus, and then Hudson White is standing at the top of the steps inside the bus.

"Fighter," he says. "It's your last chance. It's now or never." He shakes his head sadly. "Don't do this to yourself, brother."

Seeing my old friend, and knowing what his life is like — the fame and the money, but also the loss of his closest relationships — gives me an unexpected sense of peace and comfort. When I start walking toward him, I see the relief in his eyes. But then I reach into my bag, pull out the quebracho, and extend it to him.

"Pippin wanted you to have this," I say. "It means a lot to her."

In utter disbelief, Hudson takes the bat. As soon as I let it go, the bus door slams shut in my face.

With a certainty I've never experienced before, I turn my back on the bus that would take me to all my childhood dreams. And I walk in the other direction.

The Second Chance

Baseball is game of failure. A player who gets out 70% of the time is an All-Star. A team that loses 60 games a year is a pennant winner. A pitcher who allows a run in every start could still win a Cy Young Award.

But it's also a sport in which there are 162 games each year. In that long season, it can accurately be said that "There's always tomorrow."

And that means baseball is also a game of second chances.

Chapter 14

As I watch the team bus drive away and speed toward the airport, I'm watching my dreams disappear. I'll never tip my cap to my father. I'll never see action in a Major League baseball game. I was given a second chance. I won't be given a third.

As Bud looks at me with obvious pride, I slowly walk back into the stadium. I make my way back through the tunnels, through the clubhouse, and back into the dugout. There on the wall, as I hoped, is the day's line-up. I stand in front of it, studying the names I know so well. Martinez. Johnson. And of course, White. And down below, at the bottom of the list of bench players: Fightmaster.

I peel the line-up card from the wall, gently fold it in half, and slide it into my pocket. At least I'll have that. It'll be the perfect gift for Pippin, if she ever wakes up.

An old, thickly veined hand on my shoulder surprises me, and Bud squeezes gently. "Baseball is one beautiful game," he says. "Like a one-of-a-kind woman who can make you feel like you've never felt before. Like you'll never feel again." After a long moment of silence, he heaves a long sigh. "But when it's over, there's no guarantee she'll let you down gently."

I can't help but smile at Bud's words. Of all the wise things he's said, I'm not sure he's uttered anything more true.

"Let's go, Bud. My family's waiting for me."

I never could have anticipated the feeling I have while driving behind Bud on the way down state highway 52 toward Sweetwater. After giving up my lifelong dream of playing in the Major Leagues —

for good, this time—I don't feel anger or resentment or crushing defeat. I feel free.

It's not that I don't want desperately to play in the big leagues. I do, and likely always will. But the moment I turned my back on the team bus and started my journey back toward Sweetwater, a giant weight lifted from my shoulders.

I'm returning to where I belong.

When we reach the edge of Sweetwater, darkness covers the town. Bud texts that he's going home for the night. I know exactly where I'm going, and point my car toward the hospital.

Minutes later, I tiptoe into Pippin's dark room, surprised that nothing has changed. She looks exactly as she has every day—every week—since the day of the terrible accident. My father, who's been a mainstay by her side, sits in his wheelchair in the corner with his eyes closed.

"Charlie?" he says. His voice croaks and his eyes remain closed. "Is that you?"

"Hey dad." I go to him and put a hand on his knee, but he doesn't move. Considering how shocked my father must be to see me, the lack of a reaction is terrifying. "You okay?"

"Bad day," he says. "Having more of them."

I squeeze his knee, unsure what to say. The helplessness is killing me. I have no doubt about my decision to be here, but it's becoming obvious it won't be easy.

"I heard the Stallions came through" I say. "The championship is tomorrow morning, right?" I hope talking about the Stallions will help him perk up. "The boys must be playing well."

"The semi-finals...shouldn't have been so close," he whispers. "Barely won without you."

I feel an intense helplessness watching him struggle for breath. The few words he's managed to say exhaust him. I feel a rush of gratitude to Bud for convincing me to return. It isn't the easy route. Dealing with whatever is going to happen is sure to be difficult. But I'm home, with my family, where I need to be.

"I'll let you two get some sleep," I say. "Do you need a ride to the ballpark tomorrow?"

My father shakes his head. "Emily...superstitious."

I kiss the top of his head and hold Pippin's hand for a few minutes before leaving. I wander the halls for a while, but end up at the help desk asking to speak with Pippin's doctor.

Pippin's status quo isn't unbearable in the short term—at least it's far better than hearing that something has gone wrong. But the longer the silence continues, the smaller the chances she'll ever wake up. At least, that's the thought I can't prevent from dominating my mind.

Part of me hopes the doctor won't respond to the receptionist's call. Maybe that would mean the doctor doesn't see Pippin's case as critical. That there's no need to respond quickly, especially late at night. I try not to read into it too much when the doctor arrives at the receptionist's desk just minutes later.

"Charlie," he says. "I'm glad you're here. How are you?"

"That depends," I say. "How Pippin's doing?"

The doctor heaves a long sigh, which doesn't seem like a good sign. "When she was initially stabilized, it was good news. But the more time that goes by..."

I don't need him to verbally confirm the thoughts I just had. I nod in understanding. "There has to be something we can do."

"We're doing all we can," the doctor says. He puts a hand on my shoulder and squeezes. "And I'm not saying things can't turn around for her. But I think, in situations like this, it's best to be prepared for the worst. It can make the shock of it all less painful, if it comes to that."

I physically recoil from the words. I didn't give up my dreams so I could come home and watch my sister die. The things we need are hope and optimism, not preparing for the worst. Pippin needs all the positive energy she can get right now and what the doctor is suggesting sounds a lot like giving up. I've never been one to give up.

"You prepare yourself all you want," I say. "I want no part of it." The doctor looks to his feet and nods. "My sister is going to wake up," I say. "Call me when she does."

I brush past the doctor and out of the room, wishing I could believe my own words.

• • •

The first pitch of the Minnesota State Amateur Baseball Championship game is slated for 9am tomorrow morning, and it's only 11pm. I'll never fall asleep with all the thoughts swimming in my head, so I go to the lumber yard and make my way back to the work space.

The harsh florescent lights dangle from the ceiling, casting a pale glow over the equipment. I look at the thin slab of quebracho that remains, but I'm afraid to touch it.

After Pippin's accident, I tried so hard to construct a bat just like hers. I took an excruciating amount of time, making sure to avoid any preventable mistakes. I measured multiple times before making any adjustments. I went over her notes meticulously, slowly. Until, inevitably, I ran into a note about the precise vibrational frequencies or the secret to optimizing the transfer of energy, and I realized all over again that I would never be able to duplicate Pippin's quebracho bat.

Now, only a thin strip remains. Enough for one more attempt. I have no option but to try one last time.

I flip through Pippin's notes again, trying to glean some little piece of information I might have missed about how to adjust the taper from the handle so it's just right, or what makes the weight distribution allow for such a fluid swing.

This time, it actually seems to work. For a moment, it makes sense. I can see the bat in my mind's eye. So I start the lathe and begin trimming the wood into the shape of a bat.

I work for hours, into the early morning. I carefully ease the tools into the wood, trying to feel what Pippin felt as she made her bat. I measure the taper to three-eighths of an inch. This time, as the clock strikes three in the morning, the bat finally looks right.

I move my gaze from the bat to a diagram Pippin drew in her notebook, and back again. Something in my stomach flutters as I realize I might have done it. The taper is exact. The shape is perfect. The weight, when I pick it up, is familiar.

I put my feet into a hitting position and bring the bat back to my shoulder. I look forward, as if facing a pitcher, and ease the barrel into a half-swing. It feels perfect. Exact. I glance around to make sure there's room, then bring the bat back and take a full swing. The barrel whips through the strike zone.

But something catches on my finger on the follow-through, almost as if the wood shifts. Panicked, I look at the handle and study it closely. A thin line snakes from the handle all the way through the thin taper and into the barrel. Maybe the crack was in the wood from the beginning, maybe I caused it when working on the lathe. It doesn't matter. The bat is cracked.

I don't feel rage or anger. Only a deep sense of sadness as I run my finger along the entire length of the crack. I lean down right where I am, sit on the hard, sawdust-covered floor, and begin to cry.

I cradle the piece of quebracho in my arms and press it against my cheek. I weep onto the wood and watch a tear slip into the crack and run down the length of it. I've failed Pippin in so many ways, but not even the accident feels like as strong of a betrayal as the destruction of her bat, and my inability to replace it.

• • •

I toss and turn, unable to sleep. I lay in bed, staring at the ceiling, trying everything I can to shut down my mind and allow myself to rest. But how can I rest? What if some sort of miracle idea comes to me for how to use the discarded quebracho and still make a perfect bat, and I miss it because I'm sleeping?

It's a ridiculous thought—that I could somehow construct a perfect bat from scraps of wood when I couldn't even do it with a full slab. The smart thing would be to fall asleep and wake up energized, so I have the ability to play the very small role I have—to lead the Stallions to the state championship for both Pippin and my father.

Just as my eyelids are finally starting to fall, my phone vibrates on the bedside table.

My head snaps to it as if I've been waiting for it. I push the button on the phone and notice the time — 3:32am — just before I see who the text is from: Emily.

I try the passcode four times before finally forcing myself to take a deep breath and push the right numbers. I open Emily's message and read:

– Oz wants to see you.

My heart pounds against my ribs as I stare at the words, trying to figure out what Oz could possibly want in the middle of the night, after refusing to speak to me for weeks.

– Why?

I sit up in bed and bounce my foot, waiting for the reply.

– He didn't say.

– He's at your house?

– Yes.

I stare at the screen, scared of what I might find at Emily's house.

– Be right there.

I climb out of bed and slip my feet into some old shoes. Still wearing the sweatpants and long-sleeved shirt I use as pajamas, I step out into the warm summer night.

Crickets chirp as I walk down the sidewalk toward Emily's house. In the distance, fireflies blink in random patterns, both peaceful and confusing. Silence hangs over the neighborhood. The humid air is warm and heavy.

Emily waits on her doorstep, under the porch light. She nods when she sees me approaching. She takes my hand and together we go inside. In the living room, Oz sits on a couch, staring at a wall.

"Hey buddy," I say. When Oz's eyes don't move from the spot on the wall, I kneel in front of him. "Your mom tells me you wanted to see me."

Oz's gaze seems to flicker, then focus on me. He nods silently and walks out the front door. I look at Emily, who shrugs and says, "I guess you should follow him."

I have to jog to catch up. "What's up, Oz? Is everything okay?" I realize the stupidity of the question the moment I ask it. Oz keeps walking. "Where are we going?"

"I have to show you something," Oz finally says. "Something I should have shown you before. You might be mad."

I might be mad? What could Oz possibly have to show me at three in the morning that might make me mad? And what makes it so important that it can't wait until daylight?

The streets are dark, giving our journey a surreal feeling. As if the whole thing is a dream. Maybe Oz will take me somewhere and Pippin will be there waiting for me. Maybe the whole day—from being in uniform for the Twins game, to being told I would start tomorrow in Oakland, to leaving my team and returning home—maybe the entire thing was a dream.

Maybe the dream has been even longer. Maybe Oz will take me to a place where I'll wake up and the last few, terrible weeks never even happened.

But reality has other ideas, and instead of following Oz to a place where I awaken to my old life, I follow him to the back of the lumberyard, where Oz pulls a key from his pocket and flashes me a guilty look.

"Pippin gave me hers to make a copy. When I started helping her."

Oz inserts the key, twists it, and pushes the door open with a creak. He leans his head back outside and scans both directions. Once he's satisfied the coast is clear, he grabs my sleeve and pulls me inside.

Another wave of grief threatens to knock me off my feet. The workspace spreads out before us. The lathe. The tools. The smell of cedar and pine, and also the fleeting scent of quebracho: nutty with a hint of cocoa. This place was a refuge for me and Pippin. Now, in the darkness, it feels dead. The cracked bat I made earlier in the night lies broken at my feet.

"I don't usually do bad things," Oz says.

I dread what I'm going to hear. I have no idea what Oz could have done that would make him act so skittish, so guilty. And I'm not sure I want to find out. I have to force the words out of my mouth.

"What did you do, Oz?" Part of me hopes Oz won't answer. That he'll lead me right back out the door and walk back to his house, as if he'd never asked to see me.

"I've never stolen anything before, I swear. And I wouldn't have, except…"

His voice trails off, unable to finish. "Except what, Oz? What did you steal?"

Oz's voice is barely above a whisper. "Money."

The thud of disappointment in my stomach is nothing compared to the overwhelming grief about Pippin that continues to wash over me in waves. Then I figure it out. Oz must be telling me this now because he knows I'll be too grief-stricken about Pippin's condition to care about Oz stealing money from the lumberyard. A flash of anger courses through me. My eyes widen and pressure mounts in my forehead.

"I paid it back, though," Oz says, sensing my temper about to blow. "So I just borrowed it, really."

I can't figure out what he's talking about. He paid it back? My thoughts fly back to my strange conversation with Mr. Edmond the last time we saw each other. Extra money had been in the till, yet his monthly numbers matched up perfectly.

"Why?" I ask. "I don't understand."

"I had to. To get more quebracho. I had to use Mr. Edmond's account at the lumberyard. I had to use his computer. His credit card on file."

I still don't understand. "Why?" I say again.

Oz takes my hand tentatively and pulls me to a corner of the workroom. We stop in front of a green, metal door and Oz looks around again, like he's about to break-and-enter. He pulls out the key from his pocket again and says, "The key works for all the doors." He twists the knob, gives me one last worried look, and opens the door.

It's dark inside, and I can't see what the room contains. But I can sense that it's a small space. No more than a large storage closet, with cement walls and floors. But the smell that wafts from the room is unmistakable. Nutty, with a hint of cocoa.

Oz flicks on a light, revealing the most amazing sight. An entire closet full of bats, each one a perfect replica of the others. A perfect replica of Pippin's design. There must be twenty of them.

"I've been mowing a lot of lawns," Oz says, walking into the closet and lifting a bat from where it leans against the wall. He hands it to me and I hold it like a fragile treasure. "So I could repay Mr. Edmond without him knowing I'd gone online and ordered more quebracho from the place in Florida."

I find it difficult to speak. "How did you...when did you make these?"

"At night, mostly," Oz says. He flashes me that guilty look again. "I snuck out after mom thought I was asleep." He shrugs, like he doesn't really understand it himself. "It's just, Pippin and I had so much fun making them. She was so excited about it, so—"

"Wait," I say. "Pippin helped you with these?"

"Just the first one. Then..."

His voice trails off and he can't make eye contact. "Then the accident," I say.

"Yeah. But I didn't mean to steal. Well, I mean, I guess I did, because I did it even though I knew it was wrong. But what if I had asked and Mr. Edmond said no? Or you said no? Or mom said no? I couldn't take that chance. I had to make more bats. For Pippin. So I could show her when she woke up. But now..."

It pains me every time Oz can't say out loud the things we both know. *But now...Pippin might never wake up.*

And it pains me to see my son feeling so bad about doing such an amazing thing. I squat low so my eyes are level with Oz's and take his hands.

"Am I in trouble?" Oz asks.

I actually laugh. "No." I look around the room, filled with what was Pippin's dream. Filled with what I couldn't give her myself. "You've done one of the most amazing things I've ever seen."

Oz chews his cheeks hard, as if holding back tears. He looks at me through shimmering eyes. He reaches out as if to take my hand, but then grabs my sleeve. "I'm glad you're my dad," he says. "I know I was mad but...I wanted it to be you."

I squeeze Oz in a hug, burying my face into my son's shoulder. There's so much I want to say, but I have no idea how to find the words.

"The bats aren't quite finished," Oz says. "They still need something."

Confused, I take the bat Oz gave me and lift it to my shoulder. I step back and give it a slow half-swing. It feels exactly like it's supposed to. It feels perfect.

"What do they need?" I ask.

Oz grabs the bat, spins it in his hands, and points to the blank barrel. "They don't have Pippin's emblem."

I set a hand on Oz's shoulder and smile. "Then let's finish them," I say.

•   •   •

I have no idea how long Oz and I work side by side, using the branding iron my father designed for the barrel of each bat. We mark them with Pippin's unique emblem. With each pair of braids encircling the distinct form of two crossing quebracho bats, Pippin becomes a little more alive. I can almost feel her presence. I know the joy she would feel at seeing us put her emblem on so many of her perfectly designed bats. But I don't feel any of that joy. Not with Pippin still in a coma.

I wonder if I'll ever again be able to feel the kind of joy I felt when Pippin would rattle off something about the physics of bat-making that I wouldn't even pretend to understand. I wonder what Pippin's doing at this very moment. I wonder if she's able to think.

At one point, around 5am, Emily texts both of us, asking if everything is okay. I reply that everything is fine and I'll bring Oz home when we're done. Then Oz and I look at each other and with silent communication, we each turn off our phones. What we're doing here feels sacred, somehow. Something too important for interruption.

Oz and I fall into a rhythm. I hold the bat steady, Oz heats the branding iron with the torch, and we bring the bat and iron together with a sizzle. We hold it for a long moment, then remove it and check our handiwork. It's a slow process that takes much longer than I expected. We work for hours, until our hands shake with fatigue and we have to squint the sleep from our eyes. When we finally finish the last bat, I hold my hand out toward Oz.

"Thank you," I say when he shakes it.

"You're welcome."

I wait, knowing it's ridiculous to wish for Oz to call me "dad" but wishing for it all the same. Oz smiles sheepishly and, as a distraction, brings out his cell phone and turns it on. The time pops up on his screen along with several missed texts, and he gasps." Oh no," he says. "You're late. The game's about to start."

•   •   •

It's Championship Day in Minnesota. The streets of Sweetwater are deserted until we get within a few blocks of the stadium. The closer we get, the more packed the road gets, with cars on each side, some even double parked so the driver wouldn't miss the first pitch. I pull into the parking lot, which is entirely full, and stop the car in the middle of the lane. No one will be able to get by me, but no one will be completely blocked in, either.

"Yes," Oz says from the passenger seat. His head is craning behind us to see the scoreboard in right-center field. "We made it."

He's right. The other team is taking infield practice, which means I have plenty of time to get into my uniform and get stretched and ready. We load our arms with duffle bags and quebracho bats and hobble toward the dugout.

As soon as I cross the threshold, I know immediately that something big is happening. Something beyond baseball. Beyond the championship.

The buzz of the fans is electric, but that's not it. It's like those things are a world away. Like anything outside the dugout is on another plane of existence. And then Emily rushes up to me and grabs the front of my jersey with both hands.

"Where have you been? Did you get my text?"

The urgency in her voice is amplified by the desperation in her hands as she squeezes my jersey like she's trying to wring it out. I can't tell if she's angry, but why would she be? She knows where I was. And her text? When Oz and I realized what time it was, we immediately rushed to the stadium. If I have a text message, I haven't seen it.

Emily interprets my silence and shakes her hands, pounding her clinched fists against my chest. The movement is desperate — aggressive, even — but her eyes are bright and her beautiful mouth is spread into a wide grin.

"Pippin woke up!" she says.

I stare at her blankly, struggling to understand her words. And then my entire mind is washed clean. It's like a tsunami sweeps through, taking every single thing with it. The championship game disappears. Every person in the stands disappears. Even Emily and Oz disappear. And all that's left is Pippin.

"She woke up?" Repeating the words is all I can manage. I look around the dugout like I expect to see her sitting in her spot at the end of the bench. She's not there, of course. She hasn't been there for weeks. "I don't understand."

Emily laughs a high, twinkling laugh. "An hour ago," she says. She puts her hands on my face like she's trying to force my attention back to reality. "They can't say for sure what will happen next, but the doctor said her prognosis just improved a hundred percent."

As what she's telling me slowly gets through to me, I feel my heartbeat quicken and rise into my neck and throat. "What are we doing?" I say. "We have to go see her."

"Not yet." Emily still has my face in her hands and she squeezes now, as if to keep me in place.

"Not yet? What are you talking about? She's awake!"

"The game," Emily says. "The championship. It means a lot to her. She'll still be there in three hours. They said she needs rest, anyway."

In the past few moments, I've completely forgotten about the baseball game. How could that possibly matter now?

Before I can think of how to reply, something in the corner of the dugout catches my eye. It's the opposite side from where Pippin would be. It's my father, in his recliner. But he's barely recognizable as my father.

The sight of him creates a war inside me. When joy is mixed with sadness, the result is a strange floating sensation. For a moment, I feel like I'm outside my body. Like the competing emotions are too much for a human brain and some part of me checks out. I'm still here, still standing in front of Emily, having just heard the best news I could imagine. And yet...

Something in the back of my throat squeezes when I look at my dad. His face is gaunt and yellow. He resembles a skeleton with thin, translucent skin pulled tightly over the bones of his face. His empty stare points at the field, but he doesn't appear to see anything at all. His lips, which I've only ever known as turned up in a smile, twitch and grimace. From his watery eyes gazing at the baseball diamond, tears slide down his cheeks. I go to him and squat next to the recliner.

"Pippin's awake," I say.

Obviously, he knows about Pippin, having been in the dugout this whole time. He nods, but there's a cringe where a smile should be, as if the motion is painful. "I know I'm not able to show it right now," he says, "but that makes me happier than I could possibly tell you."

I put my arm around him and I'm shocked by the frailty of his shoulder. His body shakes, but I don't know if it's from the pain or if he's fighting back tears. After several moments, he breaks down in earnest, hiding his face in his once-strong hands.

"I can't stay," he says, and I fight my own tears with everything I have.

"I know." It's obvious from his appearance and it's obvious from the way the players are looking at him with deep concern. But the implications of his leaving the championship game are terrifying.

My father keeps his eyes on the field and manages a strained smile. "I do love being at the ballpark," he says. "I do love baseball."

I would sit next to my father forever and be perfectly happy. But he groans and leans forward, his movements emphasizing the words he has to work so hard to say.

"It's time, Charlie. Take me home."

· · ·

I drive slowly. With every little bump, I can almost feel the stabbing pain shooting through my father's body.

"I've always wanted to die in my own home," he says. His voice is barely above a whisper, and it's still colored with agony. "But that won't happen, now, of course." His breath is deep and labored. With extreme effort, he manages to cover my hand with his. "Let's go see your sister."

The hospital parking lot is just around the other side of the building. I park, then hop out quickly to make sure my father doesn't try to get out before I can help.

I didn't need to worry. His limp form slumps in the front seat, his eyes vacant, as though the last of his energy was used to take in Sweetwater Ballpark in all its glory. When I open the door, he doesn't move. I set up his wheelchair, then slide my arms under him and ease him into it, shocked and terrified once again by the lightness of his body.

I push him through the automatic front doors and look for the information desk. My father's head hangs to the side and his expression doesn't change. "I'll be right back," I say, and squeeze his hand, which makes the edges of his lips twitch in something like a smile.

I speak to someone at the front desk, which doesn't take long. In a small town like this, there's not much red tape to deal with. I have a brief conversation with a doctor, in which I force myself to say what my father asked: that he not be revived if his heart or breathing stop. Then, accompanied by a nurse, I push my dad's wheelchair into an elevator, down a hallway, and into the same room as Pippin.

I stop when I see her. I can feel my father's breath catch in exactly the same way as mine. Pippin's eyes are closed. The breathing tube is out, which in itself makes her look more human, more herself. But other than that, she looks just like she has for weeks. She could still be in a coma, for all I know.

"She's just sleeping," the nurse says, reading my expression. "It's the best thing for her recovery right now, so let's try to let her. I'm sure she'll be awake again before long."

She gestures to the other bed in the room so I steer my dad to it and help him onto it. It seems like I should get used to it, but every time I pick him up I'm surprised by how much weight he has lost. He's literally withering away.

I think of rolling his bed toward the window, but Pippin's bed is blocking the way, and besides, his bed is too short to see out, even if it was inclined. But I crack the window open an inch. Just enough to hear the public address announcer giving the starting line-ups for the championship game. When he gets to the third batter for the Stallions and the name called isn't mine, my father and I both hold perfectly still. Neither of us says anything.

"I wonder," my father says softly, "if we could find a radio in this place."

The nurse leaves without a word and comes back a minute later with an old AM/FM radio. I take it and plug it in while the nurse inserts a line into my father's arm. Morphine, I realize. To keep him comfortable.

I ignore the implications of that and fiddle with the dial until I find the station broadcasting the state championship game. The fact that it is starting without me feels surreal. But I ignore the spark inside urging me to get back to the field, and focus on my father.

"I have something to show you," I say. "Don't go anywhere." He attempts a smile at my gallows humor and I run back out to the car, grab the quebracho bat from my bag, and bring it inside. When I get back to the hospital room, I take it by the barrel and extend the handle toward him. He's too weak to take it, so I kneel beside the bed and hold the bat with the emblem facing us.

My father smiles and I recognize contentment, but not joy.

"Will you sit with me for a while?" His voice is barely more than a whisper. I move a chair from the corner and bring it next to his bed. He takes a deep breath. "So," he says. "You came home."

So much has happened in the short amount of time since I left the Twins. "Yeah," I say. "I came home." I think back to the moment I watched the bus carrying Hudson White and the rest of the Twins to the airport, leaving me behind. "Because of you and Pippin," I say.

My father's brow crinkles, pulling the skin tight on his hollow face. "And Oz," he says.

"Yeah. Oz, too."

"It shows maturity," he says, slowly. "You proved that you understand what it means to be a father. And to be a brother. And a son."

"What do you mean?"

The pauses in my father's speech worry me, but I wait as patiently as I can as he gathers himself. "Sometimes, when you love someone, you have to make sacrifices for them. You have to take a supporting role. Maybe even sacrifice your dreams and all the accolades that come from achieving them."

I don't respond because I don't know if I'm as noble as my father says, but I don't want to shatter his vision of me, whether it's accurate or not.

"But I have to wonder," he says. "Why did you leave in the first place?"

I've considered that exact question a few times since I left the Twins. What was it that made me leave my dying father and comatose sister to play in the majors? What could possibly have that kind of control over a person? The answer, when it came, wasn't easy to accept. And I wasn't sure I'd ever admit the truth to my father. But as we sit together now, I finally come clean.

"When I was young, I always thought there must have been something I could have done to make mom stay. But I didn't do it. And she left us. And it made me wonder if you'd leave too."

I see the pain in my father's eyes, but it isn't the cancer. It's the look of a man learning he's been unable to protect his son from life's hardest moments, despite his best efforts. I don't want to continue, but it's too late now.

"And then I thought, no father would leave his family if his son was a Major League baseball player. If I could do that, if I could achieve that, you'd be so proud of me..." I shake my head, realizing the futility of my quest. "It was the only way I could be sure you wouldn't leave us, too."

My father's hand flutters. He's trying to move it, but has no strength. I want to help, but don't know how. So I wait while my father uses every ounce of strength he has to lift his hand and set it on top of mine.

"You don't have the slightest clue how much I love you, do you?" he says.

I wipe a tear from my cheek and lean close so I can make out my father's words through his raspy breath. "I never cared if you played in the majors, Charlie. I only wanted that because you wanted it. I wanted it for you."

The words hit me hard, and create a mixture of regret and freedom. "All I wanted..." My father takes several long breaths before continuing. "All I wanted then was the same thing I want now. To spend time with you. To sit with my son and listen to a ballgame."

I'm torn between his request and my promise to Pippin that I'll help the Stallions win. As if reading my thoughts, my father pats my hand softly. "The boys will pull it out. And if they need you in the late innings, the ballpark's right around the corner."

I'm not sure I share his confidence in my teammates, but I'm not about to leave him. Or Pippin, even though she's still asleep. So I turn up the radio loud enough for us to hear, but soft enough that it won't wake Pippin, and together we listen to the play-by-play.

•　•　•

"Do you remember your fifth grade Little League team?"

After nearly an hour of silently listening to the play-by-play announcers call the state championship game—now 3-2 Stallions in the fifth inning—I'm startled by my father's voice. It's stronger than before, as if he's been gathering strength over the past hour, just for this conversation. It's still raspy and weak, but I can understand him.

"We were sponsored by some gas station, weren't we?" I say.

My father tries to laugh, but the pain of the movement cuts it short. "I'd forgotten. I was thinking of when your teammate with the blazing fastball hit you with a pitch during practice."

"Yeah. I still remember how much that hurt."

"Until that day, that would have been the end. You wouldn't have stepped back into the batter's box." My father's lips turn up with the smallest of crinkles. "But that day, completely on your own, you did step back in."

"I remember. I hit a single up the middle on the next pitch."

"You showed courage. Determination. In that moment, you grew up a little."

Cheering slides through the window, filling the room with a sound so familiar, yet so out of place. It dies away, and in the long silence that follows, the game moves into the sixth inning...

"And then there was the Hayfield game during your senior year," my father says. A half hour has passed since he last spoke and I wonder again if he's been building the strength to speak that whole time.

"We were ranked first in state," I say. "Until they beat us."

"You were the last out. A strikeout, with the tying run on third."

"Ouch. That one still stings."

"After the game? When you cried in my arms? I couldn't remember ever feeling so close to you. My son. My baby boy. Leaning on his father for support. I knew it was hard for you, but it was one of the best moments of my life."

As another quiet burst of cheering fills the room, I think back on the moment my father was talking about. I try to relive it over and over, that feeling of safety and love in his arms, the only safe haven in the world. The play-by-play announcer takes the game into the seventh, the Stallions still clinging to a one-run lead.

"The day you were promoted to Triple-A," my father says some time later. "I told you we didn't have to meet up for Major League baseball games anymore, like we had every month. You were one step away. You'd need to focus every ounce of energy on the game."

"You had to have known I'd still make our games," I say.

"Yes," my father whispers. "Because you knew how much they meant to me."

A crackly voice tells of a long home run against the Stallions, and they fall behind 4-3. My father takes another deep breath.

"People might say a relationship based on a sport is superficial. But they're wrong." He takes several more deep breaths and fights a groan. "Through baseball, I've come to know you, Charlie. And you should know, you've been a great son. You've become a great man. No matter what, I never, never would have left you. You've been everything to me." Through tears and weakness and the cancer that's ending his life, my father squeezes my hand and says, "You're my only son."

I struggle against the tears. I fight the knot in my throat so I can tell my dad he's been the best father in the world. That he means more to me than I've ever been able to say; than I ever could say. But, as the Stallions give up another home run, now trailing 6-3, I instead bury my face in my father's shoulder and sob.

"You should go," my father says, long moments later. "I've monopolized you. The team needs you, and you made your sister a promise."

I know it's true. I can't stand to leave the last two hours in the past, but my father is right. "I'll come right back," I say, kissing his forehead. "As soon as the game is over. I'll come straight back here."

My father manages a smile, although I can see the anguish behind it. "I'll be here," he says.

As I head for the door, my father's voice stops me, stronger than it has been since we entered the hospital.

"Charlie," he says.

I turn slowly, fighting the feeling that whatever words come next could be the last I ever hear him say.

"I'm proud of you, son," he says. And I let the words wash over my soul.

．　　．　　．

I take a few steps toward the exit of the room, but I don't make it that far. From behind me, a voice stops me in my tracks. It's pure, light, and surprisingly strong. It's not my father.

"Charlie?" Pippin says. "Is that you?"

I'm at her side without even realizing I've moved. I stroke her tangled, red hair and touch her cheeks and forehead, trying to believe what I'm seeing: Pippin. Alive. Awake. Okay.

"Pippin," I say. All the words I want to say inundate my mind at once. That I'm sorry for hitting her with the bat. I'm sorry I left for the Twins. I'm sorry I wasn't here when she awoke from her coma. But I don't know where to start, and the only thing that comes out of my mouth is, "Pippin. Pippin."

"I know who I am," she says, grinning. "Quebracho didn't knock everything out of my brain."

"Oh, thank God," I say, burying my face in her hair.

"Where were you going?" she asks.

I look in her eyes, trying to find some sign of recognition or understanding. "The championship game," I say. "We're losing. I'm so sorry. I know I promised you...I'm leaving right now to try to help—"

"No," Pippin says, cutting me off. "You can't."

I follow her gaze to my father. He's lying in bed, not even able to turn his head to look at us. I realize Pippin's right. My father is dying, as anyone can see. I need to be here with him. I stand over his bed, looking into his eyes, trying to see past the pain. He swallows, clicks the button for another dose of morphine, and takes a deep breath.

"No," he says. "It's okay." Although he can't move his head, his eyes dart toward Pippin, then back to me. "I'm in good hands. You go give your little sister that championship."

I look at them both, lying in their hospital beds, but headed in different directions. Toward different futures. But one thing that unites them is their irrational love of the Stallions. Their desire to break the streak and bring home a championship for Sweetwater.

I don't know if I can give them what they want. Baseball isn't an individual sport and the game is nearly over. But as I watch them watching me, I know I have to try. No matter what might happen, I have to try.

I smile at them both and try to sound as confident as I can. "Okay," I say. "Let's go win the Stallions a state championship."

Sacrifice Bunt

The Sacrifice Bunt is the epitome of team play. Unlike the sacrifice fly, in which a batter often tries for a home run and settles for an out that results in a run, the sacrifice bunt has no such potential. A true sacrifice bunt, as opposed to the drag bunt, has no purpose but to advance the baserunner. The bunter is typically—indeed is expected to be—thrown out at first base.

The player willingly gives up the enjoyment of hitting and the potential for glory in the name of the team's greater good.

Chapter 15

As I speed into the parking lot of Sweetwater Ballpark, I crane my neck to see the scoreboard. The Stallions are still trailing, 7-5 now, and they're batting in the bottom of the eighth inning. I double park, snag my bag from the back seat, and sprint toward the entrance.

As soon as I set foot in the dugout, Mack spots me and his eyes bulge. "Blake," he yells. "Charlie's going to take this one."

A kid I barely recognize mopes back to the dugout as I grab a quebracho from the bat rack and jam a pine tar-stained helmet onto my head. Emily and Oz both look at me questioningly. I nod but don't say anything. My focus on the game says enough.

Duane stares at me from his spot on the bench. Slouched lazily with his hat crooked and wearing tennis shoes, it's obvious he's still not playing. He appears to be the only one. I can't figure out if I should feel bad about that or not, but I don't have time to deal with him right now. The game is on the line.

I study the scoreboard and scan the bases. A runner on first. One out, bottom of the eighth, down by two. A home run will tie the game. With two outs still available, Mack has decided now is the time to pull out all the stops. He could wait for the ninth to have me pinch-hit, but there's no guarantee anyone will be on base. A solo home run wouldn't be enough, no matter how far I might hit it. It's now or never if the Stallions hope to win a state championship.

I dig my left spike into the dirt, getting a strong hold. I bring the quebracho close to my face and lean my cheek against it, trying to feel Pippin's presence in the wood. As I step into the batter's box, I look to the hospital.

Since I know Pippin and my father are on the third floor, I can narrow down the possible windows, but I have no idea which window is theirs. I face the third floor windows, lift the batting helmet off my head, and raise it in salute. I'll never tip my cap from the batter's box of a big league stadium, but something about doing it here feels more personal anyway.

I replace the batting helmet and smile with the knowledge that I've found my "why."

The first pitch is low and outside and I take it for a ball. But even the act of not swinging raises my confidence another notch. I saw the ball so well it looked almost like a beach ball coming in. I tracked it perfectly, right from the pitcher's release point. I knock the bat against one of my spikes, then step back into the batter's box.

The next pitch is a curveball and I recognize it so early I know exactly how much it will break and where it will end up. Low and in, out of the strike zone. I take it for ball two.

Now's the time. The perfect hitter's count. I can look for a fastball, knowing the pitcher won't want to fall behind 3-0.

But a fastball doesn't come. The third pitch is another breaking ball, again out of the zone. And with a crushing feeling, I realize what I—and Mack—should have known was coming all along.

They aren't going to give me anything to hit.

Disappointment starts in my temples and slides all the way down my body, making me slouch in the batter's box as, expectedly, another slider bounces to the catcher. Deflated, I walk to first base.

It's the worst possible scenario. I missed the opportunities for three at-bats and the Stallions trail late. The other team was able to take the bat out of my hands with a semi-intentional walk, and now I can't do anything but hope my teammates come through.

They don't. As I watch from first base, the next batter strikes out and the following one grounds weakly to the second baseman, ending the inning with no runs scored. The game heads to the ninth with the Stallions still trailing by two, and my opportunity has passed.

The third baseman brings my glove out to me with a shrug that suggests there's nothing more I could have done. It doesn't make me feel any better.

The second pitch of the top of the ninth gives me a chance to contribute something. A sharp ground ball skips up the middle, past the pitcher, and nearly into center field. But I read the bat angle early and get a good jump. I launch my body horizontal and feel the smack of the baseball in the webbing of my glove. As quickly as possible, I slide onto one knee and fire the ball to first base, beating the runner by a half-step.

The crowd roars, but I worry it's too little too late. I can make all the diving plays in the world, but if the Stallions don't score at least two runs when our turn comes in the bottom of the ninth, we'll finish second, the streak without a championship will remain intact, and I will have broken my promise to Pippin.

Worst of all, there's nothing I can do about it anymore.

I try to build a wall around the negative thoughts and focus on the game. The next batter hits a screaming line drive, but it's right at our center field for the second out and it looks like the Stallions might be able to hold the deficit at two.

As I catch the ball and finish tossing it around the horn, something flashes in the corner of my eye. It doesn't take long to realize where it's coming from: the hospital. Third floor.

The sun glints off the window again and I watch the pane of glass slide upward. A moment later, a mop of red hair leans out the window, accompanied by the frantically waving hand of my little sister.

I laugh out loud at what she's doing. Since she and my father are listening on the radio, they know about the semi-intentional walk. They know I must be feeling like I failed Pippin. So she opened the window and waved at me. My kid sister, looking out for me.

The third out of the inning comes on a long fly ball that our right-fielder hauls in at the wall, but it barely registers. My mind is reeling so fast, it's like I wake up from a trance to realize I'm sitting in the dugout in the bottom of the ninth, and the Stallions need two runs to tie, three to win.

•　　•　　•

I'm up seventh, if it comes to that. Theoretically, if things work out perfectly for me, it could be the ideal game-winning scenario. But my experience being stranded in the on-deck circle with the Twins is still fresh in my mind.

Watching my teammates' at-bats—and not being able to do anything to help—creates one of the most helpless feelings I can imagine. I stroll, purposefully, slowly, to the end of the dugout and sit by Emily.

She's beaming. The knowledge that Pippin is awake has spread to everyone in the stadium. For those who know her, it's like a drug. It lifts everyone in the dugout.

"The thing about baseball," Emily says, taking my hand in hers, "is that you never can tell what's going to happen."

Right on cue, our lead-off hitter, using a dark red quebracho bat, smacks a single up the middle and Emily nods approvingly. The next Stallion hits a ground ball that bounces off the third base bag and trickles into left field, giving us runners on first and second with nobody out. The dugout roars to life and I feel butterflies in my chest.

The way I get to the on-deck circle is ordinary. A strikeout, an RBI single—putting us down by only one run—followed by another strikeout. But what happens then—with runners on first and third with two outs, down by a run—is anything but ordinary.

I swing a weighted bat in the on-deck circle, wondering if our centerfielder, Josh Hansen, will end the game with a double in the gap and a Stallions victory, or end the game with an out and a Stallions loss. Or one of the many possibilities in the middle, which would mean I would get to hit.

"Time!" Mack yells from the dugout.

Hansen, who's busy digging his back foot into the batter's box, cocks his head as he looks at his coach, but then he walks quickly toward the on-deck circle, where Mack stands next to me. Mack continues to frantically wave him over, which seems like overkill until I realize he's not waving at Hansen, but at our third-base coach. The coach turns to look behind him, then turns the other way. When he realizes no one is there, he jogs to meet us in the on-deck circle.

"Strange situation," Mack says when we're all together.

"How's that?" the third-base coach says.

Mack chews his gum loudly for several long seconds. Finally, he nods to himself and says, "If Hansen gets a hit here, you need to hold the runner at third."

"Makes sense," the third-base coach says. "Small park like this, we don't want to take the chance of him getting thrown out trying to score from first. Not with Charlie up next."

"I don't mean him," Mack says.

"You don't mean who?"

"I don't mean the runner at first. I mean the runner at third. Make him stay there."

"What?" Hansen and I say at the same time.

The coach stares at Mack for a second, then his brow crinkles like he's trying to understand, then his mouth drops open a couple inches. "You want me to hold the runner who's already on third base? He could walk to the plate, and he's the tying run."

"I understand that," Mack says.

"Then why in the world wouldn't we score him?"

Mack chews his gum even faster. He looks to me, apparently thinking I'll be more understanding of his crazy scheme. "Think about it. We've used up our entire bullpen. Last inning they hit three of the hardest balls they've hit all game. If we go to extra innings, we lose, and that's a fact. We're not looking to tie this up. We need to win it right here, right now."

"I agree," I say. "But that starts by getting the runner home from third."

Mack shakes his head hard. "Can't do that."

"Why?" I ask.

"Think it through. Say Hansen here hits a single. What would happen? If we play it normally."

I motion out to the field like I'm orchestrating the action as I talk. "The run scores from third. Depending on where the ball is hit, the runner from first either gets to second or third. So we've got two on, two out, a tie game, and I'm up with a chance to win it."

"Exactly," Mack says. "And what happens then?"

It hits me like a sledgehammer. Mack isn't crazy. He's exactly right. "They walk me," I say. "Just like last time."

"Precisely," Mack says. "And you remember what happened after they did that last inning."

"They got out of it with no runs."

"Meaning we'd likely go to extra innings without any pitching. And we'd lose." He looks at all of us in the circle and nods in certainty. "Unless Hansen hits it out of the park, the only way we can win this thing is if they have to pitch to Charlie. "

Hansen and the third-base coach still look skeptical. "He's right," I say. "No matter what, unless Hansen hits it out of the park, we have to keep that runner on third. That is, if we want me to have a chance to hit."

Finally, Hansen and the coach start nodding. It's crazy, but it's the best option. "I guess I just can't get out, then," Hansen says, and he strides back toward home plate.

The third-base coach looks at Mack and lowers his voice. "Do you have any idea what people will say? Holding the tying run when he's already at third base? It's probably never happened in the history of the game."

"There's probably never been a situation that warranted it," Mack says. "But there is now."

"Let's play ball!" the umpire yells from his spot behind home plate.

The third-base coach jogs back to his spot and takes the base runner aside. He puts his arm around him and walks up the left field line a few feet to explain the unusual situation without being overheard.

Then comes the moment of truth.

Hansen, to his credit, does his part. On a first pitch fastball, he drives the ball over the second baseman's head and into right field. But that's when the chaos starts.

The runner at third keeps his foot planted firmly on the base, as planned. Almost immediately, the entire stadium of fans erupt. They scream at the runner and wave their arms frantically. Several put their hands on their heads in utter disbelief. They must think the Stallions have decided to throw the game. To not send a runner who's already on third base and could score so easily? It's unheard of.

Meanwhile, the runner who was at first rounds second base, and that's when I realize the flaw in our plan. No one told the runner at first what was going to happen.

As he should, the runner continues past second and toward third base. There's no need to check to see if anyone is still at third base because…well, why would there be anyone at third base? It would make no sense.

But there is someone at third base because he hasn't moved an inch since the ball was hit. I put my hands over my face, realizing we now have two players standing on third base.

I peek through my fingers and watch the chaos continue. The third-base coach frantically waves the runner back to second base. He's half way there when he realizes Hansen has rounded first, saw no one at second base, and sprinted there.

The next twenty seconds are a cluster of baserunners going every which way and the fielders on the other team going back and forth between run-downs, trying to end the game by tagging someone out.

They end up with Hansen in a rundown between first and second. They close the gap with each toss until finally, one more throw from to the second baseman will end it. Hansen sprints with all he has, but it's futile. The ball beats him, and he's stuck. The second baseman reaches up for the toss…and drops it.

The toss was a little high, but it was still an easy play to make. An easy out. At least, in professional ball. I forget sometimes that these guys are accountants and insurance salesmen. They don't exactly spend a lot of time practicing run-downs.

Somehow, each Stallion baserunner has found a safe place. The bases are loaded and I'm up. It wasn't exactly how Mack drew it up, and we had to risk everything to get here, but we got exactly what we wanted in the end. The guy who could be playing in the Major Leagues right now, with an at-bat to win it all for the Stallions. And this time, there's nowhere to put me.

· · ·

The quebracho feels strong and smooth in my hands. Thousands of people are on their feet, now understanding why the runner remained on third base. The plan, so close to backfiring, has already become legendary. The talk spreads through the crowd like wildfire. People will tell the story for years about the day the Stallions held a runner on third base—a runner who was already at third base!—and the other team was forced to pitch to the professional.

Everything is in my hands now. It's time to be the hero.

I close my eyes for a moment before stepping to the plate. My time with Bud has taught me many things, and I realize now that all of them have to do with introspection. Now isn't the time to hurry up to the plate and get it over with. Win or lose, hero or goat, I need to be in this moment.

Slowly, deliberately, I make my way to home plate and dig my back foot into the dirt. Everything I've been through, the entire road of my life has brought me to this moment.

My mother leaving us.

My full decade in the minor leagues.

My return to Sweetwater.

My father.

Emily.

Oz.

Pippin. More than anything, Pippin.

When I think of my little sister, awake in the hospital and watching from the window, a strange sensation comes over me and causes me to hesitate. I suddenly find it impossible to step the rest of the way into the batter's box. Despite all the risks the Stallions took to get me here, I can't force myself to step up and finish it. Instead, I remove my foot from the batter's box and ask the umpire for time.

He probably thinks it's a dramatic ploy, or maybe an attempt to rattle the pitcher, but it's neither. When he reluctantly grants me a time out, I quickly walk back to the dugout, acutely aware of the stares of everyone in the stadium. Suddenly, the talk turns from the unconventional base running move to why the superstar is walking off the field at the most important moment of the season. The most important moment of the last fifty seasons of Stallions baseball.

I go straight to my bag, pull out my cell phone, and start a video call while my teammates look on incredulously. It doesn't take long for Pippin's curly red hair to fill the screen.

"Charlie, what's going on? You're up! Right now!"

"I know, Pip. But there's something I have to ask you. Something important."

"Charlie! There are five thousand people wondering what the heck you're doing right now. What could be so important?"

I feel my teammates staring at me, so I duck out of the dugout where they can't hear me. With fans craning their necks to see what I'm doing, I look back to Pippin's face on the screen.

"There's something I need to do, Pip. I think it's the right thing, but I can't guarantee it'll result in a Stallions win. In fact, there's a good chance it could ruin everything."

"Okay," she says slowly, trying to understand.

When I tell her of my plan, she's quiet for a long time. The crowd is getting anxious and I hear the umpire's voice yelling into the dugout, asking where I am. He's demanding a hitter. Right now. When I look back at my phone, Pippin looks older than she normally does. Not in the number of years she's been alive, but older in maturity. Finally, something like a smile eases its way onto her face.

"Remember when I said there were those three things that could make me feel happy?" she says. "Making quebracho, winning the science fair, and the Stallions winning a championship?"

"Of course."

"Well, that was a lie. There's something else. Something that would beat all three. And that's for my big brother to come home and be with me." She wipes at her eyes and I realize she's crying. What she's saying—what she's allowing me to do—can't be easy for her. She sniffles and continues.

"You're the thing that makes me happiest, Charlie. You've already made me the happiest I can be, just by being here with me. Just by coming back home. So whatever you have to do is fine with me. As long as you promise to come see me as soon as it's over."

I wish I could tell her how impressed I am by her. I wish I could tell her how much I love her and admire her and am grateful for her. But Mack's voice booms at me from the entrance to the dugout, so I just say, "Thanks, Pip. I'll see you soon."

"Finally," Mack says when I enter the dugout. "What the hell was that? Actually, don't answer that. Just get up there and win us a state championship."

He points to the field. To home plate, where success and glory await. But instead of walking out there, I find Oz and look straight at him. I wink, which makes him smile. At the sight of my son smiling at me, I feel like I could do anything.

"I'm really sorry Mack, but I can't hit."

Mack stammers and stutters and tries to find the words, before finally settling on, "What! What in the world are you talking about, Fightmaster?"

"Duane is going to hit for me," I say, still looking at Oz, whose confusion matches everyone else's.

After a long moment of universal shock, Mack finally shakes his head like he's just been stunned by a punch in a boxing match. "Duane Jones is not going to hit for you. I don't know what you think you're doing, but if you don't get out there right now, I swear I'll…"

Mack can't seem to think of exactly what he'll do, and I take the opportunity to motion to Duane to get up. I don't know if his hesitation is from disbelief or terror, but eventually he grabs his spikes from his bag and puts them on in place of his tennis shoes. He stares at me the entire time, like he's waiting for me to take it back and start laughing at him.

"You can't do this, Charlie," Mack says. "The season's on the line. The championship."

"I'm sorry, Mack, but there's nothing you can do. I'm not going up there to hit, and Duane is the only hitter left on the bench."

Duane is wide-eyed as he approaches me. He moves tentatively, like he's sure I'm about to change my mind. Instead, I raise the quebracho bat toward him. "Take this," I say. "And look for the inside fastball. They think they can jam you, but they can't. Not with this bat."

Duane swallows hard and stares at the bat, then at me. "Why? You hate me."

"I don't hate you, Duane. I realized recently that I just didn't know you." Something about the crease in his brow makes my throat hurt. "I know we've had our differences, but I believe in you. I know you can do this."

I'm not sure if it's my words or the bat in his hands, but he starts to look more calm. The fear is gone, replaced by determination. When the umpire yells once more, he takes a deep breath and walks onto the field.

I stroll back to the threshold of the dugout, where Oz waits for me. My son studies me intently, as if trying to read what went through my mind to make me do all I could to help my biggest enemy. To let him have the chance at glory.

I feel lighter than I have in a very long time.

When Duane hits a first-pitch inside fastball down the left field line for a double, scoring the winning runs of the state tournament, I don't see it happen.

Instead, I'm smiling at my son.

• • •

The Stallions swarm the field, jumping up and down in a mosh pit of celebration near home plate. I watch with a feeling of calm pleasure as Oz sprints onto the field and leaps on top of the pile, a smile the size of a baseball glove spread across his face.

From the pile, a couple of my teammates wave frantically for me to join them. But I have other celebrations to get to. I grab my keys, wallet, and baseball bag, then head for the exit.

"Tell them we'll be right there," Emily says.

I can't contain the joy. I kiss her lips, say, "I will," and quickly jog to my car.

I could probably throw a baseball from the parking lot of the baseball stadium to the hospital parking lot, but the drive seems to take forever. I just want to be there. I just want to see my sister's joy, my father's pride.

I park, enter the hospital, and take an elevator to the third floor, but it's all a blur. As I jog toward room 312, the post-game show on the radio echoes down the hallway. The announcers are raving about Duane. How he came through in the most clutch situation possible. How he brought a championship back to Sweetwater.

"Pretty amazing, right?" I say, bursting into the room. "You guys heard it, right?"

Pippin is sitting up in her bed, looking over at my father. The expression on her face is unreadable, but one glance at my father is all it takes to understand. I can't decide whether to look at him or avert my eyes, which are quickly filling with tears.

"When did it happen?" I ask Pippin.

I still can't discern her expression. Tears flow freely down her cheeks, but at the same time she seems unable to contain a smile.

Strange as it is, I think I understand. Warm tears run down my cheeks, but the pain I expected when this moment inevitably came isn't there. In its place, a wave of peace sweeps over me.

"Just a few minutes ago," Pippin says, sniffling.

"Did he hear…" I'm not able to finish my question, but Pippin understands.

"All of it," she says, nodding and smiling even bigger beneath her tears. "He knew the Stallions won, and he knew what you did."

"Really?"

"Yep. It was all the radio guys could talk about. *'Duane Jones is going to hit for Charlie Fightmaster. And Fightmaster just gave him his bat! What a sign of teamwork!'* They were a little over the top about it, I thought."

I think of my father, in the hospital bed with his daughter, listening to the play-by-play as his son became an adult. He died the way he had lived—on his own terms and after he had known his children were going to be okay.

Pippin slowly drops her legs over the side of her bed and I help her over to our father's body. We each take one of his hands. I gaze at the wrinkled hand in my own. I don't want to look at his face—something about the angle of his head and the droop of his lips seem lifeless. But his hands—the hands that threw countless baseballs to me as we played catch, and slapped my back each time we embraced in a hug, and shook my own hand firmly in congratulations after a baseball game, whether I'd played well or poorly—these hands still look the same. And they're my father's hands.

I take his hand, and Pippin's hand, and I press them against my cheeks. We sit like that for a long moment. Then my little sister and I say goodbye to the man who raised us.

·   ·   ·

When Emily and Oz arrive, they already know. Not wanting them to be taken by surprise by my father's passing, I texted Emily as they were on their way over from the stadium. So they enter quietly, reverently. I can see the same struggle in their eyes: trying to navigate the mixture of joy and sorrow.

"I'm so sorry," Emily says. "For both of you. For all of us. He was a great man."

We all nod silently. Some of us look at my father's body while others avoid our eyes. "At least he got to see the Stallions win it all," Pippin says.

"Yeah," I say. "Thanks to your quebracho bats."

"Do you really think it made a difference?"

"Absolutely. There's no way Duane would have gotten a hit without it."

Pippin giggles. Her red hair is greasy and her eyes are puffy, but I don't think I've ever seen her look so beautiful.

I want to wrap her in my arms and never let her go. Never allow her to face the sadness and fear and uncertainty that await her when she leaves this place and discovers that her life has changed so drastically. Again.

"Oh, I almost forgot," I say. "Dad wanted me to bring this to you."

A moment of pain follows the words, and it takes a moment to figure out why. But then it hits me. The words make it sound like my father is still with us. How could he have wanted me to bring something to Pippin if he wasn't still with us? It suddenly feels like more than a gift, it has transformed into a final connection to our father. Slowly, I reach into my baseball bag and remove a perfect quebracho bat.

Pippin reaches for the bat tentatively, almost reverently. She carefully takes it and spins it so she can see the barrel. Her giggle returns as she looks at the braids wrapped around two crossing bats, and the words **Fightmaster Bat Company-M1PF**.

"What's it mean?" she asks.

"Model 1, Pippin Fightmaster. Dad designed it, just like you asked him to."

Pippin stares at it again. "It's perfect," she says.

We sit in quiet admiration for a long time, studying the details of the emblem. Pippin sneaks several peeks at me, only to look away as soon as my eyes meet hers. I can't figure out what's going on in her mind. Surely more than I can comprehend. After all, she's just woken up from a coma, she's lost her father, and she's realized her dream of a Sweetwater Stallions state championship—all in the last few hours. How could it not be overwhelming?

But something about the look she keeps giving me is beyond sadness at the loss of our father or excitement about the championship. More than anything else, her eyes seem scared.

"When I get out of here," she finally says. "Do you think we might be able to make more bats? Or…"

She can't force herself to finish the question, and now I understand why. She isn't just asking about the bats. She's asking about my plans. She doesn't know about my three day Major League career, or the fact that I left before I ever saw the field. The fear in her eyes is fear that she might have an empty house waiting for her, with her father gone and her brother off chasing his dream once again.

From an inside pocket of my baseball bag I remove the folded Twins line-up card. I wipe some infield dirt off, clearing the names of everyone on the Twins roster for that game. There, at the very bottom, hastily written, is *Fightmaster*. When I hand it to Pippin, her brow forms deep crinkles as she tries to figure out what she's looking at.

"Wait," she says. "Is this...how did you get this? This is..."

"It's a long story," I say.

I crouch next to the hospital bed and run my hand through Pippin's gnarled hair. I study her beautiful, scattered freckles and her perfect, crooked teeth.

"And I'll tell you all of it. But for right now, all you need to know is that we can make as many bats as you want, Pipsqueak. For as long as you want to make them. Because I'm not going anywhere. And that's a promise."

The Perfect Game

In Major League Baseball history, hundreds of thousands of games have been played. Fewer than 25 perfect games have been thrown, and nobody has more than one. And while it's true that the pitcher must be uncommonly dominant for the entire game, there are always near misses for batters, spectacular plays by defenders, and questionable calls by umpires.

Even in the midst of the most dominant individual performance in the sport, baseball remains a team game.

Chapter 16

"Hurry, Charlie! We're going to be late!"

I hear the words, but don't obey right away. I stare at my sister, in awe of how quickly her recovery is taking place. Sure, there are still nightly headaches, some dizziness and nausea when she forgets to take her medications, but considering the fact that her survival was in doubt just a week ago, I can't believe how well Pippin is doing.

She sighs a deep, exaggerated puff and puts her hands on her hips. "You're doing it again."

"Doing what?"

"Ah, staring? Like some creepball?"

I laugh out loud. It's good to have my little sister back. "Sorry. I'm ready. We can go now."

"Finally. I can't wait to see the look on Skyler's face when quebracho beats her out for first place. We absolutely can't be late for the awards ceremony."

During the drive to the middle school, Pippin is silent. She stares out the window, tapping her foot incessantly.

"Hey," I say from the driver's seat. "No matter what, we both know yours is the best project actually done by a seventh grader. Anyone who knows me knows I definitely couldn't have done yours for you."

A brief smile is all I get from her. "Maybe. But as long as she's the one who gets to walk up on the stage and hold the first place trophy, none of that matters."

I'm happy to see Emily and Oz standing outside the main entrance of the school, waiting for us. "Good luck, Pippin," Emily says as soon as we're within earshot. "I just know you're going to win."

Oz looks like he wants to say something, too, but squeezes his mom's arm a little tighter instead.

Soon, we've filed into the auditorium, found our seats, and listened to a long-winded speech by one of the judges about how this year's State Science Fair Competition has featured some of the best projects he's ever seen out of middle schoolers. The comment draws an exasperated look from Pippin, but nothing more. Then the judge hands the microphone to Mr. Lauritson to name the winners.

He starts by announcing the tenth place finisher. After five names are called—none of them Pippin's—Pippin shuffles in her seat and begins wringing her hands. When her name doesn't appear in the next three, I start to panic too. Up until now, I've been hoping not to hear her name. If she's going to have a chance to beat Skyler, she can't come in third. But now I worry she hasn't even made the top ten.

"Now for our top two finishers in the state of Minnesota," Mr. Lauritson says. His smile is encouraging, but he's probably supposed to stay neutral, and would have forced a smile either way. "I think all the judges who studied these projects agree that we've never seen the likes of them, and deciding between them was extremely difficult. However, in the end, one of them stood out for its ingenuity, in-depth research, and mature ideas."

"Oh shoot," Pippin says beside me. I noticed the use of the word "mature" as well. Obviously, Mr. Lauritson is sending Pippin a message—that he knows the winning project wasn't done by a middle school girl named Skyler.

"The second place winner is...Skyler Shepherd!"

"Ohmygod, ohmygod, ohmygod," Pippin says, bouncing in her seat now.

I burst out laughing when the two adults next to Skyler stand and begin walking with her to the podium to accept the award, until Skyler realizes what's happening and gestures them back to their seats.

"And this year's champion of the Summer State Science Fair is...Pippin Fightmaster for her project on the various properties of quebracho wood in the use—"

Pippin's screeching in my ear prevents me from hearing anything more. And as the audience cheers her accomplishment, I know that starting at shortstop for the Minnesota Twins couldn't hold a candle to being here while my socially awkward, funny-looking sister cries tears of joy and holds her science fair trophy high over her head.

·   ·   ·

I stay off to the side and watch Pippin graciously accept the congratulations of dozens of people. It's long overdue. I've had plenty of recognition in my life. Plenty of awards and popularity and attention. And for what? Being able to hit a baseball? It's time Pippin gets some well-deserved recognition for her brilliance, perseverance, and integrity. Things that should be worth a lot more.

Oz tugs on my sleeve. "Can we come over and celebrate with Pippin?" he asks.

"Of course. Maybe you could take her home and I'll stop and get an ice cream cake on the way. You know how she loves ice cream cake."

"Done," Emily says, and she leans over and kisses me on the cheek.

Pippin makes her way toward the exit, still accepting handshakes and occasional hugs from people I've never seen before. I don't even try to hide my smile as I make my way out of the auditorium to go find some ice cream cake.

"Get back here, Fightmaster," a craggy voice says from behind me.

A hooked hand grips my shoulder and I turn to find Bud Crawford. I shake Bud's hand firmly.

"I'll see you there," I say to Emily as she steers Oz and Pippin toward the exit.

I watch them for a few steps—Pippin wiping tears from her cheeks and continuing to thank people for their congratulations—before turning back to Bud. "It's been quite a ride, hasn't it Bud?"

"You didn't screw it up too bad in the end."

I wonder what Bud's plans are for the day. The thought of him walking home alone to an empty house makes me sad. I nearly invite him to my house, but something about Bud's posture—fidgety and still uncomfortable in the presence of others—makes me think he might need some time alone. After so long on his own, learning to socialize must be exhausting.

"Thanks for everything, Bud," I say.

The old man nods, not making eye contact. "You did okay. Finding perfect harmony, that is."

I smile my thanks. "At the plate? Maybe. But we both know it doesn't come so easy in the rest of life."

Bud simply looks at Emily, Oz, and Pippin as they disappear out the front doors. He nods his head approvingly and repeats, "You're doing okay."

I kick at the dirt for a moment. "So what's next for you? I was thinking we'll need a good hitting coach next year."

Bud shudders and I try to figure out why. Maybe the thought of being around people so much? Or the thought of repeating the frustration of trying to teach an ignorant ballplayer about harmony. "I guess we'll see."

I put my hand on the old man's shoulder and Bud nods without looking at me—acknowledgement that he understands my gratitude. "And you?" Bud says, changing the subject. "Sticking around with the kids, then?"

"Yeah, I guess. But that's secondary. I have bigger reasons to stay."

"Oh? Bigger than your family?"

"Way bigger," I say. I look to the sky and squint, as if calculating something. "I went deep forty-eight times this summer. If I play for another fifteen years, I just might have a shot at your record. I'll be the new Mr. 500."

"Ha!" Bud roars. It's the first time I've heard him laugh and the sound is music to my ears. "You didn't learn a thing, did you Fightmaster?"

I chuckle too and shake Bud's hand one last time. "See you in the spring then? In a Stallions uniform?"

Bud nods again, and this time risks a quick moment of eye contact. "Before spring would be fine too," he mumbles. "If you wanted to bring the family by. You don't have to, of course," he hurries to add. "Just, if it's convenient."

A cool breeze rustles the leaves of a nearby maple tree. "Tuesday evenings work well for us," I say. "Let's make it a regular thing."

Bud swipes at his eyes and clears his throat roughly. "Better bring food," he says. "I don't want you stealing all of my lefse."

I pretend to consider the offer for a long while.

"It's a deal," I finally say.

· · ·

It's 3pm. The Twins are at home against the Rangers. They'll be taking the field in about four hours. It's a two hour drive to Minneapolis.

I'd better hurry.

I text Emily to let her know I won't be able to come home right away, and can she hang out with Pippin and Oz at the house? I can tell by the tone of her text that she's confused—what's more important that going home to celebrate Pippin's success? But she doesn't ask too many questions, so I speed toward Minneapolis as fast as the Escort will take me.

I could call Hudson, or even text him. But that would make it too easy for him to say no, and I can't have him say no.

I don't have a plan for how to get into the stadium. I'm hoping to be able to tell a security guard that I was on the team for a brief time, but when I try that, the guard looks at me like I'm crazy and stands his ground. Fortunately, Hudson is late—as usual—and approaches just as I'm about to give up on this particular guard and try another one.

"Fighter?" he says. "What are you doing here? Don't let Skip see you. He's not exactly a big fan of yours these days."

"No?" I say, slapping his hand in our familiar way. "Managers don't like when their players quit the team right in front of them?"

"Ha! Not so much." He looks around as if trying to find something. "What are you doing here?"

"I need a favor," I say. "It's important."

When I tell him what I have in mind, Hudson gives me the same look the security guard just gave me — the one that's certain I'm crazy.

"Man, you know I can't do that. You know how much money they'll fine me?"

"Seriously, Hudson? You're worried about money? Fine, whatever. I'll pay for it. Let me know how much it is and I'll pay for it."

"You could never afford it, Fighter."

He's right, and I have no answer to that. But thinking of what this could mean for Pippin convinces me to make one more stab at it.

"Think about Ayesha," I say.

"Ayesha? Fighter, don't even try to —"

"What if Ayesha had one thing that would make her happier than anything else in the world. What if you had the power to give it to her — and you knew someone who had the power to help. Wouldn't you do every single thing you could to make that happen?"

Hudson shakes his head, but it doesn't mean "no." I can tell. He's shaking his head at the fact that I'm getting through to him.

"Look, I know you've only met Pippin that one time. I know she's not Ayesha. She's not your flesh and blood. But she's my Ayesha, you know? And she's had so much go against her, so many disappointments." I'm surprised at how strongly I feel about this. Strong enough to keep groveling, apparently. "I almost killed her, do you understand that? I'm begging you, please, as my friend. Do this one thing for me, and I'll never ask for another favor for the rest of my life."

We're both quiet for a long moment. I try to think of how else I could convince him, but I've done what I can. It's up to Hudson now. He keeps shaking his head slowly. "You know I can't guarantee what'll happen. I haven't been swinging the bat so good lately."

"I have complete confidence in you. Just do me a favor, will you? Swing out of your shoes for me."

Hudson barks out a laugh. He stares at the ground for so long I start to wonder if he's going to answer. Finally, he stands and starts to walk past the security guard and through the entrance.

Over his shoulder, he says, "Fighter, you have no idea the size of the favor you owe me."

• • •

The sun is getting low by the time I make my way back to Sweetwater and catch up with everyone back at the house. It makes me happy to see Emily bustling around as if she lives here, and my throat tightens when I notice Oz slouched in my dad's recliner, pushing buttons on the TV remote control until finally landing on the Twins game. I see Hudson in his position in center field and feel my heart rate increase. I just hope he hasn't changed his mind.

Pippin sits on the floor, holding a quebracho bat in her hands, studying it from every angle. She waves me over and I lower myself onto the floor next to her.

"So I was thinking," she says, and I prepare to feign understanding of whatever comes next. "Due to quebracho's unique shape, maybe we should adjust the positioning of the trademark in relation to other bats. I'm thinking it could be toward the end, maybe centered four and an eighth inches from the inverted cup."

I enjoy watching Pippin acting like herself again. I can see the difference in her demeanor since her luck has started to turn. So far, in addition to having her big brother around, her Stallions have won the state championship and she took home first place in the state middle school science fair. All of that has gone a long way to counter the loss of our father. But I still have high hopes for what's to come. Hopefully in just a few minutes.

Emily slices the ice cream cake and gives a piece to everyone, but I don't touch mine. I'm too busy watching the Twins game, wondering if Hudson will actually do what I asked. What I begged for, if I'm honest. But if he comes through, it could be life-changing. For all of us.

"Why aren't you eating your ice cream cake?" Pippin asks, leaning over as if she's very interested in a second piece.

Before I can answer, Oz says, "Wow," and all of us follow his stare to the television.

"Guys!" he says. "Is that..."

On the screen, Hudson is in the on-deck circle dabbing a pine tar rag onto a bat. It's crazy to think I could be in that dugout right now.

"Hudson White is seriously using one of our bats," Oz says.

The bat Hudson finishes preparing and carries to the plate is so uniquely shaped there's no confusing it for any other bat. It's so strange, even the announcers take notice.

"Turn it up!" Pippin says.

"Shhh!" Oz says, and cranks up the volume.

"....a little bat-making outfit there that created this unique design. White hasn't used it in a game, but he says batting practice today went exceptionally well with it. Maybe the change will help break him out of his recent slump."

"No way," Oz says, and Pippin giggles. I can only stare at the screen as my old friend comes through beyond anything I could have expected. First, he stares at the bat, long enough for the cameras to move to a close-up of him. He's been on TV enough times to know exactly what camera is on him and where it comes from. He looks right into the camera, holds the bat next to his face, smiles a big, bright smile, and points at the barrel. He moves his hand down to the taper like a game-show host showing off a prize. Then he bounces his eyebrows and mouths the word, "Quebracho."

Although I'm guessing nobody outside Sweetwater could understand what he said, what happens next doesn't need interpretation. We all watch in complete silence as he steps back into the batter's box and launches the first pitch to straight-away center field. It short-hops the wall as Hudson flies around the bases. He sprints around second and dives into third base head-first, beating the throw by a half-second.

The announcers are beside themselves, talking about the bat more than they talk about Hudson White and his broken slump. As White stands and swipes the dirt off his jersey, I put my hand on Pippin's shoulder, never looking away from the screen.

"Well Pip, I'd say we better get started making more bats."

Eight Months Later

It was a cold, snowy winter, even by Minnesota standards. Emily says she didn't mind because she wouldn't have been able to enjoy nice weather anyway, with how many hours she was putting in at her new office. As one of only two lawyers in town, her business has taken off immediately and kept her busy. But not too busy to spend time with me, Oz, and Pippin.

Pippin has been giving me a hard time recently about proposing. She says it's obvious we're in love, there's no one else in Sweetwater for me to date, and besides, I'm getting old. I haven't taken the plunge yet, but I have to admit I'm getting more comfortable with the idea.

It's a mid-April night, after the Sweetwater Stallions began defense of our state title with a comfortable 7-2 win in the season opener. I'm cuddled next to Emily on the bench atop the scoreboard after the lights have long gone dark. It's not anything like the Green Monster. It's less dramatic, less impressive. But it feels a lot more like home.

Oz and Pippin play on the dark field, tossing baseballs high into the air and trying their best to catch them. I'm reminded of the thought I had just before I destroyed the quebracho bat: that our circles of people who really care for us are so small, and that fact makes life meaningless. And I realize now just how wrong I was.

Maybe it's true that what happens to us only impacts a handful of people. Maybe only one or two people will be devastated when we're gone. But as I sit beneath the stadium lights with my family, I have a hard time understanding why I ever thought that made things meaningless. All the meaning I could possibly imagine is right here with me tonight.

That's the nature of a circle, I guess. Circles are connected, protected, and full.

I stand and balance on the scoreboard bench. "Be careful," Emily says. "The last thing he'd want is for you to fall and break your neck doing this."

"True. Especially since he's the one who told me to do it."

I pull the container with my father's ashes from my large jacket pocket and remove the lid. "Hey guys!" I yell down to Pippin and Oz. When they look up, I toss the ashes into the wind and let out a loud cheer.

Pippin and Oz, realizing what I did, mimic my howl. For a few magical moments, my father's ashes float in the breeze while the four of us celebrate. Then the ashes drift away and there's silence as we all watch the peaceful night, each alone in our thoughts.

Finally, I sit back down next to Emily, nodding. "No fuss. Just like he would have wanted."

"And at the ballpark for eternity," Emily says. "Also just what he would have wanted." After several more leisurely moments, Emily says, "Who do you think Bud will tell his secrets to next?"

"No idea. But I feel sorry for whoever it is."

"No you don't," Emily says, punching my shoulder.

I can't help but laugh. "No. I don't. I wish I could do it all again."

After a few moments of watching the kids resume playing on the field, Emily asks, "So what do you make of his 'perfect harmony' thing now? Do you buy it?"

I consider my answer seriously. I think about the obstacles I've faced as well as my successes. I think about all the moments that have passed me by, and those I've been able to actually live.

"I think it's possible," I say. "At least, in any given moment. And if we can't find harmony here and now, in this moment, then we never will. Because the moment we're living is the only one we'll ever have."

Emily gazes at the field, then up at the stadium lights. "When did you become such a deep thinker?"

"The day you took me to see some crazy old man."

Crickets start chirping in the nearby fields and the first fireflies begin dancing beyond the stadium wall. "So?" Emily says.

"So what?"

"Is there perfect harmony in this moment?"

I watch Pippin chase after a baseball with pure happiness on her face—and I realize the vulnerability of knowing I can't protect her from life. I think of my father and accept the truth of his death. And I watch Emily as she watches Oz and realize my family is the reason for everything I do.

"I don't care what you call it," I say. "But if you're asking me if I love my life in this very moment?" I close my eyes, breathe deeply of the late spring air, and hear the beautiful sound of my son hitting a baseball with the bat he made with Pippin.

"Perfect harmony doesn't begin to describe it."

The End

Acknowledgements

This story has been a labor of love for me, but it wouldn't have been possible without the help and support of many people. Thanks to my writer's group members, Sheala Henke, Amy Rivers, Ronda Simmons, Sara Roberts, and Laura Mahal. Even through the craziness of 2020, you've been a great help. Also, a special thanks to writer's group member David Sharp, whose reading of my early drafts and insightful feedback helped beyond measure.

As always, credit goes to Reagan Rothe, my publisher at Black Rose Writing. He and his team—Christopher Miller and Justin Weeks—have made the process seamless and as stress-free as possible. I look forward to many more successes together.

My wife, Anne, continues to be my greatest support. I love our life together and don't tell you nearly enough how grateful I am for you. And thank you to my daughters, Maya and Lily, for being yourselves, which is exactly who I hope you will always be.

About the Author

Joe Siple is the author of *The Five Wishes of Mr. Murray McBride*, a #1 Bestseller in several countries and winner of multiple awards, including being named "2018 Book of the Year" by the Maxy Awards. Siple lives in Colorado with his wife and two daughters.

Note from the Author

Word-of-mouth is crucial for any author to succeed. If you enjoyed *Charlie Fightmaster and the Search for Perfect Harmony*, please leave a review online — anywhere you are able. Even if it's just a sentence or two. It would make all the difference and would be very much appreciated.

Thanks!
Joe Siple

Thank you so much for reading one of **Joe Siple's** novels. If you enjoyed the experience, please check out Book One of the *Mr. Murray McBride* series for your next great read!

The Five Wishes of Mr. Murray McBride by Joe Siple

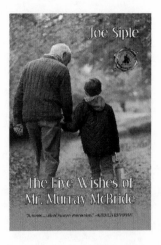

2018 Maxy Award "Book Of The Year"
"A sweet...tale of human connection...
will feel familiar to fans of Hallmark movies."
–*Kirkus Reviews*

"An emotional story that will leave readers meditating on the life-saving magic of kindness."
–*Indie Reader*

53092601R00144